DOG STAR

Susan Waller Miccio
www.susanwallermiccio.com

FRONT COVER: Illustration by Karen Chamberlain

DOG STAR

Susan Waller Miccio

Dedication

To the memory of
Ch. Patchouli Panda of Alan-Li
"Patches"
born May 28, 1991
who slept in my lap or at my feet while I wrote
and passed away in my arms on March 8, 2000

Acknowledgments

Delmarvans and others who know the tri-state peninsula where this book is set will doubtless note that I have taken geographic liberties. While place names and locations of major towns, roads and features are accurate, I have invented or moved lesser features to suit the needs of the narrative. The aptly named Murderkill River exists, but don't go looking for Swann's Pond or the graceful house called Swann's Nest.

My thanks to: David Kintsfather of Kutztown State College who coached me on filmmaking; "Lypps" (Herring Creek's Lyppizon Man) and owner Joan Maloney who helped me understand the personality of the Chesapeake Bay Retriever; Jim Rementer of the Lenape Language Project, The Delaware Tribe, for suggesting Teke's name; Anne Arundel County (Maryland) K-9 Officer Keith Baumann and "Bubba," whose courage and drive to work inspired me; Kipsyll "Kippy" Schurman who coached me on bass-fishing in the ponds of lower Delaware; Bill Cassell, Delaware State Police (ret.), who told me with stake-out stories with a rural flavor; David Mick of the Milford Delaware Carlisle Volunteer Fire Co. who explained body recovery; Bob Reynolds, native Delawarean, who has regaled me with tall tales over the years; Brian McCarthy, Forensic Investigator from the Delaware Office of the Chief Medical Examiner, who briefed me on forensic procedures; Roy W. Miller, Fisheries section of the Delaware Division of Fish and Wildlife, who educated me on Delaware's ponds; Doris Willing of Bridgeville Delaware who gave me a tour of her chicken houses; Lt. Tim Winstead, Public Information Office of the Delaware State Police, who patiently answered my questions about police procedure; Corp. Brian Anderson, K-9 officer of the Delaware State Police, who cleared up my questions about tracking and apprehensions; Allison Turner, Biological Technician at Assateague Island National Seashore, who monitors the herd of Chincoteague ponies, and Arnie Rausch who deputized German-speaking friends on my behalf.

Finally, thanks to my crew of "readers"—Andrea Struble, Kate Widdowson, Mary Bundy, Lisa Hylton, Donna Zammetti and my Mom, Nora Waller, who passed away before she could see this book in print.

Chapter One

The big Chessie leaped from the dock onto the deck of the 50-foot skipjack moored alongside. He halted on his mark, posed a forepaw on the bowsprit of the sailing vessel, and lifted his gaze. The sunrise momentarily gilded his eyes, and coppery highlights glinted from his chestnut coat. After a dramatic pause, he turned to face the camera squarely.

"Cut!" a guy in a plaid flannel shirt called out.

"Good boy, Teke!" called my friend Peg, rising from a crouch in the bow of the *Mary T. Deale*. She wrapped an arm around the Chesapeake Bay Retriever, hugging him, and scratched his chest energetically with her other hand. Teke's tongue lolled in pleasure. Peg looked up and waved at me where I stood gawking with the rest of the spectators.

Talking and gesturing, plaid-flannel-shirt, trailed by a man with a camera on his shoulder, moved five paces further along the shoreline eyeing the angles back to the *Mary T.* Following directions inaudible at my distance, Peg positioned Teke on the dock and, once again, disappeared from sight aboard the skipjack.

"Roll film," said plaid-flannel-shirt. "Speed," replied the camera guy. "Action."

Teke loped down the dock, bounded aboard the skipjack and struck the pose, precisely as before.

"Cut," plaid-flannel-shirt called out. "Good head shot. That's a wrap, everybody. Take a break, Peg. Hey! You guys with the bounce cards, come with me!"

Peg stood in the bow and stepped over to the dock. Teke followed and fell into place at her left heel.

"That was great, Peg," I said when they reached me. She shrugged slightly, but I could tell by her shining brown eyes glued on the dog, now sitting calmly at her side, that she was proud of Teke's performance. I leaned over and roughed up the thick, wavy coat over his shoulders. Teke replied by offering me one of his huge paws, which he left resting in my hand.

"So, what happens next?" I asked as I tickled Teke's webbed toes.

1

"Well, we're going out on the river to do some shots of Teke retrieving. But, first, Steve – he's the director over there - wants to shoot some background scenery around here," she flipped her hand toward the lighthouse behind her, "while the light is good." Half a dozen guys with bounce cards—which, Peg explained, are light reflectors—were trailing Steve the director toward the lighthouse.

Like the *Mary T. Deale*, one of the last of a fleet of oyster dredging sailboats on the Bay, the nineteenth century Hooper Strait Lighthouse is a key attraction of the Chesapeake Bay Maritime Museum. In its heyday, the hexagonal cottage perched atop iron pilings was screwed into Hooper Strait, and a lens in the cupola atop the cottage shone out over the Bay.

I had arrived at the museum grounds in St. Michaels Maryland at first light to cheer on my best friend, Peg Beauchamp, and her Chessie, Teke. Today was Teke's first outing as spokesdog for Delmarva tourism.

Tourism fuels the Delmarva economy. Lying between the Atlantic Ocean and Delaware Bay on the east and the Chesapeake Bay on the west, Delmarva is a peninsula. Though carved up among three states— Delaware and the Eastern Shores of Maryland and Virginia—Delmarva is an area where people share a culture and economic interests different than those of the Bay's urbanized Western Shores. From May through September, millions of East Coast city-dwellers flock to Delmarva's clean beaches, glitzy slots, quaint rural towns, pristine wildlife refuges, and tax-free outlets.

As his breed's name indicates, Teke's kind is native to the Bay country. In 1807, so the story goes, two Newfoundland dogs named Sailor and Canton were shipwrecked in the Bay. Their descendants were intermingled with other breeds and eventually developed into the Chesapeake Bay Retriever, one of only a handful of breeds to originate in North America. With its strong hindquarters and thick oily coat perfectly adapted to retrieving game birds in the cold waters of the Bay, the Chessie is a consummate water dog and Maryland's State Dog.

A Chessie's hard-headedness can challenge a trainer. As a puppy, Teke had been no exception. But Peg is a brilliant trainer and Teke's many titles in obedience, agility and tracking competitions were a tribute to her technique and the highlight of her career—until now.

2

When Delmarva's three states banded together to announce a talent search for a spokesdog to star in commercials promoting Delmarva's tourist attractions, Peg decided to audition Teke. Over two hundred canine competitors turned out to vie for the job. Teamed with Peg's professionalism, the local appeal of the handsome 95-pound sporting dog worked to Teke's advantage, and he won over the competition paws down.

"I had no idea this was going to be such a big deal," Peg whispered as we watched the crew and spectators converge on the lighthouse.

I didn't know how much Peg was making from this job—there are some things even close friends don't ask. However, judging from her excited plans for a new training building, I had assumed the contract was lucrative. Peg had been drooling over one of those spacious metal buildings for the better part of a decade.

"Listen, I want Teke to take a nap. He's been up half the night. Want a cup of coffee?" she said.

"Noticed my teeth chattering, eh?" I replied. Mornings on the water are always chilly. Peg and I both sported rosy cheeks, runny noses, and numbed fingers.

"I left the Tibbies in the car, Peg," I said. "I was afraid they'd bark when they saw Teke. I'll meet you back at the RV." Peg nodded and she set off briskly with Teke at heel.

The "Tibbies" are my Tibetan Spaniels, Senge and Dawa—pronounced SEN-gay and DAH-wah. Most people look at them and say, 'Oh, look at the cute Pekes.' And I reply, no, they are Tibetan Spaniels, the ancestor of the Pekingese, from the land on the roof of the world, Tibet. Then, I coach them to look closer and notice that the monkey-like faces are not flat like a Peke's but have a nice, blunt muzzle, that they are neither as small nor bow-legged as a Peke but medium-sized with a good length of leg, that they don't have coat to the floor but mid-length silky hair. As I walked the dogs to Peg's RV, this familiar scene replayed twice.

Peg's home away from home is an RV with a house unit mounted onto a van frame. The house unit includes a small kitchen, a miniscule bathroom with toilet and overhead shower, and a bedroom tucked into the back. Another bed occupies the claustrophobic loft over the driving compartment. Peg had removed the table and benches in the "dining area" to make room for dog crates. Like many people active in dog sports, Peg and her dogs take off most weekends in warm weather, driving hundreds of miles to compete in an event.

Senge and Dawa had known Teke since puppyhood. In fact, he had been their canine nanny on many occasions. As we climbed into the rig, they greeted him with typical Tibbie enthusiasm. Eyes bugging, they streaked from one end of the RV to the other, jumping on and off the bed, teasing Teke to catch them.

Peg flattened herself against the kitchen counter and lifted the cups of nuked coffee out of danger. Not that flattening was needed. Peg's tall body lacked any bulges. Always the natural athlete, she remained lean and muscular no matter how much she ate or how little she exercised. It has always annoyed me.

The Tibbies soon wore themselves out wild-dogging and flopped down to pant. Having stoically endured their antics, Teke crept into his sheepskin-lined crate, circled and settled down for a nap. Peg squatted and scratched his ears for a moment before latching the crate door. Recovered, the ever curious Tibbies took up positions on Peg's bed to observe the goings-on through the window at the back.

Mugs in hand, Peg and I left the RV and strolled down to the lighthouse to watch the filming. As we made our way through the small crowd of down-vested and sweater-clad spectators milling around, Peg stopped to chat with a few people she knew. A couple of well-wishers from Peg's dog training classes hugged her and gushed over Teke's performance. Peg turned when someone tapped her on the shoulder.

"Hey, Dr. Lynch," Peg said when she turned to a sturdy woman with a square, ruddy face and cropped, sun-bleached hair. "This is a surprise."

"I read about it in the *Observer*. It's not everyday one of our patients becomes a movie star," said the young veterinarian from the practice where Peg and I take our dogs.

"Did you see him work? What did you think?" Peg asked.

"He really looked good. Perfect in fact. You've done a good job with him," Dr. Lynch replied.

4

We talked a while longer before Peg and I left her to continue toward the lighthouse.

"I like Dr. Lynch. I think she brings some updated ideas to Doc Twilley's practice, " Peg commented. I agreed.

"You know, I didn't know there was anything about today in the paper. I guess Grace Bishop put it in her column."

"Speak of the devil," I said.

A familiar shock of white hair bobbed above the crowd ahead. Grace Bishop covered community events for the social column in the local paper. Whether it was a benefit dance, Chamber of Commerce dinner or fireman's carnival, Grace was there. She'd been around forever. More importantly, Grace was a dog lover who wrote dog-related stories for her paper. As always, scribbling on a steno pad, she was undoubtedly taking notes for a story about Peg and Teke for her column. We chatted amiably for a while about how well Teke had performed in the morning's shoot. Grace asked several questions about how Peg trained Teke to repeat the required moves over and over flawlessly.

When another well-wisher drew Peg aside, Grace wedged her talon-like fingers in my bicep and shot me a meaningful look. "Did you see who's here?" she hissed.

"Ow, Grace, that hurts," I protested and yanked my arm away. "Who?"

"Evelyn Hitchens," Grace said, sneering, "I can't believe she had the nerve to show up."

"Well, nerve isn't something she lacks," I said sarcastically, massaging my arm. I scanned the crowd but didn't see Evelyn.

Grace snorted. "Nothing but a puppy mill. That's what she is," she proclaimed.

I shrugged. "Maybe so." I had no proof that Evelyn ran a puppy mill, where dogs are bred indiscriminately and puppies sold for profit, without concern for their health or well-being. But I knew she had proven herself a disagreeable woman at the spokesdog tryouts—loud, pushy, and insulting to the other dogs and their owners.

"The way she showed her ass, pardon my French, at that last audition was…" Grace suddenly stopped talking. She abruptly turned her head toward the parking lot. "What the hell's going on over there?" she demanded loudly.

Everyone in earshot turned to the direction of her stare to see Peg running flat out across the dead winter grass toward the parking lot. She disappeared behind a Three Guys Productions vans.

Nothing could make Peg move that fast except the final run in a national dog agility championship or a dog in danger. I thrust the coffee cup at Grace and sprinted for the van. I could hear Peg sobbing. My heart choking me, I rounded the van to find her on her knees. Her body shielding and restraining him, Teke lay on the ground next to the van's rear wheel.

"Get a vet! Get a vet!" she screamed at the gawkers.

Chapter Two

I was still shaken hours later when I turned into the gravel and sand lane to Swann's Nest. No, that's not some realtor's corny name for a suburban development. My name is Abigail Forrest Swann—Abby for short. My people have lived on this land in the little state of Delaware for a couple hundred years, and Swann's Nest is the house my ancestors built here. The house is situated on a slight rise on a V of land between Swann Creek and Cattail Branch, a rivulet that feeds the creek. About a mile downstream, Swann Creek flows into the Murderkill River 15 miles upstream from where the river slides gently into the Delaware Bay.

Every time I drive up the lane as it winds along the course of Cattail Branch, I love to catch that first glimpse of the Nest in the clearing. In 1785, Daniel Swann built the main two-story and attic, three-bay Georgian house on 250 acres he bought during the land turnovers following the Revolution. Constructed of brick laid in the Flemish bond pattern, a decorative design called a belt course encircles the structure between the first and second stories. Beneath the roofline, a richly carved cornice crowns the walls.

My ancestor had attached his elegant house to one end of an earlier, humbler dwelling on the site. The kitchen of the older two-room, frame structure, now modernized, remains my kitchen, while the larger room in the old wing is my all-purpose room that architects like to call the great room. Above the great room is the original bedroom under the eaves, its one dormer window looking toward the creek, accessed by a narrow, steep, closed stair winding around the fireplace,

The Nest sits on a small lawn surrounded by woods. A large carriage house and diverse small outbuildings, also constructed of brick and dating from the late 18th and early 19th centuries, are scattered around the clearing.

Long before the first Daniel bought the land, an enterprising Swedish colonist, whose heirs would eventually build the old frame house, received the land in a grant from the Duke of York. This fellow had promptly dammed up the meandering woodland creek to create a millpond to power a grist mill. By Daniel's time, the 17th century mill had fallen down, but Daniel rebuilt it to grind corn and wheat for the new republic's farmers. He later added a sawmill to cut the oak and pine in the surrounding forests into building lumber. The mills are long gone, along with the vast tracts of forest that fed them, but serene Swann Pond is still there. A walk of a few hundred yards through the woods up creek from the house, the Pond is visible from the Nest's second story windows on the west side.

This is where I grew up and where I returned after my father, one of many Daniel namesakes in the family, died two years ago last January. When I left Delmarva for college, I stayed away for years. Maybe growing up in an old house surrounded by antiques steered me to study decorative arts. But it was a freshman course in Asian art that launched me toward what I thought would be a scholarly career in some university's Art department or perhaps a curatorship in some museum's Asian department. Then, while I was in graduate school, I met Brian.

A dealer of Japanese objects from Seattle, Brian Forrest was knowledgeable and urbane. He argued persuasively that I could be far more successful as an entrepreneur than a scholar. I was impressed with his business sense and not a little attracted by his tall, blond good looks. When he offered me an opportunity to be his East Coast partner, I was thrilled. Eventually, he offered me his name, too. I took it. Big mistake.

I spent my post-college years in D.C. —Washington that is—busily growing my business, "Abigail Swann, Asian Antiquities" which eventually became "Abigail Forrest-Swann, Asian Antiquities." Brian may have been a rat, but he was a smart rat. The business was successful. Much as I would have liked to drop the Forrest after the divorce, I was already well-known to the trade by that name. So, I compromised and dropped the hyphen instead.

After I inherited the Nest, I'd commuted back and forth to D.C., spending the weekdays in the city and most weekends at the Nest. But the summertime trip, along with millions of other city-dwellers, became unbearable. I spent hundreds of hours of my life in a line of traffic, inhaling exhaust fumes, as I crept eastbound on U.S. 50 toward the toll booths at the Chesapeake Bay Bridge. Once over the Bridge, I risked life and limb dodging crazed urbanites in their headlong rush for the beach until, at last, I turned off on the peaceful back roads leading to my Nest.

It eventually dawned on me why they charge a toll only on the eastbound span of the Bridge; only a fool would go the other way. So, I moved back home for good. That was a year ago. Once settled back at the Nest, the tension of city life gradually let go. I soon felt like I'd never left home and, moreover, I never wanted to leave again.

Though too petite to see out the car window, Dawa and Senge knew they were home. Dawa raised herself to a sit. Beside her, Senge began to squirm and whine. It didn't take canine psychics to figure it out. The familiar crunch of gravel under the tires would tip off even an olfactory-impaired human. Still, the Tibbies could no doubt smell the tulip poplars, hollies, sweet gums, and loblolly pines in the woods, the freshwater branch to the right and, finally, the musty old brick of the Nest—each a signpost to noses a thousand times more sensitive than mine.

Senge was already standing at the kitchen door, woofing impatiently, as Dawa and I crossed from the former carriage house, now part garage and part workshop, to the kitchen wing. I could hear the phone ringing as I turned the key.

"Abby?" asked Peg, as if the Tibbies would answer the phone. Not that they couldn't, it's just that they wouldn't bother.

"How's Teke?" I replied.

"He'll be OK. Bruised up some. Nothing broken, nothing bleeding, nothing internal. I just got home from Doc Twilley's," Peg said in one breath and then paused. "I just can't figure out what happened. He was running across the parking lot when I saw the Three Guys van back up and knock him down. How did he get out of the crate and out of the RV?"

"Well…" I hesitated, wondering whether I should mention the suspicion that had grown in my mind on the drive home. "When I got there, the door to the rig was standing wide open and the crate was unlatched."

"What? I *know* I latched his crate," she said, punching out the word 'know.'

My mind skipped back to the scene earlier that day. When Peg had yelled for a vet, Jackie Lynch had shown up within a few seconds.

While she examined Teke, I had rushed to the RV, where I'd left Senge and Dawa on Peg's bed. I was terrified that they, too, were running loose.

Miraculously, the two Tibbies were standing just inside the RV's open door. Gasping more from terror than from my sprint, I'd knelt and hugged them tightly while they licked my ears. When I leaned back to look lovingly at them, their wrinkly foreheads told me that both were clearly upset. Dawa trembled. Hugging them one more time, I'd noticed the door to Teke's crate was also open. I remember being puzzled, but there had been no time to think about it. I had to get back to Peg and Teke.

Kissing the Tibbies' heads, I stood up to leave but, as I turned to the door, I'd felt the soft but firm touch of a Dawa's petite paw on my calf. But when I looked down, she was staring not at me but at Teke's crate. She stepped toward it, then looked up at me and back to the crate. Then, she stretched forward to sniff something on the floor in front of the crate. Bending over, I picked up and pocketed what Dawa had shown me and, carefully latching the RV door behind me, I ran back to where Dr. Lynch and Peg still knelt over Teke.

Dr. Lynch had said Teke didn't appear to be badly hurt but she wanted to get x-rays. While she and Peg were loading him in the vet's Jeep for the trip to the clinic, I retrieved the contents of my pocket and examined them in my palm. It was three pieces of dried liver.

"How the hell did the crate get unlatched?"

"Huh? I'm sorry. What'd you say?" I asked, momentarily confused. I didn't wait for her answer. "Peg, did you know Evelyn Hitchens was there today?"

"You're kidding," Peg said with a snort.

"I didn't see her, but Grace told me she was there."

"I can't stand that Hitchens woman," Peg said, "She treats her dogs awful."

"Mmmm," I said noncommittally. Peg had known Evelyn Hitchens for all the years I'd lived in the city. All I knew about her was that her behavior during the spokesdog competition showed her to be a person who cared more about herself than her dogs.

Dawa delicately touched my calf with her paw. I looked down. She was motionless, her deep brown eyes glittering.

"What is it, little girl?" I asked, puzzled.

"Abby? You there?" Peg said, drawing my attention away from Dawa. "Could you watch Teke tomorrow morning? Dr. Lynch said he'll probably be stiff and sore for a day or so, so Steve called off filming for the day. But I need to go back over to St. Michaels to pick up the RV. I don't want to drag Teke over there and I don't want to leave him home alone either," she explained, needlessly. By now, she should know that the Tibbies and I love Teke. No explanations required.

"Oh, sure, no problem. Bring him over," I said. "How'd you get home yesterday, Peg?"

"Dr. Lynch drove us home after she'd finished examining Teke. I offered to call somebody to come get me, but she insisted. She seems real nice. I'm so glad she was there." She paused. "I just don't understand how Teke got out of his crate."

While Peg said good night, I glanced down again. Dawa was still staring at me with magic eyes. Senge whined and scratched at the pantry door.

"OK, you guys, I get the message. Dinner time."

"I love your new sign, Abby," Peg said as she motioned Teke through the kitchen door the next morning. Teke sauntered to his bed in the corner, a large plaid pillow stuffed with cedar shavings, while Senge bounced around him and Dawa gently sniffed his injured leg.

My new sign, at the end of the lane, proclaimed that Abigail Forrest Swann—Asian Antiquities—formerly of the Nation's Capital was now operating from a Delaware backwater. Well, almost operating. Most of my inventory was still boxed up in the carriage house, but soon it would be en route to the space I'd leased in an antiques mall in Rehoboth Beach, a resort community on the ocean.

Enticed by Delaware's tax-free shopping, tourists and retirees flocked to the shops and malls along the resort coast. I'd decided to tap that market. Hopefully, my loyal and well-heeled clientele from the city would continue to seek me out as well. They could also find me on the internet, where my web site would soon be up. I only hoped to make enough income to pay the upkeep on the Nest. Two-hundred-year-old houses are like a drain down which to pour your money.

"Breakfast?" I asked as I opened a package of scrapple, deftly removing and flicking the nutrition statement into the trash without looking at the fat content. Why torture myself?

"No thanks. I ate," said my svelte friend, "Tea would be good though. I'll get it."

"So, how's Teke doing?" I asked while slicing a slab of scrapple.

"A little depressed. But he's lucky not to have been hurt worse." She hit the button on the microwave.

"All that muscling protected him," I remarked and slid the slab into the frying pan. Peg nodded in agreement and took her mug of hot water out of the microwave.

As an urban sophisticate, I would have turned up my nose at the suggestion of eating scrapple. However, while grocery shopping soon after I moved home, a hunk of the gray meat with the unfortunate name called to me from the refrigerator case. I succumbed and took it home. I thought I'd died and gone to heaven when I bit into that scrapple sandwich, the first since childhood. Now I rationed myself one sandwich made of the local delicacy—a term I use facetiously–per week.

"Well, I'll take him for a walk around the pond later on. He'll like that and it'll keep him limber."

She nodded again and plopped into a chair at the kitchen table, dunking her Earl Grey bag and watching me as I moved a box of carefully packed 19th century Imari dishes to one side of the table. While she contemplated the color of the tea, I lifted a dish with a lovely chrysanthemum pattern from the box.

"What are you thinking, Peg?" I asked as I automatically ran my hands over the dish, in search of tiny, invisible imperfections best detected by touch.

"I'm thinking somebody went in my RV and let him out."

Dawa touched the back of my calf. I reached down and scratched her head. I'm well-trained.

"I think you may be right about that," I said, carefully placing the Imari dish on the kitchen Hoosier and taking out another encased in its protective wrapping. "Peg, you don't use liver on Teke, do you?"

Understanding that I was referring to the small bits of liver some dog trainers use as an incentive and reward, she shook her head 'no,' still staring into her mug. "Teke has never been food-motivated," she said, "The only reward he wants is his toy *du jour*."

"I didn't think so," I said, removing the bubble wrap from the dish and placing it gently next to its companion on the Hoosier. I reached into my jeans pocket and dropped the three pieces of desiccated liver onto the table. "I found that bait right outside his crate when I ran back to check on the Tibbies."

She stared at the liver.

"I think somebody's trying to hurt Teke, Peg."

She nodded.

Chapter Three

There's a saying among fanciers of the Tibetan Spaniel that Tibbies are like potato chips—you can't have just one. It appears to be a fact. "Only" Tibbies are a rarity. Most people who discover this uncommon breed soon find themselves with a pair, a trio and so on. In fact, one day while surfing the net for information about Tibbies, I discovered that a special collective noun, evocative of their personality, has been coined for Tibbies. Lions live in a pride, whales in a pod, geese in a gaggle, and Tibbies in an attitude.

Everyday, my attitude and I head down to Swann's Pond. It's only a short stroll through the fenced woods surrounding the Nest down to Cattail Branch, over the footbridge, and through the piney grove to the south gate. Then we take the farm lane that skirts an adjacent field out to Swann's Pond Road. Across the road, we're on park land. A short cut through the state-owned woods brings us to a path encircling the pond. Oh well, I guess it does sound complicated but it's really only a twenty-minute stroll.

In the 1950's and 60's, Delaware acquired a number of privately-owned ponds and made them into state-run fishing areas. This suited my parsimonious grandfather, Poppop Benjamin, just fine. He never stopped complaining about the cost of maintaining Swann's Pond. The state's offer was a good deal for my family. Besides stocking the pond with game fish, the state repaired the deteriorating mill dam, replaced the bridge over the Creek, cleared the underbrush, and improved the woodland. Eventually, they also cleared a walking trail around the pond, paved a small parking lot and added a boat ramp and picnic area. In summer, they mow the grass and maintain a portable toilet on site. So, now the Swanns have the use of the pond without the headaches of owning it.

After Peg left for St. Michaels and I polished off my scrapple sandwich, my attitude and I headed for the Pond. I let the dogs run free in the fenced woods between the house and the gate. Though Teke wanted to hang back at first, Tibbies do not take "no" for an answer. With Senge attached to an ear and Dawa tugging at his tail, they soon propelled him into a suitably energetic pace and then, leaving him behind, dashed ahead.

A Tibbie rarely travels in a straight line willingly. Instead, they "jink" with rapid fire changes in direction—forward, then reverse, then flank—always twirling, charging and retreating. Today was no exception. Teke did not join in the jinking but trotted along sedately while I brought up the rear.

At the gate, the dogs panted patiently while I attached their leads. As we turned down the farm lane toward the Pond, the ill-mannered Tibbies trotted ahead, as their independent natures demand. while the well-trained Teke walked at my heel. The sun was still low in the eastern sky, pinking the low scudding clouds. March had been windy but mild and dry so far. Today's calm was a relief.

The farmer who leased the land, Tim West, had taken advantage of the good weather. Lime lay on the field like a dusting of snow. I assumed Tim would plow soon and wondered what he planned to plant in this field this year. I hoped it wouldn't be boring soybeans. Corn makes a prettier field, and I love to listen to it whisper while it grows.

After a few token barks at the cows and calves in the distant pasture, we crossed Swann's Pond Road, and the Tibbies followed the footpath I'd worn through the woods around the pond. We descended the slope to the trail at pond's edge.

I use the term "slope" advisedly. Shortly after moving home to the Nest, I was given directions to a get-together at someone's house. Told to follow a certain road up a hill and turn into the driveway at the top of the hill, I traveled the entire length of the road, back and forth, half a dozen times, passing several driveways but no "hill" of any description. I then saw another car filled with people I recognized as fellow guests, select and turn into a driveway. I have since learned to refine my eyesight to identify any elevation, even as little as one foot, as a "hill."

Even ponds are shallow in such flat country. Though a pretty pond, Swann's depth is only six or seven feet with a nine-foot trench at its center. On this breezeless morning, the pond's glassy surface was relatively deserted. I spotted one Tracker deep in a cove, its angler standing at the bow trolling the shoreline for bass. While the dogs sniffed a rotting log, I paused to watch the fisherman cast into the lily pads.

He's hunting a lunker, a female fat with eggs, fanning her nest, I thought. The dogs concluded their investigation and we left the cove.

A green canoe passed in the opposite direction, only the dip of the paddles marking its passage. Songbirds were calling high up in the pines. I clutched at my chest but was irritated to discover I'd left my binoculars hanging by the back door instead of around my neck. When we came to the bridge over the creek where it enters the pond, I told the dogs to "sit," which they did, panting happily. I leaned against the railing with my eyes closed, face lifted to the sun. A walker startled me out of my daydream with a "cute dogs" remark. I murmured thanks and we continued on our circuit.

Teke seemed to be walking more comfortably by the time we returned to the Nest. He'd even pricked his ears and grown still when he spotted some Canada geese, year-round residents of the pond site, foraging near the picnic tables. I was pleased that his spirits seemed to have brightened.

Back home, a cup of tea at my hand, I settled down in the dining room where some pieces that I'd kept in storage were arrayed on dining table, still in their boxes. I was looking forward to spending the morning unpacking and studying them.

Dawa and Senge took up positions in the deep window seat gazing out over the yard. In Tibet, Tibbies were watch dogs. Patrolling the walls of monasteries and rooftops of the homes of the well-off, they alerted the human inhabitants and giant Tibetan Mastiffs below to the approach of strangers. To this day, all Tibbies love to climb to the highest possible point and watch for intruders. Bred for an altogether different purpose, Teke was content to leave the watch-dogging to the Tibbies. He circled and settled on the hearth.

Dawa trilled and Senge growled at something they saw outside. I pushed back my chair and joined them at the window, peering through the old, wavy glass.

"That's just our geese," I said to the Tibs, scratching their ears. The pair of Canada geese stops by every morning to see what the songbirds have left behind on the ground under the feeder. They hang around all year, apparently feeling no need to migrate with other Canadas, in the relative comfort of the vicinity of Swann's. I assume they are a bonded pair, a married couple so to speak, since I have never seen them apart, and they produce a quantity of goslings every year. Senge grunted in reply, sighed and dropped his chin onto the window stool. Dawa, less tolerant of other creatures on her turf, whether furred or feathered, continued to peer fiercely at the geese.

I returned to the dining table where I powered up my laptop and dislodged an object from its foam peanuts. "Ah." I exhaled the word, not even realizing I'd been holding my breath, as a lovely bamboo okimono emerged from a covering of thick brown paper. The reclining puppy with its drop ears and chubby cheeks just fit my cupped palm. I remembered vaguely hearing another dealer of orientalia say that these puppies were guardians placed beside the beds of Japanese children to keep away whatever evil lurked in the night.

This was the first puppy okimono I had ever acquired. I observed it closely as is my habit by training and inclination. It seemed in excellent condition with only one or two mild imperfections in the caramel-colored polish of its surface. When I turned it over, I saw the signature cartouche on a forepaw but did not recognize it. Mentally recording the ideogram, I consulted a couple reference books from the floor-to-ceiling bookcases at either side of the fireplace but could not find the artist's name.

I tapped some notes about the object into my laptop while I contemplated what price to ask for it. A few minutes later, I was still studying it, forming a theory about its age, when Dawa patted my calf.

"What do you think of this, Dawa?" I asked, placing the okimono on the carpet. She crouched in front of the puppy. Gently placing a forepaw on either side of it, she curled her slippers, the long hair that grows from a Tibbie's toes, around it. She held it tightly while she sniffed. I had no fear she'd cause any damage. She looked up and smiled by stretching her lip away from her lower teeth, the way Tibbies do. I nodded.

"I think you're right, little Moon," I said to her, my eyes resting lovingly on her for a moment. Sometimes I called her Moon, which is what Dawa means in Tibetan. I'd named her that because of her creamy white coat with caramel-colored patches, like a late summer man-in-the-moon. Senge, ever jealous, ran over to sniff the okimono, too. I'd called him Senge, which means Lion, because I'd read that Tibetans bred their small dogs in the image of Buddha's spirit-lion. In Buddhist imagery, the lion following in the Buddha's footsteps symbolizes the triumph of peace over violence. When Senge was a puppy, he'd been at my heels every moment. But Senge was not the least bit leonine in his personality. On the contrary, he was a huggy bear.

"Yes, definitely late Edo period, 19th century." Rescuing the okimono from Senge's curious less-gentle nose, I placed it on the fireplace mantel next to a pillow vase bearing the hand-painted image of a Tibbie. Since Dawa and Senge had come into my life, I became increasing unwilling to part with objects that look like Tibbies or, for that matter, most any dog. When I run across them in my work, they inevitably end up on a mantel or library table or bookcase somewhere in Swann's Nest. The Nest has become a temple to dogs.

"It's probably supposed to be an Akita or some other Japanese breed but it sure looks like a Tibbie puppy, doesn't it? I think it's a keeper." It would be fun to just deal caniniana, I mused as I returned to my work, assuming I could ever find any doggy objects that weren't "keepers."

Doubtless thinking that I don't have enough sporting dog prints on the walls, Teke hoisted himself to a stand and sauntered to my side where he plopped beside my feet. I scratched his head until he seemed asleep and then went back to work.

Around three o'clock, Peg stopped by to pick up Teke. The Three Guys people wanted him back at St. Michaels in the morning to shoot the delayed retrieving scenes. To make sure Teke was up to the repetitive swims on the river as well as the rest of the shooting schedule, she had made an appointment with Doc Twilley to check him over. She rattled off the remainder of the shoots: Friday–on the Boardwalk in Rehoboth Beach Delaware. Monday–an amusement park in Ocean City Maryland. Tuesday–dolphin-watching at Cape Henlopen State Park. Wednesday– wild ponies at Assateague National Seashore in Virginia. Thursday– NASCAR™ at Dover International Speedway and a C-5 Galaxy at Dover Air Force Base, both in Dover Delaware.

As I planned to deliver some stock to my new "shop" in the antiques mall in Rehoboth Beach on Friday, we agreed to meet on the Boardwalk and, afterwards, make a short run to Lewes for the annual Ladies Shrimp Feast at the fire hall. As the limited number of tickets to the popular get-together sold out a year in advance, we'd been planning this outing for over a year.

I stood in the yard until Peg and Teke disappeared around the curve in the lane, headed for Doc Twilley's, on the other side of Swann's Pond about three miles away. Turning back to the house, I paused with my hand on handle of the old pump by the kitchen door. I pulled it up. It emitted a hollow sucking wheeze. I pushed down hard, and the spout coughed air. Was what had happened to Teke just a stupid prank or had someone deliberately tried to hurt him? Did Evelyn Hitchens do it to get back at Peg because Teke won over her dog? Would she do it again?

Chapter Four

As I arranged objects in my booth at the antiques mall in Rehoboth, I tried not to think about the elegant little shop I'd left behind in D.C. I kept reminding myself that I hadn't really come down in the world but had deliberately chosen a simpler lifestyle here in "slower, lower Delaware." Unlike the hectic, urbanized northernmost county, where most of its three quarters of a million people live, Delaware's two southern counties remain predominantly rural in character and, with the exception of tourist-choked roads on summer weekends, relatively slow-paced.

When I left the antiques mall that Friday afternoon, I was fairly pleased with my booth. Casting a critical eye over the scene one last time, I approved the asymmetrical but balanced arrangement created by the forms and textures of the objects chosen. Two Edo six-panel paper screens from the 18th century, with their colorful idealized depictions of Japanese landscape, flanked my allotted space. A century-old Tibetan carpet in blue and red, a near twin to the larger one beneath my dining table at the Nest, formed the backdrop. Two embroidered silk kimonos hung on artfully arranged branches at one side. My display cases were sparely but tastefully furnished with objects as diverse as woodblock prints, a 19th century Satsuma incense burner, several lovely pieces of Chinese export porcelain, and a contemporary Tibetan thangka, each object carefully labeled with its purpose, origin, age and price.

I nodded goodnight to the elderly gentleman who watched over the dealers' booths and customers' parcels and set off for the Boardwalk. As I strolled, I window-shopped. Rehoboth's side streets were lined with storefronts selling everything from chic beachwear to cheap souvenirs. I wondered when I could afford to move shop to one of these charming alleyways. By the time I reached the Boardwalk, the day's filming was wrapping up.

Lucky for the actors working with Teke, the day had turned out to be more-or-less mild. Still, when I arrived, the local actors portraying a family of Washingtonian or Philadelphian tourists, were pulling on fleece sweats over their cheerful summer outfits to ward off the chill breeze. For their sakes, I hoped the director hadn't asked them to take a polar bear dip in the ocean. Peg, with Teke asleep beside her, was sitting on a Boardwalk bench eating French fries from a cup.

"Can I have one?" I said, parking next to Peg and thrusting my fingers into the cup before she could reply. What are friends for? I gobbled the first fry and went back for two.

"Yum," I said through a mouthful of salt-and-vinegary potato deep-fried with the skin on. I remembered the days before the locally famous fries were franchised, the days when you could get them only at the beach. They still taste better seasoned with salt air, I thought. "I'm starved. How'd your day go?"

"Great. Teke was perfect. He did four different scenes. Playing Frisbee with the actors, running down the beach, buying cotton candy and flying a kite. He's bored now, though," she said, stroking the big head pressed against her thigh, "There's a lot of sitting around doing nothing while they set scenes up."

"Buying cotton candy?" I asked, lifting an eyebrow.

"Yeah, weird, right? They had him stand up against the counter and the girl put the cotton candy in his mouth." She shrugged. "We just do what they tell us to do."

"So, are you done? Can we go?" I was impatient. My mouth was all set for shrimp.

"Yep, we're done. Let me just check on what time I'm supposed to be in O.C. tomorrow. Back in a minute." While Peg talked with the director, I inhaled the remaining fries. I was tempted to lick the cup but, glancing around sheepishly, thought better of it.

"OK, let's go," she said, returning to the bench and shouldering her backpack full of dog toys, treats, water bottles and portable water dish. "He says he wants us there at six in the morning. I guess it will have to be an early night for me." She hooked a lead onto Teke's collar.

I followed Peg's pickup north on Del. 1. We turned left, then right, then left onto successively narrower country roads, passing flat fields that stretched to the woods on the horizon. Those unfamiliar with the web of back roads in this part of Sussex County have to navigate by the sun, the odometer and landmarks. Needless to say, the lack of signage among endless look-alike corn and soybean fields sometimes impeded fire and paramedic crews. So, the state had recently assigned road names and erected signs to improve emergency response, but the road by Peg's house remained unmarked.

After a few miles along Peg's road, known variously to the locals as Old Chapel or Browns Chapel Road or by an obscure route number that I'd forgotten, we turned into a gravel lane flanked by century-old walnut trees. At its end stood a neat farmhouse the color of cream with hunter green trim.

Peg had bought the quintessential 19th century Delmarva farmhouse on five acres several years back. From the vantage of my second floor apartment in upscale Georgetown, I thought my high school buddy had lost her mind and told her so. The rundown relic possessed absolutely no architectural interest that I could see—just a poor farmer's modest dwelling abandoned to the field mice. The four-room main section consisted of a parlor and dining room on either side of the center hall downstairs and two bedrooms and a 1930's vintage bath upstairs. A single story wing off the back of the main section housed a hopelessly primitive kitchen.

Peg claimed that the back section was the original home place, far earlier than the rest of the house. Sure enough, she was proven correct when demolition revealed a walk-in fireplace, walled up in the 19th century, that spanned an entire wall. Restored at immense expense, it was now the centerpiece of her country kitchen.

What had originally attracted Peg to the derelict property was not so much the house but the outbuildings. Now neatly painted to match the house, Peg had seen their potential as kennels and training buildings even when they were half fallen down. Hardworking and resourceful, Peg had rehabbed the outbuildings first, and only later turned her attention to her own comfort. Over the years, she had transformed the mundane house and run-down structures into a cozy country home for herself and her dogs, and she did most of the work herself—a feat for which I admire her.

As we pulled up, we heard Peg's two other dogs, an Australian Shepherd called Bits and a Golden Retriever called Dapper, barking in the runs adjacent to the kennel building out back. Teke leapt from the truck and raced to the kennel to greet his brothers.

The dogs come first, of course. So, while Peg was out in the kennel fixing their dinner, I paid a visit to the bathroom to repair the damage. A glance in the mirror revealed straight, shoulder-length blonde hair, darkened by winter gloom and tousled by ocean breezes. A quick brushing found the part and settled it back into its customary lack of style. A swipe of rose blush on each cheekbone and a dab of dusky lipstick restored the illusion of life, while a generous application of mascara set off my best feature. I vainly admired my green eyes and thick lashes for a moment before skipping back downstairs. Pulling on my sheepskin-lined denim jacket against the evening cool, I went out onto the back porch just as Peg was walking in from the kennel building.

"Everything OK?"

"Sure. They scarfed down their dinner and settled for a nap. Teke's tired. Me, too," she said, disappearing into the mudroom. "Cripe. I look like hell," I heard her say behind me as she caught a glimpse of herself the mirror hanging by the back door. "Give me a sec."

I perched on a porch bench, my arms wrapped around, to wait. When she emerged a few minutes later, she had changed into a fresh button-down shirt, tucked neatly into her jeans, and restored order to her short blunt-cut hair. When we were kids, Peg had had a remarkable head of long, thick black hair, but she'd gone prematurely white by her thirtieth birthday. Eventually, she gave up on the coloring routine and settled on a practical short cut. The silvery effect was very attractive in contrast to her otherwise youthful appearance.

"It's going to be cold tonight," she said, zipping up her parka and flicking off the house lights.

"You need lipstick," I remarked as we walked toward her truck.

Using the side mirror, she quickly applied a coral shade to her lips more-or-less by feel since the daylight had faded to a streak along the horizon. We climbed into the pickup and headed for town. By the time we arrived, it was dark.

The Ladies Shrimp Feast began in reaction to the all-male Oyster Eat at a rival volunteer fire company in a neighboring town. By the time we reached Station No. 2, the fire hall in Lewes, many of the 450 female ticket holders had already staked out places.

Going to one of these local events always brings to mind the time I brought my then fiancé, now ex, Brian home for the first time eight years ago. Brian was a city boy. Before our engagement party, my father had drawn him aside and solemnly warned him, "Be careful what you say to people down here, son. Everybody knows everybody, and most of them are related to each other." It's true. By the time Peg and I had found a place to sit, we'd run into three of her cousins and re-told the story of the filming four or five times.

Like any other fire hall feed, food was plentiful. Nine hundred pounds of spicy bright pink-orange shellfish, heaps of ham and egg salad sandwiches and gallons of clam chowder were fast disappearing. But unlike other fire hall feeds, there was some serious partying going on, too. Reveling in a night away from husbands and kids, the women washed down the food with canning jars of beer and wine coolers and then danced off the calories.

As always, the shrimp were delectable. We ate them as fast as we could peel them, tossing away the shells, pausing only to dunk in sauce laced with hot horseradish, and washed them down with a swig of beer.

I spotted Grace. As a fixture at all these events, she knew everyone. Pausing to jot a few notes for her column in her ever-present notebook and to take the occasional, tasteful photo of grinning feasters, she was plying her way around the room. When she spotted us, she stuck her hand up and headed for our table. Eating and drinking never stopped Grace from talking. Between shrimp, she ticked off a who's who of the women present. Delaware's salt-of-the-earth female Governor topped the list followed by the leading entrepreneurs and professionals. She wrapped up with mutual acquaintances and relatives.

"So, how are the commercials going, Peg?" Grace demanded.

"Good. I'm happy with Teke's performance."

"Is he fully recovered from the accident?"

"Yeah. Just some bruises and temporary soreness. He's his old self again."

"Oh that's good. Did you ever find out how he got out?"

"Well," Peg paused and glanced at me, "Off the record, we think someone let him out deliberately, but we don't know who."

If Grace was shocked by the news, she didn't show it. Without missing a beat, she observed that "that bitch" Evelyn Hitchens had to be behind it. Peg shrugged and Grace plowed on.

"So, have you seen any of the commercials yet?"

"No, but they say the first one will be ready soon. Are we back on the record, Grace?"

"But of course," Grace replied with a flourish of her hand. She rubbed her fingers on a towelette and took up her notebook, pen poised, "So where have you filmed so far and what's next?"

By nine-thirty, the party was just getting started. Unfortunately, the next day would be an early one for Peg and Teke, and she started making noises about leaving. Reluctantly, we declared success and bid farewell to our fellow revelers. Outside, bundled up and waddling toward Peg's truck, we ran into Phil Hughes and a friend.

I'd liked Phil from the moment Peg introduced him to me. He had a good sense of humor and adored his dog, Ham, a German Short-haired Pointer. In fact, Ham is why Phil and Peg met. Phil is a Delaware State trooper. About a year before, Peg had helped train Ham and two other K-9's to detect explosives. Ham turned out to be so good at sniffing out bombs that Phil and he are called in whenever a threat is received or a dignitary's visit necessitates a precautionary security sweep.

Phil and Peg had liked each other in a dog friend kind of way but dawdled around until they finally started going together seriously about six months ago. Unlike me, Peg had never experimented with marriage and, at 33, remained technically uncommitted. Still, Phil and she had been exclusive ever since they started going together. She seemed very happy.

Phil grabbed Peg for a hug. At 6'2", he towered over her 5'8". His bear-like body enveloped her wiry one. I was slightly jealous that his green eyes were prettier than mine, but, all in all, I had to admit he was an attractive man with his reddish blond hair and mustache. He had a great laugh.

Phil introduced us to his friend and fellow trooper, Dave Griffith.

"Call me Griff," the friend said, sticking out his very large hand.

25

Phil explained that Griff and he had just come from the Oyster Eat in Georgetown. Both were attired in colorful flannel shirts, jeans, work boots and ball caps. This was the *de rigueur* dress for the Oyster Eat, worn even by the upstate lawyers who descend on the Eat in stretch limos.

Given that Georgetown was several miles away, I knew this "chance" meeting had been pre-arranged. I shot a glare at Peg. She grinned sideways but avoided eye contact.

"I heard this was the first year in a long time they actually got real Chesapeake oysters. How were they?" Peg asked.

"Real good," the men chorused, adding a few lip-smacks for emphasis.

"Was the place packed?"

"Oh yeah. About a thousand I'd guess," Phil said, "shoulder to shoulder. I heard they brought in a hundred bushels of oysters."

With a history of sixty-plus years, the Oyster Eat is a longer Sussex County tradition than the Ladies Shrimp Feast. It has even earned a designation by the Library of Congress as a "local legacy" event. The men don't just drink beer, smoke cigars and eat succulent steamed oysters tossed down the length of the tables from buckets and pried from their shells on the tip of an oyster knife. They also form and reinforce political and business alliances while tapping their toes in the two-inch bed of sawdust underfoot.

"Any problems?"

"No, just the usual drinking and whooping it up. Good bluegrass band tonight, wasn't it, Griff?" Phil said in an obvious attempt to draw his friend into the conversation.

Griff nodded. "You ladies want to stop for coffee?"

I already felt like a balloon ready to burst and was in no mood to add a full bladder to my discomfort. However, it was obvious that I would be outvoted. A game was afoot. So, we piled into Phil's Blazer and headed away from the development-gone-wild Coastal Highway into the old section of Lewes.

Lewes is the oldest town in Delaware, first settled by the Dutch in 1631. Situated on Delaware Bay just north of Cape Henlopen, where the Bay joins the Atlantic Ocean, the town remained a sleepy fishing village for three and half centuries. Over the past few years, it has worked to reinvent itself as a tourist destination. As the western terminus of the Cape May-Lewes ferry, Lewes strives to emulate its chi-chi counterpart on the New Jersey side of the Bay with antique shops, boutiques, eateries, historic homes and sport fishing charters within walking distance of the town center.

Though quiet in the off-season, a few places stay open to entertain browsers and those of us who enjoy beach walks in the winter sun and wind. One such place, a coffee house on Second Street, was enjoying brisk business from post-Eat and post-Feast revelers seeking a place to wind down.

"Phil says you're a dog trainer. How'd you get started in that?" Griff asked Peg when we'd squeezed around a small table, cappuccinos in hand.

Peg sipped. "I've always competed in obedience with my dogs. When I got out of college, I worked in a medical lab but I hated it. The only time I was happy was when I was working my dogs. Other people were always asking me to help them train their dogs, too. So I decided to try it as a business. After a while, I made enough money to quit the lab. That's all I've done since then."

"This dog you're working with now, I hear he's something else. A Chessie, right?" Griff asked.

"Yeah, a Chessie. He is special." Peg's face lit up as it always does when Teke's the subject. "I'd like to take credit, but it's really all Teke. He's the easiest dog I've ever trained. I only have to tell him once. Like, I'll show him some object, a milk jug for example, and I'll say to him, 'Teke, this is a milk jug. Now remember that.' Then later, I'll say, 'Teke, go get the milk jug.' And he knows exactly what I'm talking about and he'll go get it."

"Teke. That's an unusual name."

"It's short for Tikam," she said, pronouncing TEE-kahm. "It's Lenape, the language of the Lenape—or Delaware—tribe. It means, 'Defend her!' Actually, Teke's full name is Ch./OTCh Welashuwill Tikam, CGC, TD, OA. Those are all his American Kennel Club titles." She grinned.

Griff's eyes widened. He understood the letters—Ch. for Champion, OTCh for Obedience Trial Champion, CGC for Canine Good Citizen, TD for Tracking Dog, and OA for Open Agility. Moreover, he understood the significance of the letters—the effort that went into earning the right to append them to Teke's name.

"What does way-LAH-shoe-will mean?" Griff asked, carefully imitating Peg's pronunciation.

"It's his breeder's kennel name. It means 'the one who swims well.' The breeder is part Lenape and she names all her dogs with Lenape names."

"Griff's in K-9, too," Phil interjected, apparently for my benefit as he was looking pointedly at me.

"Oh?" I murmured, nodding in a socially acceptable manner.

Griff pulled his wallet out of his back pocket, fished out a snapshot and slid it toward the center of the table. Flanked by two little girls, a handsome German Shepherd smiled toothily from pricked ear to pricked ear.

I warmed instantly. "What's his name?"

"Thor," he answered. "And those are my twins, Alie and Leia. They're seven," he added, retrieving the photo and tucking it back in his wallet.

"Cute kids. Nice dog," Peg commented.

"Thanks."

"Does Thor sniff out bombs, too?" I asked.

"Thor is cross-trained—which means he can do all police work—but his specialty is tracking."

"Oh? I thought they used Bloodhounds for that," I said, sipping my coffee.

"Well, yes, that's right, but Bloodhounds work a different way," Griff explained. "A Bloodhound can scent discriminate—you know, track a specific person based on that person's scent on some clothing or other object. Thor just follows the freshest human scent. It's my job to find a place to start him, like a place where a suspect was last seen."

"Is it true they love to work more than anything?" I asked.

"Yeah. Thor is just a normal, friendly dog at home. A real goof in fact. But when he gets in the cruiser, he changes into a different dog.

He's all business. Totally focused. He just goes nuts when I say, 'Let's go get bad guys.' He can't wait to get on the job and he hates it when I leave the house in uniform without him, like when I have to appear in court."

"Has he actually caught a lot of criminals?" I asked but I was thinking, not bad looking.

He nodded. "He's had twelve apprehensions in three years on the job." He slid the wallet into the back pocket of his jeans, which my sidelong glance told me were nicely and tightly fitted. "Do you have dogs, too?"

I smiled and fished in my handbag for my wallet.

"He's good-looking," Peg remarked an hour later, en route back to her house.

"Yeah, nice Shepherd," I said blandly, just to irk her.

She didn't take the bait but pursued her thought. "Nice build. Gorgeous blue eyes. And that prematurely silver hair is very attractive." She mugged in the rear view mirror and primped her own silver hair. I smiled. "Quiet but kinda witty," she continued. "Phil says he's a good guy. He used to be a teacher—some kind of science, I think—but decided he wanted to be in law enforcement. So, he just up and quit teaching and went to the academy."

My brief marriage to Brian, aka the rat, had left me fairly well turned off men. Not that I don't appreciate looking at them, and Griff was certainly decent to look at. And, I had to admit I'd had a distinctly favorable reaction to a man who pulls out a photo of his dog. In an hour's conversation, I had learned that he's a little older than me—39 to my 33. Like me, he's divorced, and the ex-wife and twin girls live in Pennsylvania. A definite point in his favor was that his eyes hadn't glazed over when I said I was a dealer in Asian antiquities. He'd even managed a couple intelligent questions about samurai. But, best of all, like me, he's a dog lover. I toyed with the idea for a moment.

"Well, we'll see," I said and changed the subject. Peg knew me well enough to leave it alone. Annoy me and I get stubborn, sort of like a Tibbie.

A cold front had passed through. It was a chilly night, but I like fresh, cool air and night sounds. I pushed aside the heavy lace curtains and cracked the bedroom window, gazing out over the lawn through the wavy glass. The wind had died and the trees were still. An almost-full moon illuminated the lawn with a silvery sheen.

In Tibet, where even the valleys lie at 14,000 feet, Tibbies kept their humans warm in the frigid nights. Like their Tibetan forebears, Dawa and Senge are consummate bed dogs. When I slid between the sheets, Dawa had already taken up her position in a curl on the pillow next to mine. Senge promptly climbed the bed stairs and joined us on my walnut four-poster. He scratched diligently at the comforter for a few moments, to fluff it just so, circled once and plopped next to me with a heavy sigh.

I stared up at the crocheted canopy, an heirloom handmade by my Great-Aunt Elizabeth, thinking about nothing, waiting for shrimp to digest and sleep to come. My hand rested on Senge's silken coat.

"She forgot to give us our bedtime biscuit," Senge mumbled with a sigh.

"Oh, Brother, all you think about is your stomach." Dawa said nothing for a moment and then observed, "That human who smelled like a cigarette had a liver treat."

"Mmmm, I like liver," Senge said, rolling onto his back and licking his lips.

"Yes, I know! I had to stop you eating that liver."

"Why did stop me, Sister?"

"Because the human dropped the liver so that Teke would follow and go outside. I had to show Mom the liver." She paused. "Did you smell Teke's back leg? It smelled sick."

"Teke is tough. All his kind are," Senge said dismissively.

"Yes, they are. But Mom is worried, Brother," Dawa replied.

"If I go and woof at the biscuit jar, do you think she will get up and give us a biscuit, Sister?"

" 'A human is always in trouble and a dog is always hungry'," Dawa quoted the old Tibetan proverb, rolling onto her back with a grunt and a sigh.

"Sh-h-h, Tibbies. Time for sleep now," I said. They settled. The okimono, which by now had found its way to the antique English washstand at my bedside, kept watch.

Chapter Five

Surprise! I pressed my nose to the wavy glass of my bedroom window. A spring snow had fallen overnight and blanketed the ground below with three inches. I was eager to get outside. My shower could wait.

The Tibbies bounded into the yard. Like the dogs of northern lands, Tibbies are well-adapted to cold. Their fuzzy undercoat acts as insulation while the longer overcoat shields them from the wet. Even their toes grow long hair, called slippers or sometimes snowshoes, to protect their paws and improve traction in rough, ice terrain.

We three enjoyed a romp through the hushed woods followed by a brisk circuit around the glassy pond rimmed with a thin crust of ice. By the time oatmeal was bubbling on the stove an hour later, the snow on the roof was melting away and the trees were dripping. That's the usual way with snow on Delmarva–short-lived.

The morning's snow was barely in evidence when I ushered Senge and Dawa through the door of All Creatures Great and Small Veterinary Hospital, Doc Twilley's clinic, early that afternoon. One other patron sat in a corner of the tiny waiting room. An invisible creature occupied the cat-size carrier next to her feet.

I nodded to her and positioned myself on the "dog side" of the room. Unfortunately, the woman's mere presence provoked Senge and Dawa to wiggle and whine incessantly since their mission in life is to convert all cat people to dog people. They persisted until I distracted them with a bribe in the form of a biscuit produced from my pocket. The cat person bucked her eyes.

At that moment, Doc Twilley's receptionist, a blond girl of about eighteen, emerged through the door labeled Exam Room 1. "Can I help you?" she greeted me as she skirted around behind the counter. I gave her my name, which she tapped on the keyboard.

"Dawa and Senge are just here for shots?" she asked, struggling to pronounce their names.

Before I could manage an answer, we all jumped. Somewhere in the clinic, a door had slammed hard. The dogs barking in the boarding kennel out back fell silent for a moment. Senge and Dawa ceased their begging for another biscuit and pricked their ears.

"I guess something fell," the girl murmured, turning back to her keyboard. I nodded but I couldn't help but notice the sound of an engine revving and the sound of tires skidding on gravel outside the clinic. A glance through the window revealed a brown Jeep speeding across the parking lot. Nothing unusual about that. Jeeps and all other manner of sport utility vehicles are ubiquitous on Delmarva, a status symbol here as elsewhere in the country.

As the Jeep pulled onto Swann's Creek Road, I noticed the black license plate with white numbers. A black license plate is a distinctly Delawarean status symbol. The lower the tag number on an antique plate, the greater the prestige. People pay vast sums of money for bona fide lower number tags, even willing them to their heirs for generations. The genuine black tag is so sought after that illegal "knock-offs" are nothing unusual either.

A moment later, Doc Twilley peeked out of Exam Room 1 and beckoned the other patient. I glimpsed a sealpoint Siamese, with stunning blue eyes, when she passed by me into the Exam Room.

When she emerged ten minutes later, I couldn't resist remarking, "Pretty Siamese. I had one the whole time I was growing up. Nicest cat I ever had. He lived to be 19," I said truthfully.

"Thanks. Cute dogs," she parried.

"Thanks," I said, smiling widely. I am extremely proud of my Tibbies.

"You can go in now," the receptionist said, motioning me toward Exam Room 1.

Doc Twilley had been my family's vet for my entire lifetime, and I'm 33. I was wondering how old Doc Twilley is when he came into the room. His white hair says 70 but his lean, muscular build and smooth movement bespeaks years less than that. He's probably about the same age as my father, I concluded. Dad would have been 72 this year. Even though I love my work, I couldn't imagine working until 72.

At 6' 4", Doc towers over my 5'5". He once told me he played semi-professional basketball in his youth. He must have been very handsome as a young man, too. Even now he is attractive, his large brown eyes and tanned skin a striking contrast to a full head of glossy white hair. Miz Doc Twilley, as everyone called his wife, had passed away about five years ago. All the local widows must be after him, I thought, as I lifted the two Tibbies onto the examining table.

Doc Twilley leaned over so that Dawa and Senge could reach his chin to bestow greeting licks. "Good dogs," he said, roughing Senge's mane and tickling Dawa's chin. When I'd first brought them back from England, he'd told me they were the first Tibbies he'd ever seen but they'd soon charmed him the as they invariably did everyone else.

"Any problems?" he asked.

"No, not really. I've noticed that Senge snores but it's just a soft, quiet snore," I remarked.

"Well, that's probably a slightly elongated soft palate. It happens in these little fellas with short muzzles. Any trouble breathing?"

"No, none," I said. "He would run for miles if I let him."

"Good. Well, now, let's just listen to these tickers," he said and applied the stethoscope first to Dawa and then Senge. Doc had never been one to use medical terms overmuch. "Sounds good," he pronounced. He then carefully felt over their bodies and peered into their ears and mouths. "Well, everything seems fine. I'll just do the vaccinations now."

While Doc was preparing the injections, I mentioned that Teke seemed to be fine in spite of the accident and that the commercials were coming along well. "He was a lucky dog—lucky not to have been hurt worse, I mean," I said.

Doc looked at me blankly and murmured, "Yes, lucky." He gave Dawa her shot. She wagged her tail.

It struck me that Doc might not remember the connection between myself and Teke. "Peg Beauchamp is a close friend of mine," I added.

"Oh, that's right," he said, thumping his head as if to say 'how could I forget that.' "You two went to high school together, didn't you? Graduated with Mike?"

I nodded. Mike was Doc's younger son. I'd heard he was a software engineer now and lived out in California. I asked after Mike and learned that his wife had just produced Doc's third grandbaby, a daughter.

"So, how's Don?" I also asked, wondering if Doc's older, wilder son had ever settled down.

"Well, you know Don," he shook his head. "It took him a while, but he finally found a place he liked–Colorado. Has a good job in financial planning. Karen and he have two boys. But I don't see either of them much. Mike gets home once a year, in the summer, but Don hasn't been home in, oh, three years now."

He turned away. "Well now, are you keeping these dogs on heartworm preventative year round?"

"Yes, every month all year," I replied, but I was thinking that it was too bad Don doesn't get home more often now that Miz Doc is gone.

"Good. Never know when those damn mosquitoes are gonna wake up," he said, alluding to the fact that mosquitoes transmit the heartworm.

"Bass will be out soon, too," I said, smiling. In addition to prints of sporting dogs and veterinary information posters, Doc's waiting room walls were adorned with citations. He and his Tracker were a regular fixture on Swann's Pond.

He smiled and his cheeks colored. "Oh, yes. I can't wait to get out on the water. Just a few more days. I'm going to several tournaments this spring." He winked at me and patted the dogs. "All done."

When I returned to the waiting room, two wiggly puppies—a Weimaraner and a mixed breed—and two cats were waiting with their people. I made out the check and handed it to the receptionist. "You're busy today," I observed, "Where's Dr. Lynch?"

"I guess she's off today," she mumbled unhelpfully. I watched as she keyed my payment into the computer and printed out a receipt and a vaccination certificate for each Tibbie.

The cold snap that brought the snow passed quickly, followed by a couple breezy but spring-like days. The dogwoods and maples sprang into bud, and grape hyacinths popped out of the ground overnight. Of course, my least favorite spring event was just around the corner—the grass would inevitably start growing lush and green, and I would have to be forced to back the lawn tractor out of the carriage house.

Doc Twilley was right on more than one score. Swann's Pond was soon busy with anglers and the mosquitoes woke up. I didn't see Doc out on the pond when I took the dogs on their morning walk, but I suspected he had been and gone by the time I got there.

I didn't see Peg or Teke either, but she called me every night to fill me in on Teke's exploits. She was elated about the shoot at Assateague Island. An offshore island far south on the peninsula, Assateague bridges the Maryland-Virginia border and has both a National Seashore and state park on it. It is renowned for its bands of Chincoteague ponies. According to a popular legend, the wild ponies are descended from horses that swam ashore from a wrecked Spanish galleon. For centuries, the sturdy animals roamed the island park's dunes and marshes, little known off Delmarva until Marguerite Henry's book *Misty of Chincoteague* immortalized them in the minds of children everywhere.

The day of the shoot had been, as Peg explained it, one of those God-given days that occasionally happens by sea, a day when the quality of light is so wonderful that it hurts your eyes. The park authorities, who'd been reluctant to grant permission for the shoot in the first place, had been adamant that the film crew not approach the ponies because they don't want the public to get the idea that it's OK to harass the animals. When the park ranger chaperone located a small band of ponies grazing, Teke was positioned on a dune in the foreground, well away from but overlooking the mares and foals. The shimmering ocean formed the backdrop. While the crew went quietly about its business, Teke sat motionless on the dune. However, one of the foals became curious and approached Teke. The crew held its collective breath.

"I gave Teke the steely eye and he didn't even blink," Peg said. "Nobody moved and, luckily, the foal's dam was busy grazing and just ignored the situation. The foal got within a couple feet and reached out his muzzle toward Teke. Then he skittered back down the dune to his mother. I don't know if they'll use it or not, but I was so proud of Teke. He's such a good boy."

Peg also mentioned that she had seen an early version of the St. Michael's commercial. When she didn't rush to volunteer any information, I asked how she liked it.

"Well, I don't know exactly. I'm ambivalent," she said.

"Why is that?" I asked, prodding.

"Oh, the photography is beautiful. Really. They show scenes around St. Michaels—the lighthouse, sailboats, the old Inn over in Oxford. And Teke is beautiful. They used the scene on the skipjack, the one you saw us shooting, and another one we shot a couple days later, where he's jumping into the water after a duck," she said.

She cleared her throat and continued, "The only thing that sort of bothers me is that, in the last scene, they made Teke's mouth move like he's talking and dubbed a voice for him. You know, like in those commercials for cat food." She paused. "I don't know why it's bothering me so much. I think it's just that Teke has such great dignity and it just makes him look like a clown."

"What does he say?"

"Oh, it's nothing that bad, really. He's sitting with Miss Maryland, Miss Delaware and Miss Virginia. They're on this sailboat, the wind in their hair like—you know—looking gorgeous and cuddling Teke. They say this bit about the beauties of the Bay. Then, right at the end, Teke says, 'And the crabs are good, too' and then he licks his lips."

"Are they going to do this in all of them?"

"They said they might, if the tourism people like this first one," she replied.

"Well, Peg, my advice is don't worry about it," I said. "They're in the business of drumming up business. And I guess talking animals are popping up in all the commercials because they sell a lot of whatever. Let's just hope they keep it tasteful—you know, no wolf whistles at half-dressed girls or anything else immature."

She groaned at the thought. We fell silent for a moment. She mentioned that the shoot in Dover had been delayed until Friday and asked if I wanted to meet her for lunch. Delaware's capital is home to Dover International speedway, where one of the state's three slots casinos, along with horse-racing and NASCAR™ races, generate mega-revenue. She knew that the film crew would be shooting at the casino and track but wasn't sure how they planned to use Teke to promote these attractions.

We made a date to meet for lunch at Tio's, our favorite Mexican restaurant, on Friday after the shoot.

Chapter Six

"Come on, kids. Time for your walk," I called. The thunder of little paws could be heard descending the staircase. "Sleepy heads," I chastised the dancing Tibbies.

Pulling the dogs' leads from a hook at the backdoor, I stuffed them in my jacket pocket and opened the door. The Tibbies raced for the gate.

Friday had dawned absolutely gorgeous—a perfect spring day. It was the kind of morning that made me want to stand still and take deep breaths because the simple act of breathing the warm, sweet air was so pleasurable. I paused to admire the purple, white and yellow crocuses that Mom had planted along the footpath to Swann's Pond many years ago. Despite the best efforts of the voles, they had multiplied ever since.

Tim West, who leases the field from me, was already out that morning, encased in the cab high atop his bright green and yellow John Deere. Deep furrows appeared in the tractor's wake. We waved to each other. A flock of gulls dipped and soared behind the tractor, harvesting the worms and other creatures the plow brought to surface in the turned earth.

Weekdays are always quiet in the park. We passed no one on the trail. Swann Pond sparkled like diamonds that morning. No pond could have been lovelier. I squinted to make out a fisherman silhouetted against the newly risen sun. He raised his hand. Must be Doc out there, I thought and waved back. Meanwhile, the Tibbies occupied themselves with more mundane matters, poking their noses here, there and everywhere.

Back at the house, another box of objects awaited my analysis in the dining room. As soon as I cut the packing tape and lifted the first flap, fond memories of three years before came flowing back. The box contained the meager gleanings of my last trip to England. I had gone with intentions of bidding on several objects at a London auction house and visiting a couple of well-known British dealers. I had come home with Asian treasures I hadn't imagined.

It had been another such lovely spring day when I paid a visit to the Devonshire home of a Mrs. Brent, renowned collector of Chinese antiquities. I had made the appointment by telephone some months in advance and appeared at Mrs. Brent's door on the agreed upon day and time. The housekeeper, who introduced herself as Mrs. Brittingham, greeted me. While waiting in the drawing room, perched on an elegant 18th century settee in the Chinese style and shamelessly feasting my eyes on an 18th century lacquered cabinet, I was startled by a small golden dog hurtling across the exquisite Persian rug. She launched herself into my lap and licked the air furiously while scrambling over my chest to reach my face.

"Emma!" scolded the flustered housekeeper, scurrying into the room a moment later. "I'm sorry, Miss Swann. Emma just loves to come greet all our visitors. Emma, you naughty girl, stop that!"

Emma, whom I surmised was a Pekingese, paid absolutely no heed to Miss Brittingham's admonitions. Having accomplished her goal of kissing me on the cheek, she circled once and peremptorily plopped into my lap, the very picture of perfection.

The housekeeper made shooing motions. Emma ignored those as well.

"It's quite all right, Miss Brittingham. She's not bothering me. She's very pretty," I said, patting the small dog's silken head.

However, Emma bounced off my lap a moment later when Mrs. Brent entered the room. Dancing on her hind legs while Mrs. Brent and I shook hands, she promptly sat at her owner's feet as soon we took our seats.

I had grown up with the dogs my father brought home and established in the kennels that used to be behind the carriage house. They were Labs and Beagles for the most part, with one Jack Russell terrier thrown in. But I had never met such a charming creature as Emma. I could not help but say so to Mrs. Brent.

"Ah yes, Tibbies are quite enchanting," she agreed, reaching down to stroke Emma's ears.

"Tibbies?"

"Yes, that's right. Emma is a Tibetan Spaniel. We call them Tibbies. Do you know the breed?" she asked.

In a reply that now embarrasses me, I blurted, "Oh, I thought she was a Pekingese."

To give Mrs. Brent credit, such a *faux pas* would have caused many Tibetan Spaniel breeders to dismiss me out of hand. But the gracious lady replied by patiently explaining some of the ancient origins of the breed and their probable ancestry to the Pekingese later developed by the Chinese. She also lifted Emma into her lap and instructed me on the physical differences between the breeds.

"She is possibly the most irresistible little dog I have ever seen," I said truthfully. "That bright little monkey face is so appealing, and her personality is so sweet." By this time, I was gushing.

"Thank you. Emma is eleven years old but still behaves like a much younger bitch. That is one of the breed's finer qualities, you know— youthful longevity. I hope to have Emma's company a few more years." She paused, observing me, and then continued, "Actually, Emma is the dowager of my Tibbies. I have a number of her descendents as I have bred Tibbies for many years. Would you like to meet them?" she asked, placing Emma onto the floor.

Looking back on the scene in my mind's eye, I see now that I fairly leapt to my feet, the lacquer cabinet and my quest for a choice object wholly forgotten. We passed through the family rooms at the back of the house and exited to a covered walkway that adjoined the main house to a smaller building in the same Tudor style as the house. This, Mrs. Brent informed me, was her kennel building. She wished to have as many of her Tibbies in the house as possible but, having so many at present, had converted the former stable into a kennel building.

I have since learned that Mrs. Brent is as well-known as a breeder of Tibetan Spaniels as she is as a connoisseur and collector of Asian antiquities. Being ignorant of that, however, I was unprepared for the onrush of beautiful dogs as we entered the kennel. I imagine there were about twenty, of all colors, and they sent up a racket of greeting, tearing back and forth between Mrs. Brent and myself. In short order, the Tibbies had sniffed me up and down, as well as their limited stature permitted, lost interest and trotted outside into the fenced grassy yard surrounding the building.

Mrs. Brent introduced me to each of her dogs by call name and registered name, sire and dam and accomplishments. In all honesty, I became quite confused but listened attentively to each biography, nodding respectfully.

One dog in particular attracted my eye for his regal demeanor. He was rather haughty when I met him, cutting his eyes away and turning up his nose at me. Smiling, Mrs. Brent explained that aloofness with strangers is not unusual in the breed. His name is Dudley, Mrs. Brent continued, a champion and her best stud dog.

"In fact, I have just received one of his offspring from the dam's owner in Scotland. Would you like to see him?" she asked but didn't wait for my answer before beckoning and leading me to another section of the building.

"This is Dash," she said handing over a dark gold puppy. I cuddled the sleepy-headed 12-week-old puppy, just awakened from a nap. In retrospect, I now know that, from that minute forward, I became completely obsessed with Tibbies.

Despite the many dogs of my childhood, I knew little about pure-bred dogs. I realize now how ridiculous my unabashed pleas to purchase Dash must have sounded to Mrs. Brent. "It is simply not possible," she said kindly but firmly. Although he was still quite young, she explained that Dash was the "pick" of his litter and a puppy of great potential as a show dog and stud. She could not possibly sell him to become someone's pet.

Coming back to the present, I looked down at the Chinese foo dog, a carved representation of a lion-like dog, that I had just unwrapped from its bubble wrap. This was the object that I bought from Mrs. Brent that day, but I barely recall our negotiations. I have rarely been as disappointed as when I walked away from Dash. I could not stop thinking about him. Everything else I'd planned for this trip had evaporated from my mind. After a restless night at my bed-and-breakfast, I phoned Mrs. Brent early in the morning. I somehow persuaded her that my desire to take home a Tibetan Spaniel was sincere and asked for her advice on how to proceed.

Ethical breeders are wary of the impulse buyer who may purchase a puppy on the spur of the moment and then tire of it just as easily. Looking back, it astonishes me that Mrs. Brent did not hang up on me. Instead, she listened to my "qualifications" as I saw them—large country home, fenced property, veterinary practice three miles away, job that allows me lots of time at home, and so on.

"Miss Swann, I must tell you that the Tibetan Spaniel is not for everyone," Mrs. Brent said.

Her remark took me aback. "I'm sorry, I don't understand."

"Well, frankly, they can be quite the most obstinate and on occasion disobedient little dogs, bent on having their own way."

"Oh?"

"Yes. One must also be tolerant of the shedding and also of the noise as they do tend to bark, though usually justifiably," she said, "The worst of it is that they will run away if you give them but half a chance and are quite clever at escaping whatever manner of enclosure you devise."

"Oh."

I suppose the depth of disappointment in that single word must have caused her to take pity on me. "Of course, for a person who has the proper temperament to deal with such annoyances, they are a delightful, enchanting breed." She paused. "Perhaps you should think it over and, if you are still interested, ring me back."

I hesitated only a moment. "I understand that you are trying to present a balanced picture, Mrs. Brent," I began slowly, "but I assure you that I am very sincere and that I am not in the least bit impulsive. On the contrary, I am a very cautious person. Even with what you have said, I am convinced that I would love this breed and I would very much appreciate your help in locating a puppy to purchase."

She hesitated audibly. "Very well then, Miss Swann, where may I contact you?"

"I'm at Trevil House on the B684," I replied.

"Yes, I know Mrs. Foxwell at the Trevil. Let me ring the dam's owner and I'll ring you back," she said and the line clicked.

So that was why, when I returned to London that afternoon, I did not head for the auction house but stopped at my hotel just long enough to collect the rest of my luggage and check out. Within an hour, I was on the overnight train to Edinburgh. Mrs. Brent had told me that the dam's owner, a Mrs. Thompson, may be willing to consider selling me one of Dash's littermates and gave me directions to her home. The next morning I found myself in a hired car dodging morning traffic en route to a village near St. Andrews.

"I have two that are not spoken for," Mrs. Thompson informed me in her soft Scottish accent, as we passed through her cottage to the back garden. "I had planned to keep them to show and breed," she added, looking at me pointedly. The point was lost on me at the time, but I now know that this was a broad hint that those destined for a show career are more costly. Not that I cared. "Do you show in America?" she asked.

"No, m'am."

"Hmmm." She sighed. "Ah well. Here they are."

Six or seven Tibbies ranging in color from cream to gold greeted me at the back door. Among them were two bright-eyed youngsters. One, a golden boy with white paws and a blaze on his forehead, was the image of his brother Dash. There must have been differences between them that made Dash the preferred puppy, but, to my unknowledgeable eye, they were identical. I was instantly in love.

At Mrs. Thompson's invitation, I sat on a bench and picked up the little male. He clamored up my chest and kissed me on the face. Between the puppy's kisses, Mrs. Thompson questioned my suitability, and I recited my qualifications and references.

"You want him then?" she asked brusquely and, to my answering nod, she quoted me a price. I agreed without a moment's hesitation. "Well, Mrs. Brent says you're all right and you seem all right to me as well, though I would prefer you show him." She paused and looked at me. I looked back with an expression of mute appeal. "So, we may as well go in then and review the contract," she said, rising and striding back to the cottage.

When I leaned over to reluctantly place my little boy on the grass, I was stunned to see that his sister was sitting on my foot and staring into my eyes with what can only be described as a hurt expression on her face. She was more diminutive than my strapping boy puppy—so petite that I hadn't felt her weight through my sturdy walking shoes—and a striking creamy white color with golden patches. She lifted one forepaw and delicately placed it against my shin, curling her toes ever so slightly so that her sharp little nails could be felt through my jeans.

Oh my, I thought, she is beautiful. I was doubly smitten.

"Oh, Mrs. Thompson," I called to her retreating back, "The little girl is very sweet, too. Isn't she an unusual color?"

"Aye," answered the lady, turning back, "She's what we call a particolor—that is, mostly white with markings of another color. She's a quiet one, not as rambunctious as the others. She's coming a bit too undershot, which is why I'm letting her go to a pet home."

"Oh dear," I said under my breath, looking from the little girl to the little boy and back again. The girl puppy's eyes never left me. She showed me her lower teeth. While Mrs. Thompson might have regarded this as too pronounced an underbite, I knew instinctively it was a Tibbie smile.

"Mrs. Thompson, I don't suppose you'd consider letting me have both of these puppies, would you?" I asked in a small voice.

I came back from my reverie and looked over at Dawa and Senge. I went to England in search of antiques, but my two most precious acquisitions from that trip were not packed in the box on the table but perched atop the sofa back. Two little babies I'd called Dawa and Senge had accompanied me on the flight home in a sherpa bag on my lap. Senge slept on, but Dawa was watching me with her magical eyes, just as she had that day in Scotland. I smiled. She smiled back.

Chapter Seven

I turned off U.S. 13 and headed toward the stadium looming ahead. This was Dover International Speedway, home of the NASCAR™ Monster Mile. I crept along, looking right and left, unsure where to go. I spotted Peg's pickup in a nearly empty section of the massive parking lot, but there was no sign of life. I spied one of the now familiar white Three Guys vans in the far distance and headed for it. A gate blocked my way, and I stopped. A man in a red, white and blue jump suit sauntered over as I lowered my window.

"Can I help you, m'am?" he said in an officially polite tone of voice, leaning over slightly to look at me.

"Yes, thanks. Um. I'm supposed to meet someone here," I said, mustering an air of confidence. "I'm with the dog star in the commercials." I don't know why I said that. It sounded stupid coming out, but it had the desired effect on the guard.

"Sure thing, m'am. Go right on through, straight ahead and then to your right. They're all over there." He embellished his directions with official looking hand signals.

"Thanks," I said, smiling, and took off.

When I made the final turn, I found my way blocked again by a large crowd that I had now come to recognize as the ever-present spectators who are attracted to filings. I parked beside a Three Guys van and got out.

Adults who are as short as I am invariably see nothing at events where crowds gather. Since we no longer qualify as children, adults of greater stature pretend not to see us from their lofty heights and remain rooted to the ground in front of us—even though our standing in front of them would not impede their view in the slightest. Offered the usual choice of mid-back and shoulder-blade views, I decided to assert myself. "Excuse me," I said politely and, leading with my shoulder, managed to gently wedge my way to the front without provoking any rude comments.

I caught sight of Peg off to the left and behind the camera. Her eyes were riveted on Teke. Teke was sitting next to a man sporting an eye-popping orange, black and white jumpsuit, emblazoned with

45

advertisement patches, and matching ball cap. A similarly decorated and color coordinated race car sat behind man and dog. It was like a scene from *Days of Thunder*. In point of fact, the driver was a Tom Cruise look-alike. I wondered if he was a real driver or an actor playing a driver.

From where I stood, I could see that the driver was speaking but could not hear what he said. He then crouched and draped his arm over Teke's shoulders. Teke delivered a lick to the man's cheek right on cue. The driver did a double-take at Teke, laughed, and, turning back to the camera, continued his speech. I saw Peg lift one finger of her right hand and Teke barked. That must have been the end of the take because the driver stood up and the crew began to mill.

I seized the moment to make my move. Avoiding a man carrying a walkie-talkie whose outstretched hand appeared to be exerting invisible control over the spectators, I sidled away from the crowd and began a flanking move toward Peg. "M'am. M'am. Can I help you?" said the walkie-talkie man. On a hunch, I blurted, "Hi. I'm with the dog star and I'm really late." I tossed back a brilliant smile and kept moving. It worked, again.

"Hey Peg," I whispered, coming up behind her. She turned and smiled hello before returning her attention to Teke. They seemed to be running through the same scene as before. Maybe the driver flubbed his lines, I thought, and posed myself to look as though I belonged.

"This here's my buddy Teke," the driver said as he crouched to drape the friendly arm over Teke's shoulders. Teke delivered his lick, and the driver did his double-take and laugh. "Ol' Teke here is friendly just like all the good people here on Delmarva. So come on down and see why folks call this the land of pleasant living. Right, Teke?"

"Woof," said Teke.

"Cut," said Steve the director. He'd shed the flannel shirt he wore in St. Michaels and now sported a NASCAR™ tee-shirt. "Great job, Bobby," he said, walking over and slapping the driver on the back. "That's it, everybody. Let's take lunch. Be back at two o'clock."

Peg called Teke over and hugged him. "Good boy," she crooned to Teke and to me she said, "Well, that's it for today," she said.

"You don't have to come back at two o'clock?"

"No, this afternoon they're just shooting some footage of the car going around the track. We already did the casino this morning," she said, fastening Teke's rolled leather collar around his neck. The speedway was only one of the attractions. The adjacent "entertainment complex" also boasted a casino with slots and Vegas-style headliners.

"So, what did Teke do in the casino?"

"They had him sit up at a slot machine and press the button, then look over at the camera," she said and rolled her eyes dramatically.

"Sounds like they're going to do another one of those dogspeak scenes," I said.

"Yeah, I guess so," she answered, attaching Teke's lead to his collar. It was clear my friend relished training a dog star but was worried that the final cuts of the commercials would make him look foolish.

Since Tio's was within sight, on the other side of the vast parking lot, Peg decided not to move her pickup. She motioned Teke into the cab. We left him settling down to a nap, curled on his favorite sheepskin, and hopped in my car for the short ride to the restaurant.

"Somebody must have paid a fortune for Bobby Craddock to come appear in this commercial. He's a top competitor," Peg said as we sat down on opposite sides of a table in Tio's.

"Mmmm," I mumbled non-committally, having no clue who Bobby Craddock was. "So, that guy wasn't an actor?" I asked and grabbed a menu, "My teeth have been set for this all day!"

"Mine, too," Peg agreed before she crunched down on a warm tortilla chip dipped in salsa. "No, he's a real NASCAR™ driver. Want to split an order of quesadillas?"

Lunch was leisurely. We chattered about our businesses. Between mouthfuls, Peg revealed that she was mulling over an estimate on a new training building. The contractor had recommended razing her old kennel building, which was really just a converted chicken house, and incorporating a kennel room within the new metal building. The plan also called for space for an office and a large mirrored room that could be partitioned into two areas so that two classes could take place simultaneously.

"Why two classes? Are you planning to hire another trainer?" I asked.

"Yeah. You." When she saw my mouth drop open, she hurriedly added, "Just kidding. No, I'm not planning on hiring anybody—not right now anyway. But I was thinking that as long as I was building, I should plan way ahead. Maybe some club will lease the space from me for classes. A couple of them have asked me about using the studio."

For my part, I confided that the mall sales had been disappointing, but then I hadn't expected to do much business in March. I hoped for an upswing as the tourist season grew nearer. Besides, flyers announcing the opening of my new location and debut of my web page would be going out to all my clients in a couple weeks.

We finished up by splitting a fried ice cream and the bill.

Back in my car, Peg asked if I'd heard from Griff. I shook my head.

"Really? I thought he would have called you by now. Phil said he was pretty impressed," she commented.

I shrugged. She dropped the subject.

I cut across the parking lot toward Peg's truck. It's hard to imagine this place is packed with RV's and campers during race weeks. Some race fans even park their rigs in the prime spots as much as two months ahead of time. But, today it was deserted except for Peg's pickup. I pulled up to the driver's side door.

Peg slid out of my car, poking her head back in with a final reminder to call her, and slammed the door. I glanced toward her as she slid the key in the door lock but then looked away and pressed down the accelerator. Just as my car moved forward, I heard Peg cry out and instinctively slammed my foot on the brake. I twisted around to see what was wrong and saw Peg's stricken face looking at me through the rear window.

I rammed the car in park, jumped out and ran to her. She was mute, in shock, just standing there staring at me. I looked over her shoulder and saw Teke's sheepskin still lay over the passenger seat where we left him napping, but there was no Teke. The cab was empty. I ran around to the passenger side. The lock had been forced and the door still stood slightly ajar.

I ran to my car and, leaning in, grabbed my cell phone and pressed "911." After reporting the stolen dog, I yelled at Peg to wait. "Don't touch anything! I'm going to get help." I slid behind the wheel and sped to the gate. The guard nodded in recognition. He waved me through, but I signaled him to the window.

"Teke, the dog star, has been stolen. Did you see anyone out in the parking lot over there, hanging around that red pickup?"

"Did you say that dog they was using was stole?" the guard asked.

"Yeah, that's right. Somebody broke into the truck. Did you see anything?"

The gatekeeper had a direct line of sight to the pickup but he shook his head. "No m'am. But I ain't been standin' here all this time. I was over there watchin'," he said, gesturing toward the small crowd that, judging from the noise, was watching a car revving its engine. "But them security cameras shoulda caught it. I'll call it in," he added.

While the guard spoke into his walkie-talkie, I glanced up at the surveillance cameras mounted around the parking lot. Fidgeting with impatience, I felt like I would explode if I didn't do something. Looking in my rear view mirror, I saw one of the speedway's private security cars speed across the parking lot toward Peg's truck.

The engine screaming escalated. I signaled to the guard that I was going through and he nodded. Creeping through the unaware spectators, I parked by one of the Three Guys vans and ran to the director. He had added a NASCAR™ cap to his ensemble, and his attention was focused on the approaching race car.

"Excuse me, Mr. Mitchell," I said, tapping him on the back.

"What?" he shouted over the noise and turned to look at me. His blank expression told me he had no clue who I was.

"I'm Peg's friend. Teke was stolen from Peg's truck just now, while we were at lunch."

"What'd you say?" he shouted, turning his ear toward me.

"I said Teke's been stolen. Someone broke into Peg's truck and took Teke." I shouted back. The shock registered on his face told me he'd heard me that time. The screaming receded into the distance as the car took the far turn. "Did you see anybody hanging around over lunch, anybody messing around her truck, anybody who looked funny? Did you see anybody with Teke?"

He shook his head and said something in reply, but his answer was drowned out by the car streaking by.

"Are you Steve Mitchell?" said a voice behind me. Turning, I saw a police officer had arrived to speak with the director and I decided to check on Peg.

Two hours later, I stopped by Swann's Nest just long enough to pack a nightshirt and a few indispensable toiletries for myself and a small bag of food and treats for the dogs. I tucked Dawa and Senge securely into their crates in the backseat. I didn't want Peg to spend the night alone. I had never seen her so inconsolable.

The sun had set when I turned off Cattail Road back onto Swann's Pond Road. The road was clear as far as I could see in both directions. I had just crossed the Swann's Pond bridge when the glare of halogen lights in my rearview mirror caused me to look up. Somebody was now riding on my rear bumper.

Idiot, I thought irritably and adjusted my mirror for night driving.

Growing impatient, the tailgater pulled out to pass me. Glancing at the vehicle as he sped by, I noticed it was a dark-colored Jeep with a lighter color soft top. As he veered abruptly back into my lane to avoid an oncoming car, my headlights fell full on his black and white Delaware tag—Number 019.

"Asshole," I said out loud. I was sick and tired of jerks doing 80 miles per hour on two-lane country roads. By the time I reached town, the Jeep had long since disappeared.

Peg let Bits and Dapper into the house. Instead of wild-dogging with Dawa and Senge, the dogs looked for Teke. Not finding him, they settled in front of the hot wood stove, their chins on their paws, their ears alternately pricking and flattening, their eyes following Peg's every movement. And moving she was. She couldn't sit still. She brought a log in from the patio and knelt to add it to the wood stove that occupied one end of the refurbished kitchen hearth. Poking vigorously, she eventually became satisfied with the fire and closed the stove.

The immense hearth was the centerpiece of her "sitting room," half of the spacious country kitchen that made up the back wing of her house. She stood staring at the objects on the mantle, a collection of Teke's trophies, ribbons, and show photos, and then absentmindedly switched on the TV next to the hearth. She hadn't said more than three words since I'd arrived and when she turned away from the hearth, the startled look on her face told me she'd forgotten I was here.

"Tea?" she asked. I didn't need to answer. She'd already sped across the room to the kitchen and clanked the kettle onto the burner.

I settled onto the overstuffed chair in front of the TV and hit the mute button on the remote.

"What did the police say, Peg?" I asked.

She shrugged. "They said they'd check it out. What else are they going to say?"

"What about the surveillance cameras they've got all over the place? Didn't they catch him on video?"

"I don't know. They just said they'd check it out."

"Did you tell them about Evelyn Hitchens?"

"Yeah, I did. They said they'd get somebody to go out to her place and question her."

"Well, that's good," I said. "You know, Peg, maybe you should call Phil. Couldn't he find out something?"

"I did. He said he'd be over later." She handed me a mug of hot water. When I got up to go the kitchen for a tea bag, the dogs' eyes followed me.

"Poor babies. They know something is wrong, but they can't understand why we are upset," I remarked.

This seemed to draw Peg out of her frenzy. She sat down on the floor in front of the hearth and drew Bits and Dapper to her side. Dawa and Senge took over her lap. She wrapped her left arm around Bits' neck and laid her cheek against Dapper's silky golden shoulder, letting the Tibbies wash her face.

I returned with my brewed tea and, sitting on the ottoman, aimed the remote at the silent TV. The six o'clock local news was on the local channel. A story about pollution of the inland bays by agricultural runoff was just wrapping up.

"Police in Dover are investigating the disappearance and apparent dog-napping of Teke, a 95-pound Chesapeake Bay Retriever, from Dover International Speedway between noon and two this afternoon," intoned the young female announcer.

"I called the station," Peg said, lifting her head from Dapper's comfortable shoulder.

"Last fall, Teke beat hundreds of dogs to be named spokesdog for Delmarva tourism. Police said he had finished filming a commercial when someone broke into his owner's truck and stole the dog. Dover police are looking for a late model Jeep in connection with this incident. Anyone with information should call 555-8777. A $1000 reward is being offered for Teke's safe return. And now, Steve, what's this I hear about the rain over the weekend?"

I punched the mute button again. "I guess they did catch something on the cameras. They said it was a Jeep."

"Yeah, and how many Jeeps are there in Delaware?" Peg said, burying her face in Dapper's ruff.

Dawa tilted her head at the TV screen, first to the right and then to the left. "Did you hear that? Someone stole Teke."

Senge broke off his cleaning of Peg's ear. "Sister, was it the stinky human who gave the liver to Teke?"

"I don't know, Brother," Dawa said. "They said it was a Jeep. A Jeep is a kind of car. The stinky human was in a car the color of cooked liver, but I don't know if it was a Jeep." She sighed and wrinkled her forehead.

" 'Even a dog knows his way home'," Senge quoted one of his Sister's many proverbs and resumed licking Peg's ear.

"I hope so," Dawa said. "But Chessies aren't as smart as we are, you know."

"What are they talking about?" Peg asked, distracted by the mutterings of the Tibbies.

"I don't know. Sometimes they just make the funniest sounds—rrr's, roo's, grunts and groans. Sometimes they sound just like the tribbles in that old episode of *Star Trek*. The breeder told me they're a talkative breed," I answered.

All four dogs lifted their heads and pricked their ears. A second later, they streaked to the patio door, barking furiously. When headlights flashed through the room, the dogs fell silent just long enough for us to hear a door slam in the driveway. The dogs resumed their chorus and dashed to new positions at the back door.

"Come on in," Peg hollered.

The two men made their way into the house slowly, surrounded by leaping dogs.

"Bits, Dapper, sit," Peg said quietly, and the big dogs planted their wiggly behinds on the floor. The Tibbies were roo'ing and dancing on their hind legs.

"Dawa, Senge, sit," I echoed. Their behinds brushed the floor for a millisecond before resuming their dance. I looked at Griff and shrugged.

"They are really cute," he said, hoisting Dawa up to his chest.

"Watch out. She'll snort on you!" I said quickly. No sooner were the words out of my mouth than Dawa stretched up and snorted in Griff's face. I pinked up. "I'm sorry. It's a Tibbie thing. They always clear their noses–the better to smell you with I guess–just before they kiss you."

"It's OK," he said, laughing and fending off Dawa's eager attempts to lick him on the mouth and nose. "I've had worse kisses. What did you say their names are?"

"Dawa and Senge. They're Tibetan names. Dawa means moon and Senge means lion," I answered.

"Hey fella," he said, placing Dawa on the floor and roughing up Senge's mane. Senge promptly dropped onto his side and rolled to present his belly for a rub. Determined not to be outdone, Dawa sat up on her haunches, placed her forepaws together, pad to pad, and began to circle them in a typically Tibbie motion. A chorus of "aw's" resulted.

"That's the Prayer Dog," I explained. "I didn't teach her that. It's just something she naturally does. I read on a web site about Tibbies that there's a legend about it. Back in old Tibet, these dogs lived in the Buddhist monasteries. According to the legend, they turned the prayer wheels in the monasteries. Prayer wheels are big cylinders mounted on spindles. Inside them are prayers written on paper and, as the cylinder spins, the prayers go up to Buddha. Anyway, that's why they're called Prayer Dogs."

Griff sat on the floor between the Tibbies and continued to scratch Senge's belly. "Are you praying, little girl?" he asked. Dawa stopped "praying," jumped into his lap, circled and plopped.

"Well, I guess you've made some new friends, Griff," Peg said. "Beer?"

Phil accepted the bottles of beer Peg offered and found a place on the sofa.

"Listen, I've got Thor out in the car. He's real friendly with other dogs. Could I bring him in?"

"Sure. Go get him."

I glanced over at Peg to find her staring at me with her eyebrows arched. I arched my eyebrows and bucked out my eyes back at her. She smiled wanly and turned away. Sure, he was good-looking—6'2" easy, good build, steel gray hair streaked with silver, the ruddy complexion of a man accustomed to the outdoors in all weather, and oh those blue eyes. Well, maybe later, I thought.

Thor made his entrance. A big boy, his tail thumped the walls, the washer, the recycle bins, the bags of dog food as he made his way through the narrow mudroom into the sitting room.

"Easy, Thor. Sit," Griff said. Thor sat and allowed the other dogs to approach and inspect. He did a little discreet sniffing himself under Griff's watchful eye. Soon, the dogs were bowing to each other and arf'ing invitations to play. Griff released Thor from his lead and they romped off.

"I'll take that beer now, Peg," Griff said.

"On the counter," she answered as she sat down next to Phil on the sofa. Phil draped his arm over her shoulder. He was somber.

"So, what did you find out?" she asked as Griff sat on the ottoman next to the chair where I had planted myself.

"Well, a couple of the boys went out to the Hitchens place. She said she'd been there all afternoon and didn't know nothing about it—you know—the usual. There was a green van parked up behind the house but no sign of a Jeep. She refused the consent search, of course. So, they left and went up in the woods a piece down the road. Sat there about an hour but nobody came or went," Phil recited and took a sip of beer.

"Are they going to keep an eye on the place? Can't they get a search warrant?" I asked.

"Yeah, we're watching the place. I don't know about the warrant yet. That may take some doing," he answered.

"Where exactly does she live? All I know is it's up behind Milton somewhere," Peg asked.

"Now, Peg, don't you go out there..." Phil started.

"I'm not going out there," she snapped and jumped up like something bit her. "I'm just asking."

Phil accepted her denial. "It's out of town on Horsey's Road. You pass the pond and turn left on the road to Cedar Neck. Go about three miles and it's a lane to the right. John Deere mailbox. Rancher back in a ways," Griff answered.

I tried to picture the area, but I couldn't remember ever being back there.

At half past midnight, I was still wide awake on my back on the twin bed in Peg's guestroom, my eyes shut tight against the glare of the security light that managed to penetrate both blinds and curtains. My stomach was churning, and my mind kept recycling the events of day.

As the men had grilled burgers in the chilly evening air, I had scared up some chips and a salad. When she discovered we were low on beer, Peg had insisted on going out to buy more. When she returned home, toting two six-packs, we ate half-heartedly, watched TV with one eye and made feeble attempts at conversation.

The phone had rung a couple times—friends calling Peg to find out what was going on after they'd heard the news on TV. She thanked them for calling but told them she wanted to keep the line open.

The dogs had had a good time at least. Thor was a big sweetie and very gentle with my little ones. Speaking of whom, the Tibbies were nestled against my legs, one on each side. For their sakes, I tried to keep still, but I was cramped in the narrow bed. I squirmed restlessly, to which they responded not at all. Something in the back of my brain was nagging at me, just beyond reach—something besides Teke's dognapping. It had something to do with Cedar Neck.

Chapter Eight

In the morning, I left Peg with a hug and a promise to call later in the afternoon. I didn't want to leave her alone, but a long-time client from New Jersey was meeting me at the Nest to view a collection of netsuke I'd acquired for her. Given my new laid-back approach toward my business, it was an appointment I couldn't afford to miss. Peg understood. I promised to return right after the client left.

Dawa and Senge were happy to be home and disappeared into the depths of the yard to run the fence line and sniff out any furry visitors who had passed in the night. I changed from my sweatshirt to a button-down shirt and added a tweed blazer. With my jeans, the outfit created an image of country gentility. I just had time to run my fingers through my hair when the door knocker sounded.

Mrs. Hale had occasionally purchased items from my D.C. shop over a period of several years. After a pleasant catch-up and brief tour of the Nest, I revealed the four fine 19th century Japanese netsuke I'd acquired on her behalf. The netsuke is an ornamental object of attire, often carved of ivory but sometimes of wood, horn or gourd. Those I offered Mrs. Hale were a collection of whimsical figures: a frog on a leaf, a fisherman with a basket, a reclining bear and a goat with kid.

Mrs. Hale was not a cagey customer. She made no effort to disguise her delight with the grouping. When I named my price, she promptly handed over a substantial and very welcome check without any attempt at bargaining. As soon as I'd waved her Lexus down the drive, I ran back to the house and grabbed the phone.

"Yup," said the voice on the other end of the line.

"Bill, it's Abby."

"Hey, Ab. Bonnie's not here right now. She went over to the store," my cousin's husband replied.

"That's OK. It's you I really want to talk to," I paused. "Don't you have some people over around Piney Creek?"

"Yeah, my Uncle John and Aunt Bessie live over there."

"Whereabouts?"

"Out Reynolds Road."

"Is that near Cedar Neck Road?"

"Yeah. It runs along the other side of the pond. Why?"

"This is really important, Bill. You know my friend Peg had her Chessie Teke stolen, right? And we think this woman, name of Evelyn Hitchens, might have had something to do with it. She lives out on Cedar Neck Road, and I thought maybe your Uncle John's farm might be near her place."

"Never heard of her. Want me to call Uncle John and ask him?" Bill offered. I agreed, and he promised to get back to me. Fifteen minutes later, the phone rang. According to Bill, Uncle John's farm backed up to the Hitchens property.

"Is your Uncle John friendly with this Hitchens woman?" I asked him.

"Naw, I don't think so."

"Do you suppose he'd mind if I went out and kinda looked around?"

"Well, meet me out there in a half hour and we'll ask him," Bill said and the phone went dead. Unless he was telling a tall tale, Bill was not a talkative guy.

It took me forever to round up my dogs. They had apparently found something fascinating in a distant corner of the yard and feigned ignorance of their names until I called "Treat" several times. Mrs. Brent was right when she said they could be hardheaded.

I sped down a maze of shortcuts along country roads lined with a patchwork of fields. I rushed by squares of rye in a green like the plastic grass in an Easter basket and took shallow breaths past brown acres ripe with fresh manure. It wasn't hard to find Uncle John's, a neat white farmhouse set among bare oaks. The driveway was lined by bright yellow dabs of newly bloomed forsythia. I parked my blue BMW in behind Bill's dark green Jeep.

Bill was standing on the porch with an older man, their hands in their pockets. In his seventies, Uncle John had the leathery skin of a man who'd worked outside all his life. His overalls and flannel shirt were clean but obviously well-worn.

"Billy here tells me you think Evelyn's got something to do with that dog that got stole up to Dover?" Uncle John said, after a nodding introduction.

"May be," I answered.

"Well, come on out back here and I'll show you where she lives," he said and jumped off the porch rather spryly for a man his age. He set us a brisk pace as we followed him along a gravel driveway past the barn and tractor shed to the first of his three chicken houses.

"That 'ere's her place over yonder," he said and pointed across the fallow cornfield toward a group of buildings about 300 yards away.

We were quiet for a minute, straining our eyes.

"Uncle John, you friendly with this Hitchens woman?" Bill asked.

"Hell, no," he said, "I went to school with her husband, Charlie. He were a couple years behind me. I liked him alright, but I ain't ever had much to do with her. She's allus got her nose stuck in the air. I don't think two words has passed a-tween us since Charlie died a couple years back."

"Uncle John, would you mind if I hang around out here for a while and just keep an eye on her place?" I asked.

"S'aright with me," Uncle John said and started walking back along the chicken house. "You just set up in this here No. 1 house. I'll git you somethin' to set on," he said, pulling open a small door and pushing in the screen door beyond it. He stepped over the threshold into the building.

I looked up and down the house. It was over 250 feet long and about 40 feet wide. At one end, the shiny feed bin that supplied the feed pans inside towered above the house's metal roof. The day's relative warmth had prompted Uncle John to half drop the 'curtains' that covered the screen windows that ran the full length of both sidewalls of the house.

Grimacing, I tried not to breathe as I poked my head in the door. The startled birds scattered again, clucking and fluttering. Clouds of feather dust rose in the hazy sunlight. I glanced to my left where a sea of white chickens extended as far as the eye could see. According to Uncle John, there were 13,000 of them in this house alone. They would live here until they reached four pounds, more or less, at about six weeks of age, at which time they would make a short, final trip to a nearby processing plant.

"I'll be right back," I said, backing into Bill in my haste to escape. "I've got Mom's scope out in the car," I croaked. Outside, I gulped the relatively fresh air. I had nothing against the birds themselves, but the odor of poultry, not to mention the overpowering odor of ammonia generated by their droppings, had always been repugnant to me. I wondered how long I could stand being cooped up with them. But I obviously couldn't sit out in the open spying on Evelyn, so what choice did I have?

I scooted back to my car. There, nestled in its case, was my late mother's prized birding scope that Dad gave her the Christmas before she died. Olivia Swann, whom everyone called "Liv," loved watching birds all her life—a true passion with her, not just a fashionable eccentricity. She would spend hours at a time gazing at songbirds at the Nest through the binoculars that always hung on a hook at the kitchen door and that hang there still. Before she became ill, she passed many happy days trekking over marsh trails in search of shorebirds at wildlife refuges along the Delaware coast, her trusty scope bolted to the tripod over her shoulder.

I ferreted my cell phone out of my shoulder bag and slipped it into my jacket pocket. Grabbing the scope and tripod, I hurried back to the broiler house.

Opening the door slowly so as not to ruffle the birds, I stepped gingerly onto the crust. That's what the locals call the hardened layer of litter and chicken droppings covering the floor. Uncle John had placed a stool next to the window opening, and Billy and he were passing time chatting about the biggest dilemma of chicken farming—what to do with the manure that many birds generate. For decades, local farmers have spread the manure on their fields. But environmentalists, backed by the federal government, now say the excessive amounts used on fields foul Delmarva's inland waters.

Listening to their conversation with a half an ear, I shed my jacket in the warm building and, not wanting to drop it on the crust, draped it over the stool. I bolted the scope to the tripod and peered through the eyepiece. After a bit of squirming and fidgeting, I found a more or less comfortable position from which to observe.

Evelyn's property came in sharp and bright. My view was from the rear and to the right of the house. The closest building to me was a large barn in traditional red, but its front faced away. The next closest was a kennel building with six, no, seven individual concrete runs extending out the back. As I watched, a black Standard poodle exited through a dog door, walked to the end of his run and stood staring toward the barn. When I zoomed in, I could even make out a rusty poop scoop leaning against the side of the building. It was a really good scope.

Beyond the kennel, I had a clear view of the back of Evelyn's ranch-style house with its redwood deck and above-ground pool. A detached two-car garage stood on the far side of the house, its front facing the house—and me. A green minivan was parked in the gravel driveway. The garage doors were closed.

I was surprised to find the property neat and clean. After all of Grace Bishop's gossip about Evelyn running a puppy mill, I suppose I expected a filthy kennel, rundown house, and junk cars in the yard. On the contrary, this was a respectable looking middle-class country home, and the kennels—what I could see of them–appeared to be clean and well kept. "You can't judge a book by its cover," I muttered.

"See something?" Uncle John asked. I nearly fell off the stool, having forgotten that Bill and he were still standing behind me.

"No, nothing yet. All quiet."

"Well, I'm goin' on up to the house. You holler if you need anything. C'mon, Billy. Bessie's gone to the store but I reckon I can scare us up a beer," Uncle John said, exiting the chicken house. The door closed behind them and their voices faded.

Since the huge fans that normally ventilated the house weren't on, I found myself trying not to inhale the foul fowl odor. From my reading, I knew that the houses harbored an unpleasant fungus called histoplasmosis that could prey on the eyes, lungs or other internal organs. My eyes squinted involuntarily. Or maybe the dreaded bird flu in the news was lurking somewhere in those beaks. I pinched my nose. A glance at my watch told me it was two o'clock. I still had three, maybe four, hours of good light.

Though I alternated between the naked eye and the scope, the surveillance business got really old really fast. When not gazing through the scope, I observed the chickens. They busied themselves aimlessly walking around on their huge yellow feet and stretching their necks to peck drops of water from automatic drinkers running the length of the house. Whenever the automatic feeder clicked on and food began to drop into the feed pans, they clucked excitedly. Poor things, I thought, cooped up like this with no life but eating and drinking. I might dislike them, but I could still pity them. Meanwhile, nothing stirred at Evelyn's.

At half past three, Evelyn's barrel-like figure appeared at the back door. Emerging from the house while still putting on a beige jacket, she trudged toward the kennel building and disappeared from view. I supposed she'd gone in through the front door that I couldn't see. A few minutes later, a black pickup with dual rear wheels and darkly tinted windows turned off Cedar Neck Road into the driveway. It pulled up to the kennel building. I zoomed in on the driver's side just as a sandy-haired man in camouflage pants, tee-shirt and ball cap climbed down from the cab. He was bearded, about 6' with a stocky build. I didn't recognize him.

He walked around to the truck bed, lowered the tailgate, and dragged a large bag of dog food off the bed. I recognized the bag; it was an expensive brand. Hoisting it onto his shoulder, he, too, disappeared into the building. He returned for two more bags. Eventually, Evelyn and the man came out of the building together and walked to the pickup. They stood talking for a couple minutes. Then, the man got in the pickup and left with a wave. Meanwhile, the woman disappeared inside the house. By now, it was five o'clock.

Fishing the cell phone out of my crumpled jacket pocket, I called Peg to find out whether she'd heard anything about Teke. She replied that no one had called. She was very subdued. For some reason, I didn't tell her where I was. Instead, I mumbled some excuses, promised to come over later and pressed the "end" button.

Outside, the dark clouds had started to build up. I remembered vaguely that the weather forecast on the radio had called for a warm front to pass through by morning, with increasing cloudiness. It was supposed to rain by Sunday afternoon.

A sound from outside caught my attention. A flock of geese, perhaps three or four hundred, was passing over, noisily honking to one another. Their U and V formations ebbed and flowed into one another. Even with the naked eye, it was easy to identify the white body and black wingtips of the Snow goose. They are a common sight on Delmarva – even more common than the gray and black Canada goose at this time of year. My eyes returned to Evelyn's backdoor but were soon drawn skyward again as the raucous flock continued its progress.

The birds normally leave their wintering grounds in Delmarva in early spring and head to the Arctic for a short nesting season, returning in late autumn. A few of the birds landed in the cornfield behind the chicken house. More followed, and the field was soon thronged with the honking white birds. Some pecked at the ground in search of vegetation, but most just preened and strutted. Though beautiful, Snow geese are vilified on Delmarva for their destructive habits. Instead of grazing like their Canada cousins, the Snow pulls up fragile wetlands plants by their roots. Luckily, the pickings on Uncle John's cornfield were limited to old husks and broken up stalks. Eventually, the geese lifted off as a single body in a deafening departure.

Time crawled by. The clouds thickened and blotted out the thin light. I heard the wind come up ahead of the front. By now, the chickens no longer held any interest for me, and I had already committed every detail of Evelyn's property to memory. Occasionally, I scanned her barnyard for signs of life but, more often, I found myself dozing.

Jerking myself awake from one such catnap, I glanced at my watch. It was half past five. Dusk was settling. I yawned and, thinking I might as well call it a day, I peered through the eyepiece one last time.

"Damn! When did that get there?" I said out loud to the chickens.

A dark brown Jeep was parked next to the kennel building. Someone came around the corner of the building, headed for the Jeep. I peered harder through the failing light. The person was wearing a hooded gray sweatshirt under a denim jacket, his head covered by the hood and bowed against the brisk wind. Evelyn followed the hooded person around the corner. They stood talking, but the person's back was to me. I stomped my foot, setting off a flurry of indignant clucking. I fiddled with the focus, trying to bring the Jeep's tag in focus. Unfortunately, the tag was on the far side, partially obscured by the rear-mounted spare. All I could see was that it was a black tag with a three, or maybe an eight, as the first digit.

What happened next wasn't really a conscious action—it was more like something bit me in the butt. I shot off the stool and sprinted out of the chicken house, birds flying and squawking around me. The door slammed behind me. Without looking, I sent up a silent prayer that it had closed. Thirteen thousand chickens on the loose wouldn't be a pretty sight.

I passed Uncle John, who was busy closing the curtains on another chicken house for the night, with a quick wave but no comment. As my legs pumped past the farmhouse, I caught a glimpse of Bill's Aunt Bessie, her mouth in the shape of an "O," illuminated through the kitchen window. When I rounded the porch corner, I slipped and my knee came down hard on the gravel. "Dammit!" I scrabbled up and, with one last burst of speed, reached the BMW.

Gravel flew as I floored the accelerator and sped out of the driveway. I must have been doing 60 when I swerved around the bend in Reynolds Road and slammed on the brakes at the stop sign. After a quick glance to the right and left, I let up on the brake and accelerated through the stop sign. I was now on Cedar Neck Road. The pond sped by to my left. Evelyn's house was just ahead. I slowed down almost to a stop at the end of her lane, staring toward the house. The security lights had come on as dusk fell, but I could see no sign of the Jeep.

"Stupid," I muttered, discouraged, "You should have known you couldn't get here in time. Oh well." The adrenalin rush drained away as quickly as it had come.

I crept ahead for a hundred feet or so, looking for someplace other than Evelyn's driveway to turn around. A small break in the woods to the right revealed a lane made by tire tracks. I switched on my headlights before turning into the gloomy lane. Just ahead, in the beams of my headlights, were the grinning faces of two men seated in the front seat of a large gray Ford sedan. I knew instantly that this was an unmarked police car and the men were troopers assigned to watch Evelyn. This was no Holmesian deduction on my part. The one on the passenger side was Griff.

I groaned and feebly raised my hand in recognition. They waved back. Obviously, they had seen the Jeep and anyone else who came to Evelyn's while I was dozing in the chicken house. I wasted no time backing out and headed back to Uncle John's to pick up my scope and apologize for scattering his gravel. I felt like a kid caught with her hand in the cookie jar.

Chapter Nine

There is nothing more wonderful than coming home to a dog, unless it's coming home to more than one dog. They make you feel like the most important person in the world—which, to them, you are. You're all they think about and live for. However, when I returned from Uncle John's farm, Dawa and Senge were more interested in where I'd been than in me. Even as I prepared their dinners, I could barely move for the little black noses glued to my jeans cuffs and socks.

When they finally detached their noses and began to eat, I stripped down, tossed my clothes in the washer and scooted upstairs in the buff. Twenty minutes later, I felt much better after showering and shampooing away the chicken odor. Don't get me wrong. I'm not some clean freak, scared of a little dirt and smell. There's just something about chickens that I can't abide. They give me the willies.

"So, where have *you* been all day?" Peg queried before I'd even unhooked Dawa's and Senge's leads.

"Neglecting my business," I shot back. She made a face and stuck her tongue out at me. I made one back.

"Go play," I instructed the Tibbies and pulled a stool up to the kitchen counter. "Any news?"

"No, nothing." When she turned to hand me a glass of wine she'd poured, I instantly regretted my sass. Her shoulders slumped and dark shadows stained her eyes. She probably hadn't slept a wink all night.

"Phil called and said Griff and he will be over after their shift," she said and turned back to the salad she was making. "Phil asked me if I knew where you'd been today but he wouldn't say why he asked. What's up?"

My face flamed. I quickly dipped my head and sipped the Shiraz. "Well, I went down and checked out Evelyn's place," I admitted.

"Really?" Peg paused in tossing the greens.

"Yeah. It turns out my cousin's husband's uncle—you know my cousin Bonnie, right?—well, his uncle owns the adjoining farm. I camped out in his chicken house with Mom's spotting scope."

"You hate chickens," Peg commented dryly.

"You got that right," I said and sipped the spicy wine again.

"Did you see anything?"

"Not really. The only dogs I saw were Poodles. Then, this afternoon, this guy drives up in a black Ford 250, or maybe 350, a dually. He drops off some dog food. About six foot, 200 pounds, with blond hair and a beard?"

"I dunno. I think she's got a couple boys. May be it was one of them," Peg said, shrugging.

"Then, later, a brown Jeep came up."

"Really?" she said and turned to me.

"Yeah, but I couldn't get the tag number. And the driver was all covered up. About your height, stocky. But I couldn't see anything else."

Peg sighed and turned back to the salad.

"It doesn't matter. The cops were there, parked up in the woods across from Evelyn's. They probably got the tag." I reached for a lettuce leaf.

Peg pushed me a plate of salad. "Well, thanks for trying."

"Griff was one of the cops. I guess he told Phil he'd seen me out there." I paused to chew a mouthful of greens. "I didn't know he did that kind of work. I thought he was strictly K-9, but I didn't see Thor."

"I dunno," Peg said as she leaned over to pull two loaves of golden French bread from the oven.

"Oh, I knew I smelled that wonderful bread of yours," I said and smacked my lips exaggeratedly.

"Well, I had to keep myself occupied all day," she said, tearing off a generous hunk and tossing it to me.

We sat down at the kitchen table and fell silent as we ate or, actually, I ate and she picked at crumbs. Only the occasional squeak of impatience from my ill-mannered Tibbies begging at our feet interrupted us. A chorus of barks and the crunch of gravel in the driveway signaled that Phil and Griff had arrived.

After a round of "heys" and the obligatory dog petting, Peg announced that the men should help themselves to salad, bread and wine. They didn't need asking twice.

A few minutes later, Griff caught my eye across the table. "So, Abby, busy day?" he asked, tearing off a second hunk of warm bread.

"Not really. Just a few hours of playing Nancy Drew," I replied.

Peg smiled. Since Griff was never a pre-teen girl, it took him longer to grasp my literary allusion. When he did, he smiled. Nice smile, I thought.

"So where were you—up in the woods like us?" he asked with his mouth full.

"No. I was cooped up in a chicken house out back of her place, across the field." I explained the family connection to Uncle John. "It's got a good view of the kennel building."

"You suppose he'd let us put a man out there?" Phil asked.

"I don't know. There's no love lost between Evelyn and him, though, so it wouldn't hurt to ask," I answered. "By the way, Griff, where was Thor? I thought you only do K-9 work."

"Yeah, that's right, usually. But today was my day off so I asked Mac, the other cop, if I could ride along with him." He paused. "What'd you see out there?"

"Well, no sign of Teke. She stayed in the house most of the afternoon. Then, this blond guy with a beard came up in a black pickup. He just unloaded three bags of dog food and carried it in the kennel, talked to Evelyn for a couple minutes and left. Then, later, the brown Jeep came up. I couldn't get a good look at the driver. I'd sure like to know who that was."

"We ran the tag," Phil said with his mouth full. He paused to chew and swallow. "Belongs to a Jacqueline Lynch with a Milford address. Know her?"

"Sure. She's the young vet at Doc Twilley's practice up by Abby's," Peg said.

Everyone sipped the wine and pondered the new information.

"Some vets will pay house calls to a breeder with a lot of dogs. Saves the breeder money and the vet time," Peg added.

"Well, that would explain why she was out there," Phil remarked.

"Well, I'd best check the grill," Peg said, pushing herself away from the table. She looked pointedly at me, obviously trying to suppress a grin. "I'm sorry, Abby, I didn't know. I'm afraid we're having barbecue chicken."

An hour later, after clearing the table, we settled down for coffee and apple pie in the sitting room. The only sound was the clink of forks on Peg's plates.

"Mmmm," Phil mumbled exaggeratedly, "Great pie, Peg."

"Thanks, but not as good as Abby's," Peg said.

"Real butter, tart apples, and white raisins," I said, wagging my fork at her. "That's all there is to it." Generally speaking, Peg was the better cook, but the superiority of my apple pie has always frustrated her. I was glad to see her muster a grin in response to my teasing.

"Something's been bothering me," I said, putting down my fork. "We've been so focused on Evelyn Hitchens, maybe we've overlooked somebody else who was at St. Michaels and maybe even some of the other photo shoots. Somebody else who auditioned and is mad about Teke getting the job. Or somebody who would stand to gain from Teke's," I stopped, horrified that I'd almost said 'death.' Instead, I blurted, "um, disappearance."

Phil picked up the thread. "Or, it might have nothing to do with the commercials. Maybe it's just somebody who wants to get back at Peg for something. Do you have any enemies—somebody you've argued with? Lawsuit or anything?"

Peg shook her head. "No, I think Abby's right. It's got to be somebody who's pissed about the commercials. But if it's not Hitchens, who could it be?"

"Did you see anybody else you knew at St. Michaels? What about those people from your training class?" I prodded.

"That was the Causey couple from Seaford, but I was talking to them when Teke got out and, besides, they didn't audition their dog."

"Who else?" Phil asked.

"Well, Jackie Lynch for one," Peg said, trying to recollect all the people she'd seen that day. "Grace Bishop. Louann from the Tourism office but she doesn't have anything to do with dogs." Peg paused again. "You know, I saw the Peppers before you got there, Abby. They auditioned their Golden Retriever, Dallas. He's a nice dog. I thought he might win because Goldens are so much more popular and well-known than Chessies. But I can't believe the Peppers would do anything against me or Teke. They seem like really nice people."

"Well, maybe they are, but it won't hurt to check it out," Phil said.

"What about Grace, Peg? Didn't she try out one of her Beagles?" I asked.

"Yeah, I think she did. But I don't think she was serious. Her dogs aren't even obedience-trained. You know Grace. She just came to the auditions because she's always got to be 'in' on everything."

"Yeah, I know. But, like Phil says, they should still check it out," I said. "Besides, Grace would get a kick out of being a suspect." Peg chuckled.

Phil pulled a notebook from his pocket and took down the names and phone numbers of the people Peg had mentioned. No one seriously thought that any of these people were suspects. We were just trying to keep Peg's mind occupied.

It was about eleven o'clock when I awakened the sleeping Tibbies and made my excuses. Peg walked out to the car with me, hugging herself against the chilly breeze.

"Are you sure you don't want me to stay tonight?"

Peg shook her head, "No, I'll be fine. Go home and sleep in your own gorgeous bed." Peg had always loved my antique four-poster.

"Listen, why don't you come over tomorrow? The Annual Antique Show and Sale at the Ocean City Convention Center is next weekend. It starts on Friday, so I've got to get the rest of the unpacking and appraising done so that I can figure out what to take."

Peg started to shake her head.

"Wait! I'm serious. Bring the dogs—all of them. They'll have a ball playing with the Tibbies. Just put your phone on call forwarding or leave a message on your tape with my number or your cell number. You won't miss any calls."

I could see she was thinking about it so I tossed in my *coup de grace*.

"We could even go over those exercises you want to teach the Tibbies," I paused to let that sink in.

With Peg's expert guidance, Dawa and Senge had earned their Canine Good Citizen titles and the right to append CGC to their names, but Peg had been pestering me to continue with their training. I knew she relished the novelty and challenge of training the small, stubborn dogs. I also knew that she secretly hoped to get me involved in agility or rally competition so that we could go on the road together. I'm not a very competitive person, but if the dogs would have fun, I'd be willing to try. With everything else going on in my life, I just hadn't been able to find the time.

Peg took the bait. "OK, I'll be over."

"Great," I said and gave her a squeeze. "See you in the morning."

Chapter Ten

I was out early with the dogs on Sunday morning. Sleep had been elusive, but I wanted to get the dogs out before the weather turned. Although yesterday's wind had died, rain from the low, heavy clouds still threatened.

Once out of the Swann's Nest gate, the dogs forged ahead, straining against their leads and kicking up sand with their hind legs. "Slow down, guys," I called. "I think Aunt Peg is right. You Tibbies need more training." We turned onto the well-worn shortcut to the pond through the woods. Senge sprinted from holly sapling to poplar stump, snuffling and marking each one, and then kicking leaves and dirt to spread his scent. Dawa maintained a more dignified pace with pauses for ladylike sniffing. At Peg's suggestion, I had once tried walking them on a coupler, one lead with two clips, but their walking styles differed too radically.

We passed through a dense piney grove where the ground was a thick carpet of soft, long needles. The sweet fragrance of the shats rose from beneath feet and paws. Turning onto the main path circling the pond, we rounded a bend and headed down a side path to a nose of land poking into the pond. The rustic bench at the tip of the nose is a quiet place to sit and observe the cove. There's always something to see—geese gliding to and fro, a lone blue heron fishing or a red-ear turtle sunning on a partly submerged log.

I wasn't disappointed. The cove was occupied by a two-legged critter standing in a bass boat and trolling the lily pads along the shore. He looked familiar, and I recognized the rangy angler as Doc Twilley. I raised my arm in greeting. He returned the wave.

Unfortunately, the Tibbies also recognized him and danced at the water's edge, rrr'ing and roo'ing. "Sh-h-h!" I scolded them. Senge swallowed his next rrr but Dawa ignored me and continued rrr'ing.

Doc must've given up on the spot because he reeled in his line. Sitting down, he ran the boat to the tip of the point where I stood and slowed to a stop.

"Mornin', Doc. How's the fishing?" I asked as the prow bumped the shore. The Tibbies were bouncing like balls.

"Hi there," Doc greeted the dogs first. "Hey, Abby. Fishin's good, real good. Ahead of a front is the best time. They're in a feeding frenzy." He paused and reached down into the well and held up a shiny fish by its gills. "That's a nice lunker—four pounds. Got that with pig 'n' jig." He returned the fish to the well.

"Say, I saw on TV that Teke'd been stolen up at Dover. Any word?" Doc asked.

"No, nothing yet. The police are investigating, but..." I shrugged to make my point. "Peg's put up a generous reward."

"Yeah, I saw that on TV. Damn crazy people in this world. Who would steal a dog?"

A quiet moment passed. "Doc, you know Evelyn Hitchens, don't you?"

He hesitated. "No, I don't think so. Should I?"

"You sure? Poodle breeder over by Milton?"

He shook his head. "Doesn't ring any bells. Why?"

"Oh, never mind. I thought she was a client of yours. My mistake."

"No, never heard of her," Doc said, shaking his head slowly. "Well, I hope they find that Chessie soon." The motor whirred into life.

"I'll tell Peg. Take care, Doc," I said and shoved the boat off with my foot. "Good fishin'."

I watched his back as he headed toward Turtle Island, the little hump-backed island at the westernmost end of the pond. He raised his hand and waved. I waved back.

"C'mon guys. It's time for breakfast and besides," I pulled my hood up and shivered, "it's starting to drizzle."

"He is a nice man," Senge observed as he woofed one more time at the retreating back.

"I don't like him. He poked me with a needle."

"Aw, Sister, Mom says the ouchies keep us from getting sick."

Dawa harumphed. " 'When an old dog howls, the other dogs run after him without knowing why'."

Senge rrr'd exasperatedly. "Oh Sister, you are always quoting those silly proverbs. Just what does that mean?"

"Think about it, Brother."

"No, Sister, you think about this for a change," Senge retorted. He rushed ahead and called back over his shoulder, "You're like the 'flea that hopped up from the carpet!' "

Dawa stared after him indignantly. "Ooh, I don't like rain," she muttered and, shaking the droplets from her outercoat, stomped after him.

I was already deep into my work when Peg's pickup passed the dining room window. I watched as she vaulted onto the tailgate and released Bits and Dapper from their crates in the pickup bed. They launched off the tailgate and circled each other at a run, joyously leaping and barking. Peg must've given a command inaudible to me because they simultaneously turned and shot toward the house. Meanwhile, I could hear the Tibbies barking up a storm in the kitchen.

"Hey, girl," I said, encircling my friend in my arms when we arrived in the kitchen a moment later.

"Hey," she said, returning my hug.

"Breakfast?"

"No, I ate already."

"Well, coffee or tea then?"

"Sure, coffee's good."

When we'd filled our mugs, Peg followed me into the dining room. Every available surface was covered with objects. She began to peruse.

"Oh, this is pretty," she said touching a 19th century Rose medallion charger embellished with flower motifs.

"Hang on, Peg. I've got something that I know you'll like." I bounded upstairs to my bedroom.

When I handed her the bamboo okimono a minute later, she oohed and aahed over the puppy figurine. Peg doesn't share my passion for Asian art. Her taste in the decorative arts runs to "country." I've often wondered that we've remained best friends for so many years despite how different we are. In college, I studied Asian art with a minor in Chinese. Peg majored in biology. While I moved away and assumed a sophisticated, urban lifestyle, Peg stayed home and lived a down-to-earth rural existence. Still, we share a fierce independence and, since Dawa and Senge bounced into my life, our love of dogs.

"I'm keeping that one," I said, nodding at the okimono. "I love it. It reminds me of Dawa and Senge when they were puppies."

Peg nodded. "Yes, you're right. They were so cute." She placed the okimono gently on the dining room table. "So this show next weekend is a big deal, right?"

"Uh-huh. Over a thousand dealers. I'm hoping to do a lot of business. I'll be taking a couple hundred objects."

"What can I do to help?" She looked around helplessly.

I soon put her to work unpacking objects and lining them up for my inspection. She helped me complete the sales stickers while I keyed in the items on my laptop. When we finished appraising and sorting a group of items, they were repacked—either into boxes to go to the show or into boxes for transport to the mall or back into storage.

We labored in companionable silence for three hours. Outside, it drizzled most of the morning. At noon, I threw down my marker. "I need a dog fix!" We both jumped up and skipped down the steps to the kitchen wing. The dogs, who had been peaceably napping, heard us coming and were instantly primed for fun.

"Look, the sun's coming out!" I said and pointed toward the shafts of pale light cutting through the panes of the kitchen door. "Outside everybody!"

The dogs needed no persuasion and were soon romping happily among the wet leaves and winter debris littering my backyard, by which I actually mean the front yard. Yes, that's confusing. Let me explain.

The longer sides of the rectangular three-bay Swann's Nest are mirror images. Each façade consists of a pedimented door with fanlight, two 12-over-12 windows on the ground level and three above. Surmounting each window, a wooden lintel and fluted keyblock are painted to simulate marble, as actual stone was unavailable in this part of the country in the 18th century, unless it came as the ballast in a ship. Set into the roof above, three dormers, each with its own fanlight, echo the three bays below and provide light to the attics.

What the family has always called the "front door" opened onto the aspect descending toward Swann Creek where it glides through the trees a short distance from the house. In the early days of the house, people and cargo traveled more by water than by road. They came ashore at the

Nest's landing and approached the house's "front door." Thus, the "front door" was so called because it received company. Functionally, however, the "front door" is today's back door and, thus, the "front door" opens onto what is functionally the back yard. On the other side of the house, what the family has always called the "back door" opens onto the carriage yard, where today's driveway is. What I call the "back door" is functionally today's front door and opens onto what is functionally today's front yard. Simple, right?

The air was still brisk, but the sun hinted of spring warmth. Bits and Dapper were running circles around the Tibbies while the Tibbies barked at them. Dawa suddenly leapt forward and grabbed Bits by the hock. Shocked, Bits twisted and yelped. Senge seized the chance to flank and attack from the other side. Grabbing the Aussie's short scruff, he hung precariously for a moment before retreating to join his sister. Dapper bounced back and forth, barking. A moment later they streaked toward the front yard, the big dogs in the lead but the small ones close behind.

Chuckling, I paused to contemplate the fresh earth smells and enjoy the yellow splashes of forsythia surrounding the carriage yard. As the barking dogs disappeared behind the house, I realized the kitchen phone was ringing. Peg, who was doggedly unloading agility equipment from her truck, jumped.

"I'll get it," I called and sprinted for the kitchen door. " 'Lo," I said into the receiver.

"Hey, it's Griff."

"Oh, hi," I replied, taken aback. This was the first time he'd called my house.

"Peg's machine said she's over there," he said.

"Oh. Yeah, she's here," I said just as Peg came through the kitchen door, "Any news?"

"No, I'm sorry, there's nothing really. We got a guy over there at Uncle John's though." He fell silent. I waited. "I was just calling," he cleared his throat, "to, uh, see how she is," he finished weakly.

I shook my head to let Peg know there was no news and said, "A little better, I think. We were just going out to work with the dogs."

"Well, that's good. OK, well…" he hesitated.

"Are you at work?" I asked helpfully.

"Yeah, Phil's out doing a sweep at a church. I'm just doing some paperwork."

"Somebody called in a bomb threat to a church?" I asked, incredulous.

"No, no. The Governor's going to be there later. She's giving a speech about the Underground Railroad, so he's just helping with the security check."

"Well, why don't you come over to the Nest when you get off? I haven't thought about dinner yet, but we can throw something together."

"You want us to bring a pizza?" he offered.

"Pizza tonight?" I mouthed to Peg. She shrugged.

"Sure. Sounds good. Sausage and mushrooms for us. Oh, and bring the dogs. Five o'clock?" I listened. "Right. See you then."

After I hung up, Peg and I inhaled some sorely needed fresh spring air for about an hour. We set up two agility obstacles—a jump and a dog walk.

First, she showed me how to work the dogs over jumps using Bits and Dapper as demo dogs. Both of them instantly followed her hand signals and sailed over the bar. When it was the Tibbies' turn, she adjusted the bar down to 8 inches since Dawa and Senge stand no higher than 10 and 11 inches at the shoulder, respectively. After a little coaxing with bits of hot dog, the Tibbies soon grasped that running at and jumping the bar is fun.

"We don't want to overdo one thing, so let's try the dog walk," Peg said after the dogs had each jumped a few times. I noticed that her cheeks were glowing. The dog walk is a series of three boards, two incline segments and an elevated segment between them. Peg explained in a businesslike voice that the object was for the dogs to climb the incline after first touching the "contact zone," a yellow-painted segment at the bottom of the incline. After crossing the top, the dogs must also touch the yellow contact zone at the end of the decline. Training them to touch the contact zones assures they don't get hurt by jumping up onto the dog walk at the wrong place or jumping off too soon, she explained sternly.

It turned out that Dawa and Senge were naturals on the dog walk. They showed no hesitancy in climbing the incline to the top, which was steep and long for such small dogs. However, they tended to pause on the crosspiece to look around and had to be prompted to continue on to the decline.

"That was really, really good for the first time," Peg said, roughing the Tibbies' ruffs. Even Bits and Dapper didn't do that well their first time on a dog walk."

"Well, it's really not too surprising if you think about it. It's their nature to climb to the highest point and survey their territory," I told Peg. "They have absolutely no fear of heights."

"That's true," Peg acknowledged. We sent the dogs off to play freely while Peg and I disassembled the jumps and dog walk and loaded the pieces back into her truck. We reluctantly returned to the house for a tuna sandwich lunch. Happily tired, Peg's dogs curled by the heating registers.

By the time Phil and Griff rolled into the driveway early that evening, Peg and I had knocked off the largest part of the cataloging and pricing. Only the dining table remained covered with small objects to be studied and entered into the ledger.

Neither Phil nor Griff had ever been to the Nest. Instead of heading for the kitchen door like everybody else, they climbed the brick steps to the formal "back door." The knocker sounded, booming through the cavernous entrance hall, just as I came out of the dining room with Peg in tow.

I switched on the pair of two-centuries-old brass chandeliers to illuminate the hall's polished heart pine floors, creamy yellow plaster walls and elegant dentil molding. The heavy door swung open easily, and two clean-cut, good-looking guys stood gawking past me into the house.

"Come on in," I said, sweeping my arm toward the impressive hall that continued the length of the house to the "front door" at the other end. Peg greeted Phil with a hug—something new for my generally undemonstrative friend. I was pleased.

"Man, this is some house. Like Woodburn," Phil said, referring to the Governor's mansion in Dover, as he gazed up at the 12-foot ceilings.

"Well, thanks. It's from the same period, but the Nest isn't as big as Woodburn and its decoration—the wainscoting and trim—is a lot plainer," I said in what I hoped was a graceful acceptance of the compliment. "Would you like a tour?" I asked. Almost everyone who comes to the Nest wants a tour. They nodded.

Closing the door behind them, I lead the way down the hall. As we walked, the men gaped at the oil paintings suspended between the doors to the dining room and parlor. "Oh, these are your dogs, aren't they?" Griff exclaimed when he paused in front of an oval portrait, the centerpiece of the hall. I nodded. Phil and he studied my cherished depiction of the Tibbies—Dawa reclining on a burgundy velvet pillow in the foreground and Senge sitting behind her, one paw resting protectively on her flank, their eyes gazing out lovingly.

"I had that done last year," I commented. The men nodded appreciatively and left the portrait to join me to the opposite end of the hall.

"This was the actual 'front door' to Swann's Nest in the 18th and early 19th centuries, a twin to the one through which you just entered," I said, pulling open the great door. "In those days, the forest was cleared all the way down to a landing on Swann Creek. Guests would approach the house from the landing, where they came ashore, and enter by this door." I pushed the heavy door closed.

"The house is two rooms deep on each floor. And now, if you'll follow me, I'll show you the parlor and dining room." I was deliberately playing the docent. Peg grinned at me, recalling house and garden tours my Dad made us lead back when we were teenagers; we would have preferred to go to the beach or listen to rock.

We progressed fairly slowly through the parlor and dining room downstairs and then went upstairs where I briefly showed the three bedrooms and mentioned that a bath, added in the 1920's, had replaced the small nursery. In each room, I pointed out the prized architectural features as well as my best antiques and cherished heirlooms. In passing, I mentioned that the door across from the bathroom led to a closed stair to the third floor where, according to family legend, the servants slept in tiny box-like rooms.

"Any ghosts?" Griff asked with a grin. It was a real nice grin, I noticed.

"Well, yes, actually," I paused for effect. "There's a woman's ghost, supposedly a servant girl named Sally, who jumped to her death from one of the dormer windows in the attic. It happened about 1825, or so the story goes. I don't know if it's true. I've never heard anything otherworldly—well, not much anyway." I let my voice drift off at the end. Peg tittered nervously on cue. We'd played this game when we were teens, too.

As we came back downstairs, I explained that, due to the ebb and flow of my family's fortunes, the house had declined into disrepair over the decades spanning the turn of the 20th century. After a brief respite in the 1920's when my great-grandfather had plumbed and electrified the house, the Depression had once again beaten down the family and the house along with it.

"The mill fell down during the Depression, and there's nothing left of it now. We sold off most of the land for next to nothing and just kept a small farm to feed the family. My great-grandfather and grandfather did all the farm work themselves. The women, too. I remember stories of my grandmother picking strawberries and digging sweet potatoes when she came here as a young wife. Times were hard. The men even cut holly out of the woods around the house, and the women made Christmas wreaths to sell in Philadelphia. That was a big industry here on Delmarva back then. My grandmother taught me how to do that before she died."

We retraced our steps to the downstairs hall and I paused at the archway adjacent to the back door. "This is the way to the great room and kitchen, which are actually a much older, two-room frame farmhouse. This main house wasn't added to the earlier structure until 1785."

"How old is this part?" Phil asked as I led them through the archway and down the three steps to the old wing.

"We don't know for sure. Dad thought it dated from 1730 to 1750. Definitely early eighteenth century," I replied as they looked around. "I pretty much live in this part of the house."

"It's a beautiful house," Griff said.

"Thanks. I'm really lucky to have it. Through all the bad times, the family managed to hang onto the home place without butchering it. So many families with old houses ripped out the paneling, pulled off the mantels and closed up the fireplaces, or even disassembled the staircases to sell. Either that or they modernized," I paused to make quotation marks in the air with my fingers, "with Victorian décor. But that never happened at Swann's Nest. When things eventually got better, my Dad was able to go to college and law school. After he married Mom, they worked on restoring the house for over thirty years. The whole time I was growing up, in fact, they were always working on some project."

"Oh look," Peg said, pointing through the great room windows that overlook the carriage yard. Outside, Ham and Thor were staring at us mournfully through the back window of Phil's Blazer. "Poor babies. Bring them in, Phil."

"Are you sure?" Phil said, gesturing around.

"Sure, bring them in. There's nothing in here they can damage, and I'll close the door the main house. The kitchen's through here," I said leading them through the next doorway. "Hey, wait just a minute. Didn't you say you were going to bring pizza?"

Ham and Thor joined us in the great room where we passed a quiet evening. Trying to keep Peg's mind off Teke proved impossible since none of us could think of any topic of conversation other than Teke's disappearance. So, we rehashed each piece of the puzzle again, falling silent when we had nothing more to say or when I presented something to eat. I'd managed to produce a salad of sorts from the vegetable bin along with the pizza delivered to the gate. Later, I checked the freezer and found a partial gallon of butter pecan ice cream–enough for dessert for four and dollops for the patiently waiting dogs.

Eleven o'clock rolled around. I begged Peg to stay, but she insisted on packing up the dogs and going home. Phil and Griff followed her out the lane. When the two pairs of tail lights disappeared into the woods, I turned off the lights, and the Tibbies and I headed upstairs to bed.

"What's that?" Senge murmured. He stared at the fireplace, his ears pricked at the sounds of the wind whirling in the chimney.

"It's nothing, Brother. Just the wind," Dawa whispered. Though curled with her tail over her nose, she was alert as well. Her eyes

searched the window panes where the shadows of branches waved across the moonlight.

"I wish they would find Teke," Senge said. "Everyone is so sad."

"You were good on the dog walk Aunt Peg brought over," Dawa said, to change the subject.

"Yeah, that was fun!" Senge enthused. "So was chasing Bits and Dapper."

Dawa smiled. " 'You become clever in that which you practice'," she quoted the proverb sagely.

"Then you must be very clever at snoring," Senge joked. "Go to sleep, Sister."

I lay awake for a while. The house was restless. The windows creaked in the wind that moaned outside, and the floor planks snapped as the temperature fell rapidly. Even the dogs couldn't settle down. Senge rubbed his cheeks against the comforter and repeatedly butted me in the hip with his forehead. Dawa circled and scratched at her pillow. When I finally dropped off, I dreamed about the suicidal servant girl Sally for the first time since I was a little girl and my uncle had teased me with scary stories he made up about her.

Chapter Eleven

The sun had been up for two hours by the time the dogs and I reached the pond on Monday morning. I'd been unusually slow getting out of bed. While Dawa patiently remained on her pillow at my side, Senge was pointedly posed Sphinx-like at the top of the staircase. He bolted downstairs as soon as he was sure I wasn't going to crawl back in bed. His nails scritched on the plank floor as he rounded the newel post headed for the great room. I gritted my teeth. Those floors are a pain to polish.

When I'd pulled on my jeans and a tee-shirt, Dawa rrr'd for me to lift her off the lofty bed. I tucked her under my arm and ventured downstairs, still barefoot and half asleep.

"Br-r-r, it's *cold* this morning, kids, "I remarked, shivering, as kibble fell from the dispenser into their bowls. "Let's wait awhile before we go for a walk."

On hearing the "w" word, Senge, who'd been dancing at my feet, froze and woofed. Dawa echoed him.

"Shush now. No barking. Later. We'll go for our walk *later, not now*. I promise," I reassured them and placed the bowls on the floor. They gobbled down their breakfast while I dawdled over mine.

Despite the chill, our walk to the pond was pleasant. The Tibbies paused to investigate a plop into the water as we crossed the footbridge over Cattail Branch. Peering over the edge of the bridge into the gurgling water below, they squeaked with impatience. Waiting for their curiosity to abate, I inspected the bridge and made a mental note to replace one of the boards. There's never any shortage of chores to do at Swann's Nest.

When we reached Swann's Pond Road, the dogs spied a painted turtle who'd found a sunny place on the warm asphalt.

"A lot of good those turtle crossing signs will do if some SUV comes tear-assing around that curve, little buddy," I said to the creature. "Let's get you on over to the other side." Holding the dogs at bay with one hand, I gently prodded the reluctant reptile across the road with a branch. We left him or her at pond's edge and resumed our walk along the trail.

At a low spot along the trail, the dogs stopped once again—this time to sniff some skunk cabbage newly emerged from the muck. While they diddled, I stared out over the pond's surface. From this vantage, I could see the northern shore of Turtle Island.

A glint caught my eye. I squinted at the tangle of partially submerged trunks and roots forming the island's shores but couldn't make out what had caused the glint. My free hand automatically went to the field glasses hanging around my neck. By some miracle, I'd remembered to bring them along this morning.

The glint turned out to be an aluminum bass boat. It wasn't unusual to see bass boats at the island, their occupants taking a break with a can of beer or a cup of coffee, depending on the weather and personal preference. But, I could see that no one was aboard this boat.

Maybe he's gone ashore, I thought and lowered the glasses. The dogs had reached the ends of their leads and were waiting, looking back with peeved expressions on their faces, as if to ask 'What's the problem?' I walked on.

The trail veered away from pond's edge into a stand of tulip poplar trees. The striated gray trunks, at least 20 inches in diameter, shot for the sky in straight, unlimbed lines. Bright green hollies dotted the gray and brown understory. Past the poplar stand, the trail veered near the pond's edge again. I glanced back toward the island. The boat was now obscured by a point of land. Scanning the island while Senge did his business, I could make out no movement, no unnatural color.

"It's not as though I can't see," I said. "The trees over there haven't leafed out yet." Senge was preoccupied with vigorous dirt-kicking, but Dawa tilted her head at me.

I collected Senge's business in one of the plastic bags I keep in my pocket for that purpose.

"C'mon guys. Let's go this way, back along the point a ways."

Leaving the familiar trail to trek through the undergrowth was novel for the Tibbies. They forged ahead, collecting an assortment of leaf litter and twigs on their fuzzy pants. As we neared the water, we picked up a narrow footpath made by fishermen. It was easy to follow.

"Hurry up, Tibbies," I said, a bit annoyed at the dogs' insistence on stopping at every bush. "Mommy wants to see something."

When the boat came into view, I could make out the blue stripes of a Tracker.

"I'm almost positive that's Doc Twilley's boat," I said to the dogs. The Tibbies were also studying the island, their shiny black noses lifted. Senge moaned, his customary expression of frustration. I scanned the island, glasses to my eyes, once more. From this distance and angle, I could clearly see every square inch of its half acre. Doc Twilley was definitely not on Turtle Island.

I groped for my cell phone. Not there. A flutter of panic rose in my stomach. Calculating how far in which direction would take me back to the Nest in the shortest time, I briefly considered backtracking and cutting through the woods to reach Swann's Pond Road just down from Doc Twilley's clinic. Distance-wise, it was six of one and half-dozen of another, but I rejected the idea. In that direction, there was no path through the woods. I would make better time along the good trails back to the Nest.

"Listen. This is important," I said, looking into the dogs' eyes. "We have to go really fast, as fast as we can—OK?" I did not doubt for an instant that the dogs understood what I'd said. Instead of heading up the slope to the well-maintained trail around the pond, I jogged along the western shore, clinging to the fisherman's path. The Tibbies followed obediently—in a most unTibbielike manner.

"You're such good dogs," I told them as we reached the end of a stretch made slippery by the rain. Peg had taught me that praise was at least as important as correction.

Though hard-pressed to go fast while watching my footing, jumping tree roots and avoiding slippery patches of mud and moss, my eyes kept returning to water on my right, searching for some irregularity in the gently rippling surface. The thought crossed my mind that Doc had fallen overboard and drowned. But I shooed the idea away. Even at its deepest point, Swann's Pond is only nine foot deep. Most of it is only six or seven feet, I reasoned, and Doc is over six foot tall and an excellent swimmer.

As I ran, scenes of the swimming lessons Doc gave me as a child flitted through my brain. That was back when you could still swim in the ponds, back before pollution spoiled them for swimming. Mom, Dad and I, Doc and Miz Doc and the boys would meet down at the pond for a picnic on hot Sunday afternoons. We kids spent most of the time in the water, churning up the muddy bottom trying to catch minnows.

A red pickup sat in the parking lot at the boat ramp. An empty boat trailer was hitched to the truck. I paused, breathing heavily, to look around. No sign of the truck's owner out on the pond. No sign of anyone coming or going on Swann's Pond Road either. People are still pretty trusting on Delmarva and often leave their vehicles unlocked, so I peeked inside the passenger side window to see if it was unlocked. Maybe there would be a cell phone inside. No such luck. Just a tackle box, a rod and a thermos in the cab. Nothing in the bed.

Meanwhile, Senge was eagerly sniffing one of the tires and, after watering it, moved eagerly to do the same to the next tire. I felt a gentle pressure against my calf and looked down to see Dawa tapping me.

"What is it, sweetie?" I asked.

She snorted loudly and raised onto her hind legs, gesturing with her forepaws and rrr'ing. Then she dropped down and, butting her nose into the gravel, sniffed loudly. Senge joined her in investigating the odorful spot.

A moment of indecision later, I tugged at their leads and headed for the road. "This way, Tibbies. No time for play right now. We've gotta hurry. Maybe we'll make better time along the shoulder, or maybe somebody'll come along and I can flag them down."

Though reluctant to leave the interesting spot they'd found, the Tibbies soon gave in to my tugging and followed me onto the smooth shoulder of the road. We were soon jogging again.

God—am I outta shape, I was thinking when we reached the junction where Swann's Pond Road meets Cattail Road. For a millisecond, I thought about cutting across Tim's field rather than continuing on to the lane. But the field was newly plowed, and running across the deep, soft furrows would be slower. So, the dogs and I bore to the right to stay on Swann's Pond Road. I figured I could speed up the farm lane to the gate and cut through the woods straight to the Nest.

Suddenly, the Tibbies, who had been following close to my heel, shot ahead of me to the ends of their 10-foot leads. I strengthened my grasp and pumped my legs to keep up with them. Sweat was rolling into my eyes when we reached the lane, but the Tibbies showed no sign of slowing down.

"Hey, guys. This way!" I wheezed, but they ignored me and forged on. "Wait!" I shouted and pulled back on their leads. But the dogs paid me no mind. They twisted and tugged on the ends of their leads like bucking broncos.

"What is wrong with you?" I shouted, exasperated, and shortened the leads to hold the straining, whining dogs in place as I approached them. Dawa barked sharply. Senge followed suit, and both dogs were soon barking as loudly as Tibbies can. I'd never heard them bark so urgently and incessantly. Both struggled against me to continue down the road.

"All right, all right. What is it? What are you so upset about?" I gave in and let the dogs out to the end of their leads. They shot toward the bridge over the dam that holds the pond. On my right, Swann's Pond stretched to the west, Turtle Island at its far end. To the left, lazy Swann's Creek meandered into the woods surrounding the Nest. Sturdy concrete abutments topped by steel guardrails flanked the bridge.

The dogs swerved to the right and began jumping against the abutment. Their urgent barks had become ear-splitting shrieks. Catching up, I peered over the rail into the bowl of the spillway ten feet below. A sheet of muddy pond water fell toward the creek, foaming on the rocks below.

"So what was that all about?" I asked sternly, turning to the dogs. They had fallen silent and stared at me, panting, their eyes slitted. "There's nothing here," I told them. Dawa whimpered and stood, her forepaws resting on the abutment.

I peered over the rail into the bowl again, this time craning my neck to see under the bridge. Nothing. I ran my eyes along the rim of the spillway. They stopped at a shadow against the concrete. Except for the ripples around it, the form was barely visible beneath the gray-green surface of the water. I glanced away, up the pond toward Turtle Island and the abandoned Tracker. A log broken loose from the shore and lodged against the spillway, I thought. My eyes were drawn back to the dark form.

My heart leapt into my throat and strangled me. "Ohmigod, ohmigod," I croaked out loud. I felt light-headed and fought to suck in more air.

With shaking hands, I looped the dogs' leads around the rail and darted to the end of the bridge. Rounding the abutment, I slipped on the dewy grass and bounced down the embankment on my butt. Struggling upright, I slogged to the pond's edge where black muck, littered with half-buried beer cans and fast food containers, tugged at my feet.

Blinking away the sun's reflection on the pond surface, I focused on the object in the water. There was no question. It was a body, face down. It had white hair.

I don't remember how the Tibbies and I got back to the Nest. I vaguely remember being frustrated because my hands were shaking so badly when I made the 911 call. I don't have a clue what I said. I remember pushing off my mud-caked sneaks and slipping on the pair of sandals I keep at the back door. I remember hugging the dogs, turning back to snatch my cell phone off the kitchen counter and then slamming the door behind me. I don't know why on earth I didn't get in the BMW, but, for some reason, I just started running back through the woods to the pond.

I emerged from the farm lane onto Swann's Pond Road only a couple minutes before a State police cruiser pulled up at the bridge. The trooper glanced at me, and I pointed to where I'd found the body. He nodded and, without words, descended the embankment. Leaning over, I rested my hands on my bent knees, gasping for air, the blood roaring in my ears.

In the distance, a siren wailed. Minutes later, an ambulance pulled in behind the cruiser and killed its siren. The two paramedics in it disappeared down the embankment, too.

When I'd regained some breath, I jogged down the road to the bridge and reluctantly looked over the rail. I hoped that I'd been mistaken, that the water and light had played a trick on my eyes, that it was just a sodden log. But I turned away again. I had clearly not been mistaken.

About fifteen minutes later, a maroon Suburban from the volunteer fire company pulled up. It was towing a small boat. The two firemen accompanying it consulted briefly with one of the troopers, climbed back in their vehicle and continued around the pond to the boat ramp. I watched as they backed the rescue boat into the water and slowly made their way across the pond toward the spillway. They maneuvered close to the body and grappled it. I turned away.

Eventually, a trooper approached me. He introduced himself as Whaley. Walking me to the other side of the bridge, he faced me away from the pond and asked what had happened that morning. I recited how the dogs and I had been out for a walk when I'd seen Doc Twilley's empty bass boat out at Turtle Island. When I couldn't spot Doc on the island, I'd become concerned and decided to head for the parking lot in hopes of finding somebody. But nobody was in the lot, and nobody passed on the road either, I told him. There was just a red pickup with an empty trailer parked in the lot, and it was locked.

"Is that Doc Twilley's pickup?"

I shook my head. "I'm not sure."

"That's all right. I'll run the tag. What happened then?"

"Well, I came around here cause this is the shortest way back to my house, down a farm lane up the road a piece," I paused to point toward the lane. He followed my point and nodded. "But when we came to the lane, my dogs were wild to get up here to the bridge—barking and carrying on. So we ran up here and, when I looked over the rail, I saw Doc up against the spillway."

"You know it's Doc Twilley for sure?"

"Well, no. I mean I didn't see the face. But I saw Doc's boat up the pond and," I faltered, "then I saw the white hair so..." My voice caught. "I guessed it was him. Doc has a full head of white hair."

Pinching away tears with one hand and brushing uselessly at the drying mud on my jeans with the other, I managed to go on. "So, I went down to the edge, but I didn't...." My face flamed, and I looked down, unable to continue. I was ashamed that I'd left Doc in the pond, that I'd been afraid to get in the water to see if he was still alive.

"There's nothin' you coulda done for him, m'am," Trooper Whaley said kindly. "You did the right thing calling us."

I looked him in the eyes to see if he was telling me the truth. He was. I nodded. "OK. Well, then I ran back home and called 911."

Another cruiser pulled up and discharged two more troopers. I turned to watch as they, too, disappeared down the embankment and joined a group of men standing in a circle. The rescue boat had been pulled on shore.

"Did you see anybody else this morning, Miz Swann—out on the pond, on the trail, on the road? Any cars or trucks?" Trooper Whaley asked, pulling my attention back to him.

"No, not a soul," I answered. "I don't understand how he could have drowned. Doc Twilley was a good swimmer."

The trooper paused. I guess he was wondering how much to indulge in speculation. "Well, it coulda been a lot of things," he finally said. "Maybe a heart attack or a stroke. Hard to say until the medical examiner determines the cause of..." A call from behind me interrupted the trooper. He asked me to wait, crossed the road and dropped out of sight down the embankment.

While I waited, two cars came up the road from Swann's Neck and stopped to see what was going on. I didn't recognize the drivers. A trooper came up the embankment and spoke with them briefly. He gestured for them to move on. They crept by, the drivers torn between craning their necks to see over the edge and staring at me.

A few minutes later, Trooper Whaley climbed back up to the road. "Miz Swann, will you come on over here, please, and tell us if this is Doc Twilley?"

Chapter Twelve

The dogs bounced on their hind legs, ecstatic to see me, when I finally came through the kitchen door on Thursday night. I tossed the morning paper and my keys on the counter and, dropping to my knees, I enveloped them in my arms.

"Gosh, I missed you guys," I said, gratefully accepting the "slurpies" bestowed on my face. They soon calmed. Senge curled himself against my thigh, happily panting, and Dawa turned over on her back, asking for a tummy scratch. I obliged her.

"C'mon sweeties. You go pee-pee and Mommy will get your dinner." They recognized the "p" word and the "d" word and scooted out through their dog door as soon as I opened it. I flicked on the outside lights and watched them through the panes in the kitchen door for a moment before turning to the tasks at hand.

It'd been a long day. I'd set up my booth at the convention center for the opening of the spring show and sale on Friday morning. I'd also spent some time strolling around to check out the competition. It seemed I would be the only dealer specializing in Asian items. That might be good, or it might be bad. Well, in any event, my booth was visually striking. I was confident that it would attract interest and hopefully buyers.

The *Observer* had been yellowing in the newspaper tube at the head of the driveway all day. Now I paused to unroll and flatten it on the counter, glancing over the headlines above the fold. Nothing of interest there.

I fetched a dipper of kibble from the dispenser in the pantry and, while pouring it in the dogs' bowls, fished out the Local section and spread it on the counter. I raised the kitchen window a crack and called, "Dinner!" The dog door flapped twice and the Tibbies dove into their kibble. Pouring a glass of skim milk for myself, I returned to the paper.

My heart flopped when my eye scanned the headline, "Milford Vet Murdered." I flashed back to the mottled, bloated face that they'd asked me to identify. I squeezed my eyes shut tightly and shook my head. The image disappeared.

The article said that the medical examiner had found that the cause of death was drowning. However, she had also determined that, before he drowned, Doc Twilley had been struck and likely rendered unconscious with a blow to the side of the head. They estimated that death occurred Sunday evening. It didn't say much else—just that the police were investigating and that anyone with information should call the Delaware State Police or CrimeStoppers.

I stood there for a moment, re-reading the article over and over. So, it was true. Thinking back, I realized that Doc must have been murdered only a mile away while we were eating pizza and ice cream on Sunday night.

I'd known, of course, that the police suspected an unnatural death. After I'd identified the body, Trooper Whaley had asked me a few more questions—when did I usually see Doc out here, when had I last seen him, did he usually fish alone, that sort of thing. He thanked me and told me I could go.

But I'd stayed. I'd needed to stay. I don't know how to describe it except as a feeling of paralysis. I'd hung around across the road and watched as a dark green Chevy Suburban parked pondside. "Medical Examiner" was emblazoned across the rear door. After a brief conversation with the troopers, the investigator took photos and conducted a brief examination of the body.

A few minutes later, two men in plainclothes, but obviously officers, had pulled up in an unmarked sedan. Within minutes, they were followed by a blue van marked Evidence Detection. A man and woman, dressed in khaki pants and blue shirts, got out of the van and consulted briefly with the troopers. A trooper, one of the plainclothes officers and the male evidence technician joined a fireman in the rescue boat and motored up the pond to Turtle Island.

Though embarrassed by my morbid curiosity, the temptation to watch was too compelling. I decided to walk out to the point. On the way, I passed the parking lot. The red pickup was open and the female evidence technician was snapping photos. A trooper had opened the thermos and was peering inside. He sniffed. "Coffee. Empty," I heard him say.

Trying to be inconspicuous, I skirted the parking lot and slipped into the woods a little further up the road. Forging a path through the tangled brush, I reached the point quickly. Across the short span of water, the rescue boat was alongside Doc's Tracker. The evidence technician was taking photos of the boat while the plainclothes officer and fireman talked. Beyond them, I could see the trooper slogging through the bare trees on the island.

After watching through my binoculars for about an hour, the rescue boat slowly towed Doc's boat down the pond to the boat ramp. With nothing to engage my curiosity, I'd suddenly felt drained, almost too tired to walk, and decided to head home.

By the time I'd reached the parking lot, a tow truck had been summoned. Its driver lounged against the door meditating on his cigarette. As I drew closer, I could see that the female crime technician inside the truck was lifting fingerprints from the dash. That was when it finally struck me that the police thought a murder had taken place. Those plainclothes officers were probably the homicide detectives.

When I'd reached the farm lane to turn for home, the medical investigator and a trooper were loading a black body bag into the Medical Examiner's vehicle. When it left, everyone shut up and turned to watch it go.

I flipped to the back of the Local section of the paper. Finally, there was an obituary for Doc. A smiling photo of him several years younger was accompanied by the description of his life's accomplishments and surviving family. He was 71 years old. The service was to be on Friday at two o'clock.

I groaned inwardly. I couldn't afford to close my booth at the show while I attended the funeral. But attend the funeral I must.

"Well, I'll just have to find somebody to watch the booth for me for a few hours," I said to the dogs who were sitting next to me with worried expressions on their faces.

When I crawled into bed an hour later, Dawa was already enthroned on her pillow and Senge wasted no time plastering himself to my side. I was exhausted, but sleep once again eluded me. Annoyed, I switched on the bedside lamp and plumped the pillows behind my back. I pulled out my latest book-in-progress, a history of India. It could be trusted to knock me out cold. But my eyes were drawn to the reflections in the wavy glass of my bedroom windows, and my mind replayed the events of the week—first Teke's disappearance and then Doc's death.

Doc's two sons, Mike and Don, and their families had arrived home on Tuesday afternoon. That night, Peg and I had taken a ham and a casserole over to Doc's house. We hadn't seen his boys since college. I had never met their wives and kids. Still, they hugged us, and we sat around the kitchen table like old friends do, catching up on what has happened in our lives over the years. Eventually, they asked me about finding the body. The telling of it to his sons was terrible. In the telling, I left out the part about his face. But I couldn't leave Doc's face out of my mind.

Eventually, my mind stopped whirring and I dozed off.

It hadn't been easy on such short notice but I'd found someone willing to work in my booth for the afternoon of Doc's funeral. The owner of the antique mall recommended one of the cashiers and gave me her number. Luckily, she was willing to meet me in Ocean City. The petite, sixty-ish woman, oddly but aptly named Birdie, had a chirpy way of talking. She seemed a reliable sort. Though she admitted knowing nothing about Asian antiques in particular, she seemed to know the basics—the difference between porcelain and earthenware for instance. After showing her my inventory book and briefing her on my discount policy, I'd left her in charge of the cash box and headed north to pick up Peg.

Peg was waiting at the end of the drive and quickly slid into the passenger seat. "Let's cut across by the old campgrounds and then up by the tax ditch," she suggested, "That'll be faster."

She was right. Twenty minutes later, we arrived at the Carey Funeral Home parking lot. It was overflowing. A black-suited attendant with a face like a small-mouth bass directed us up the block, where I eased the BMW into a nonexistent spot.

The funeral home was a Georgian Revival homes built at the turn of the 20th century. From the moment the bereaved enter through the two-story white colonnade, they are made to feel they are sending the dearly departed off in style. The last time I had passed through Carey's ornate portico was for Dad's funeral, and the time before that was Mom's. I experienced an uncomfortable sensation of *déjà vu*.

The parlor was packed. As a pillar of the community for many years, Doc's funeral had attracted a large crowd to pay its respects. Peg spotted acquaintances and gently guided me toward them. Unluckily, we were waylaid en route.

"Abby Swann! How the – are you?" exclaimed the woman, substituting a snort for the omitted implied expletive. That was her only concession to propriety. Her too-loud voice caused heads to turn. She imposed an exuberant embrace on me.

Not that Lorraine Parsons is unfeeling. She's just one of those pragmatic personalities who accepts what is and makes the best of the situation. Doc may have been her long-time employer and friend but, in Lorraine's mind, his funeral was as good a time as any to catch up on the gossip. She wasted no time cutting to the chase.

"So, was it awful when you found him?" she queried, her florid face mere inches from mine bore a false expression of empathy.

My eyebrows shot up involuntarily. This was brazen even for Lorraine. Over Lorraine's shoulder, I saw Peg roll her eyes.

"Well, yes, Lorraine, it was awful," I replied sarcastically. My tone of voice left the 'What a tactless question' comment barely unsaid. I turned pointedly to the two women with Lorraine. One I recognized as Doc's youthful receptionist, whose name I couldn't remember if I'd ever known it, but I'd never seen the short, red-haired, twenty-something girl with them.

I extended my hand to the redhead, "We haven't met. I'm Abby Swann."

"Oh, I am sorry," piped up Lorraine, "This is Katie Adkins, the other vet tech, and you know Debbie Masten, the receptionist. This is my cousin Abby and this is Peg Beauchamp."

"*Distant* cousin," I corrected. "Hi, Debbie. Nice to meet you, Katie."

Lorraine brushed aside the interruption. "Abby lives in that big old house at Swann's Pond."

The redhead shook hands limply but she said nothing, eyes downcast. Shy, I thought.

"Hi," said Debbie, "I've seen you at the office. Your dogs are real cute."

"Thanks."

"They ever find that dog of yours that got stolen?" Lorraine piped at Peg as if Teke's disappearance were a cheery topic of conversation.

Peg and I shook our heads, but Lorraine wasn't really interested in Teke. Not missing a beat, she resumed the interrogation. "So, how did Doc look when you found him? Could you see where he'd been hit?"

"For heaven's sake, Lorraine," hissed Peg.

I glanced toward the closed casket at the other end of the parlor. Several mourners, having no body to evaluate the mortician's skill, leaned over the many sprays and bouquets to study the florist's art and the donors' names. I was aware that the family sat just out of sight of the crowd, in an alcove to one side of the casket.

"No, Lorraine, I couldn't see anything like that," I lied. "He just looked, well, lifeless—nothing like the nice man I'd known all my life." I looked at Lorraine, whose jaw hung slack and mouth gaped slightly, and then back at the casket. "I'm going to go say something to Mike and Don."

"That woman is a pain in the butt," Peg muttered when Lorraine was out of earshot.

"I know," I conceded and shrugged, "She's been that way all her life. She just wants some tidbit she can go around telling people so she can feel important. Look. There's Dr. Lynch sitting in the third row."

Peg looked in the direction of my nod. Jackie Lynch had not dressed for the occasion—just her usual jeans and shirt. But as we passed, we could see that her eyes were red and sunken into a swollen, blotchy face. Peg arched her brows. I shrugged imperceptibly.

When the service concluded, a long line of cars and trucks with their headlights on slowly formed behind the hearse and family limousine. We crept out of town and up the highway the short distance to the cemetery at Barratt's Chapel. Peg and I hung back, in the shadow of the simple 18th century brick edifice, rather than follow the crowd to the gravesite. As the crowd began to disperse, we filed past the family seated by the flower-covered casket one last time and headed toward my car. I was hoping to hurry home and check on the Tibbies before going to Doc's house, but I was dismayed to turn a corner and run into Lorraine and Debbie, squashing cigarette butts under their feet. The other vet tech, Katie, was nowhere around.

"You really shouldn't leave those things there," I said, glaring at the butts defacing the venerable chapel's manicured pathways.

"You're right," Lorraine said with a sheepish pretense that I didn't believe for a second. She poked at her butt with the toe of her shoe until it was more or less obscured in the turf.

"Sheesh, Lorraine," I said, shaking my head and continuing on. Ignoring the hint, Lorraine tailed me with Debbie bringing up the rear.

"Are you going over to the house, Abby?" she asked from behind me.

I nodded.

"Yeah, us too."

I rolled my eyes mentally. I wondered if the two of them were traveling together. Were they just co-workers or related in some way? There seemed to be too much difference in age for them to be close friends. Debbie was a quiet kid, barely out of her teens. They couldn't have much in common.

"Debbie, who are your parents? Maybe I know them," I asked, to kill time and keep Lorraine at arms length.

"Oh, she's my cousin Ted's kid. Her Mom was Cindy Holloway," Lorraine answered for her.

I nodded. The names were vaguely familiar, but they weren't from Lorraine's mother's side, which is how she and I were related. "You been working for Doc long?"

"A couple years, since I graduated," Debbie said quietly.

"Do you like it?"

"Yeah, I guess," she said without much enthusiasm.

We walked in silence for several more yards. "Do you know what's going to happen to the practice, Lorraine?" Peg asked.

"Not a clue. Dr. Lynch has been doing the surgeries we had scheduled, but we cancelled all the appointments. Maybe the sons will sell it, but I really don't know. 'Course, business has been falling off for some time."

"Really?" Peg said.

"Oh yeah. You know, what with Doc getting on in years. Some of things he did were, well, kind of old-fashioned. People wanted the latest medicine. Plus, they got fed up with Doc. And that new practice out on the dual is closer for the people who live in town than coming all the way out to Swann's Pond."

The "dual"—pronounced dool as in drool—was local parlance for a four-lane highway where the northbound lanes are separated from the southbound lanes by a broad swath of ground. The rival practice was on U.S. 113, one of the main routes that traverse southern Delaware.

By now we had reached my car. "What do you mean by people getting fed up, Lorraine?" I asked, aiming the key at the door and pressing the unlock.

This time it was Debbie who piped up. "Because Doc was so cranky all the time. And he yelled at Dr. Lynch a lot and would criticize her in front of the patients. He pissed off a lot of people."

"That doesn't sound like Doc," Peg said.

"No, I know it doesn't if you haven't been around him for a while. He used to be the sweetest man," Lorraine said, shaking her head sadly. "But he'd changed in the past couple of years—well, ever since Miz Doc died really. You remember Betty, the receptionist before Debbie? He fired her for nothing, right in front of a full waiting room. And he's hollered at me and Katie lots of times. And, Jackie Lynch, well, she put up with a lot. That's all I can say."

"You know, Lorraine, this just doesn't sound right," I said, "I had the Tibbies in for their checkups, and he seemed fine. Then, just last Sunday, I saw him out at the pond fishing. He seemed just as nice as ever." I was sure that Lorraine had a lot more to say. I waited.

She shrugged. "He never changed toward the animals—he still took care of them all right. Or, if he was off fishing, he was OK. It seemed like it was just in the office that he'd show his ass. Moody as hell. You never knew who he was—Jekyll or Hyde—from one minute to the next. I tell you, I've been with him for twenty years, but I'd had it up to here myself," Lorraine emphasized her point with a gesture above her head. "He got so he couldn't stand some people, and some people couldn't stand him back." She paused for a breath.

"But I figured I'd try to hang in there. He had to retire sometime and then maybe Dr. Lynch would buy the practice. She's really nice to work with. And she wanted to buy in, you know. She had plans to update the facilities and the equipment. She was the one talked him into getting computers. Then, a year or so back, she tried to buy in. They were talking about it for a while, but I guess Doc changed his mind and decided he wasn't interested anymore. Or, maybe she couldn't afford it. I don't really know the details. Anyway, whatever the reason was, the deal fell through. But ever since then, he'd holler at her that she was incompetent and stuff like that, and nitpick every little thing she did. But, as far as I can tell, she's a good vet. She didn't deserve all that crap. I don't know why she took it as long as she did. There's plenty of places for a vet to work."

I shook my head. "Well, I'm sorry to hear all this. I had no idea. Maybe he was going through some kind of depression after Miz Doc died." There was a collective pause. "Well, we'll see you out at Doc's house." I lied, sincerely hoping that we could avoid her once we got there.

As I pulled onto Rt. 1 headed back toward the Nest, Peg said, "I wonder if his boys knew any of this was going on."

"And, if he thought Jackie Lynch was such a terrible vet, why didn't he just fire her?" I added.

"Yeah, but she sure acted upset for somebody who couldn't stand him," Peg said quietly.

Chapter Thirteen

I didn't know whether I was coming or going the rest of the weekend. I finally rolled into the carriage house at one o'clock Sunday night, well, actually, it was Monday morning.

"We're home," I said to the Tibbies, who were clawing at the car door to get out. They'd stayed over with "Aunt Peg" but they were glad to be back home, too.

After the funeral, Peg and I had passed an hour of subdued conversation and food consumption at Doc's house. Lorraine wasn't in sight—thankfully. Then, we rushed by the Nest to pick up the Tibbies and their overnight bag.

"You'll be much happier here with Aunt Peg," I'd assured them as I prepared to leave them in her care. Peg's offer to dogsit the rest of the weekend was welcome. I'd been worrying about leaving Dawa and Senge at home alone for long periods while I worked at the show. Dawa and Senge would help Peg keep her mind off Teke, too. But the Tibbies weren't convinced. Dawa's eyes seemed twice their normal size and Senge's worry wrinkles had tripled in number.

"Mommy will stop by on her way to and from work, and you'll have Bits and Dapper to play with all weekend," I said trying to reassure them, and encircled them both in my arms.

"OK, OK, enough already," Peg chastised. "You're getting them all worked up. Better to come and go without a lot of fuss."

"I know, I know," I said and kissed them each on top of their heads.

Peg pushed a bag containing a smoked turkey sandwich and a fruit drink into my hand. "Now go," she said, shooing me toward the door. "They'll be fine with me."

A last glance at them over Peg's shoulder and I was out the door. I relieved Birdie at half past four in the afternoon. She'd done a good business in smalls. I thanked her sincerely, tucking an extra $10 in her pay, and told her I'd be in touch next time I needed help. The smalls continued to sell well all weekend, but the big ticket items, though invariably admired, were passed by. When all was said and done, the bottom line was a bit less than I'd hoped for.

I'd noticed that business was brisk in every other genre—from country furniture to the tiresome but ubiquitous baseball cards. As I drove home with the sleeping dogs on the seat beside me, I wondered whether diversifying my stock would help my business. I promised myself I'd think about that some more when I was a little less brain dead. For now, I just wanted home and bed.

The Tibbies streaked for the kitchen door and jumped up and down while I fiddled with the key. I looked up. The crescent moon was a slash in a black velvet sky. Something hunting or hunted crashed in the undergrowth in the woods behind me, and Senge gave a sharp, impatient bark.

"God, Senge, give me a heart attack why don't you!" I said crankily as I stabbed the key at the lock. The door swung open a crack. The only problem was I hadn't unlocked it. It was already open.

"I know I've been tired and rushed but I *know* I closed and locked that door," I whispered to the dogs. I pushed the door inward.

Before I could stop them, the Tibbies bolted door and disappeared inside. Stunned, all I could think was that an intruder still in the house would hurt them. Grabbing the baseball bat I kept just inside the kitchen door, my hand reached for the light switch but hesitated. I'd always laughed about stupid people in horror movies who creep around in the dark when a perfectly good light switch is at hand. Instantaneously, I concluded that the benefits of being able to see outweighed the possibility of alerting an intruder to my presence. If he's still here, I reasoned, he undoubtedly heard me come up the lane.

The light nearly blinded me. I looked around frantically. No unwelcome surprises in the kitchen. Vaguely, my tired brain registered the fact that the dogs weren't barking. If a stranger were in the house, they would bark.

"Dawa, Senge. Come," I called in my command voice. No response, not that any Tibbie owner would reasonably expect one unless there were something in it for the Tibbie.

"Dawa, Senge. Come. TREAT!" I hollered, my voice quavering. This time their non-response terrified me. Most of the time, calling the "t-word" induced them to obey.

Oh God, I prayed, staring into the dark cavern that was the great room beyond the kitchen. My moment of paralyzed panic passed and, hefting the bat in my right hand, I rushed into the great room. Flicking the switch, the trio of schoolhouse lamps threw the long room into a warm glow.

An unearthly shriek from the dark beyond the archway to the main house stopped my heart. It was Dawa.

"DAWA, SENGE. COME!!! NOW!!!" I screamed, sprinting through the great room toward the main house, bat at ready. I heard Senge growl and then whimper. Luckily, the switch for the hall chandeliers is on the great room side of the archway. I bolted up the three steps between the two sections, flipped the switch and plunged through the door in one smooth motion. Grasping the bat two-handed, I hunched like a tennis player waiting for the serve, knees flexed, ready to launch in either direction. Glancing left, I saw only the closed "front door." I craned my neck to look up the stairs disappearing above me into the darkness.

Still clutching my weapon high, I lurched forward toward the center of the hall. "Senge! Dawa!" I shouted. Another whimper turned me right. As I swerved into the darkened dining room, I swiped the switch as I passed. I missed.

My feet flew out from under me, and the floor smacked my back hard. I may have been flat on the floor, windless and dazed, for several minutes, but, looking back, it was probably only second or two. I clawed for the bat that was no longer in my hand. Dawa shrieked again. I hoisted myself to sitting, frantically trying to focus my eyes and brain. I had rolled over onto my knees and was struggling to get a leg forward when pain exploded across my shoulders. My chin struck the hardwood, and the bat crashed next to my head.

My ear is wet, I thought hazily. Oh, Senge is licking it. I lifted my head and he transferred his ablutions to my nose. I pushed up onto my knees.

"OK, OK, Senge. Thank you, those are nice kisses, but I'm all right," I mumbled into his mane as I balanced on one wobbly arm and hugged him with the other.

"Dawa, where are you, precious one?" I asked and sat back on my heels. I saw her sitting straight ahead of me. "Are you OK?" I held out my arms, and she tiptoed to me. The vise gripping my heart loosened.

Rubbing my chin and testing my jaw, I wondered whether my teeth had been loosened by the impact. I stood slowly, wincing at the sharp pain in my right shoulder, and swept my eyes over the room. My dogs were safe, but I was terrified that the intruder was still nearby—hiding somewhere in the house or on the grounds.

Gritting my sore teeth to keep them from chattering, my eyes swept the room. I turned and peered out the doorway again, back down the hall, my ears straining for the slightest sound—a breath, a footfall, a creaking floorboard or a rasping hinge. All was silence save for Senge's snorting and sniffing and Dawa's gentle whining.

Shaking violently, I rested my forehead against the doorframe. Dawa roo'd behind me. I turned to find her standing on her hind legs, stretching to reach the dining room table with her forepaws. Next to her, Senge was vigorously butting his nose into the Tibetan carpet.

"What is it, guys?" I said. Dawa barked the impatient little yip she reserves for scolding me. There on the table, beyond reach of her paws, lay a rolled leather collar with two tags. I leaned over the table, my hand poised in mid-air, and read the tag. It said, "Teke. Peg Beauchamp, RR 2, Box 81, Milton DE. 302-777-3191." A folded up piece of paper was next to the collar.

Though hurting too badly to think straight, I had sense enough to caution myself to think very, very straight.

"Get a grip, Abby," I growled. The Tibbies looked up and tilted their heads at me.

"Listen, guys, he could still be here, in the house or on the property. We've got to get out and we've got to call somebody for help. And I'm afraid to touch anything because it could be evidence," I whispered. "Maybe I should read the note anyway. No. *No.* Better to leave it until I can get help. Come on, guys. Help Mommy out here. Follow me, OK? Dawa, Senge, heel."

Maybe some dog angel was smiling down on me or maybe the Tibbies sensed my absolute terror. Dawa and Senge, otherwise as typically independent as all their breed, uncharacteristically and promptly obeyed me. Abandoning their investigation, they came to my side. At first, I turned toward the back door, the shortest way out of the house, but changed my mind when I realized how far through the pitch black yard I would have to go to reach the carriage house. I kicked myself mentally for not replacing that floodlight that burned out. But, in the space of the second that I stared at the back door, I realized that it, too, was slightly ajar.

The panic rose in my throat again. "Come on, guys, let's go back through the great room. Nobody's in there. Come on. Heel for Mommy."

Once in the kitchen, I attached leads to the dogs' collars with trembling fingers, retrieved my bag and keys where I had dropped them at the door and sprinted across the yard to the carriage house. Locked into my car, my Tibbies safely at my side, I sped out the lane and turned onto Cattail Road, made the left at Swann's Creek Road and screeched to a stop at the bridge. I made the first call to 911 and the second to Peg.

Within ten minutes, the first trooper arrived where I waited on the bridge. I followed him back to the main gate at the head of the driveway. Another trooper met us there. They assured me that whoever had left the collar was probably long gone and, under police escort, I returned to the Nest.

About fifteen minutes later, Peg's pickup pulled into the yard where I stood with a paramedic who was earnestly trying to convince me to go to emergency room. The Tibbies were glued to my legs. Peg and Phil climbed down from the cab and hurried over.

"I'll go in tomorrow and get an xray," I promised the paramedic, "but I'm not going to emergency now." The paramedic persisted. "Yeah, yeah. I know," I said, brushing him off. "I could have a fracture or something, but it doesn't feel that bad." I rolled my shoulders.

"It'll hurt like hell tomorrow, ma'm," he commented.

"Probably will. Thanks for your help."

The paramedic shrugged and knelt to gather up his equipment.

"What happened?" Phil asked.

"Came home and somebody was in the house, in the dining room. He knocked me across the back with my bat and got away." I cringed as a bolt of pain shot through my neck.

"You should have gone to emergency," Peg remarked.

"Yeah well."

"He was aiming for your head and missed," Phil commented. "You're lucky."

"What about the collar? You said on the phone that Teke's collar is here," Peg asked.

"I don't know. I... ."

We turned to watch two cruisers pull up. Griff got out of the first, raised a hand, and turned to unload Thor from the backseat. The officer from the other approached and shook hands with Peg. She introduced him as Glen Insley, the detective in charge of Teke's case. I explained what had happened. I added that I was absolutely certain I had thrown the deadbolt when I left that morning.

"Well, let's go inside and see what this note says. Griff can get started on a sweep of the grounds," Insley said and we returned to the hall outside the dining room.

Peg stared at the collar still lying on the dining room table. Excusing himself, Glen Insley spoke quietly for several minutes with the officers who searched the house. He returned to where we were waiting.

"Well, Miz Swann, Miz Beauchamp, they've searched the entire house and the outbuildings. Everything is secure," he began.

"The third floor, too? And the basement?" I asked.

"Yes, m'am, top to bottom. Nobody's here. From what you say, I'd guess what happened is he came in through the front door here," he said, pointing to the 'back door,' "which has sustained some damage consistent with breaking and entering, and left the collar and note in the first room he came to, the dining room here. Then he must have decided to check out the rest of the house and threw the deadbolt on the kitchen door. Maybe he was exiting when you drove up."

"I'm going to get Thor started from the dining room and see if he can pick up a trail," Griff said. "Hey Thor, c'mon boy, let's go get the bad guy!" Thor pricked his ears and responded with a leap and a deafening bark. "Good boy. C'mon boy, get 'im!" Thor soon found the same spot on the carpet next to the table that Senge had been sniffing. He began moving toward the great room.

"Did you notice anything missing, Miz Swann?" Detective Insley asked.

"I didn't look. All I could think about was getting out fast." I said.

Peg was still staring at the collar on the table and the folded piece of paper next to it. Insley noticed. "Well, let's see what it says," he said and walked to the table

Chapter Fourteen

"You know, Peg, what I don't understand is why Doc's rod and tackle box were in the truck while he was out on the pond. And the thermos was empty," I said, squeezing my arms around my knees as we sat staring into the fireplace.

"Strange," she agreed, sitting on the floor next to me, staring into the fire. Her eyes were sunken.

"Yeah."

"It's like he'd already been out on the pond and went back out for some reason," Griff said from the Queen Anne chair behind us.

I glanced back. His face was hidden in the shadow cast by the chair's wings. The flickering firelight illuminated Thor twitching in a dream next to the chair. I turned back to the fire. The grandfather clock in the hall outside the parlor chimed five o'clock. The stars would soon fade.

The house, its doors having stood open to the outdoors through the coldest part of the night, was like an icebox when the police finally left at four o'clock. As I'd closed the door on the last officer, I suggested we lay a fire in the parlor and snuggle up until the old oil burner could overcome the chill.

The Tibbies were perched in the window seat adjacent to the fireplace, visible only as silhouettes against the wavy glass. Dawa's head rested on Senge's side. They were awake, their eyes glittering in the light.

The floorboards in the hall creaked as Phil entered. "Here's the coffee," he said a moment later, setting down a tray with four mugs on the coffee table.

I rose stiffly to turn on the table lamp next to Griff's chair. "Thanks, Phil. Did you find everything all right?" I said. I sat on the adjacent camelback sofa and reached for the cream.

"The other strange thing is that the boat was found up the pond and the body was found down the pond." Griff said, picking up the thread and reaching for a mug.

"I assumed the body just floated downstream," I said.

"He hadn't been dead that long—the body would've sank where he died so he had to have died where you found him. Bodies don't float until the gasses from decomposition...." He trailed off and sipped. "Besides, there isn't that much current in Swann Pond."

"The medical examiner ruled he died by drowning. So he was alive when he went in the water, even though he'd been bludgeoned," Phil added as he seated himself next to the coffee table.

"So, he either went overboard where I found him and the killer took the boat back up the pond to Turtle Island. Or, he went overboard somewhere up the pond and swam down the pond to where I found him."

"Right. But it seems unlikely to me that the killer would have attacked him and pushed him overboard right there by the bridge, in broad daylight. A car could have come along at any second," Griff said.

"Well, if he went over up the pond and could still swim, why wouldn't he swim to shore?" Phil asked.

"Doc was an athletic man, despite his age, and he'd always been a good swimmer." I replied, glancing at Peg. She was staring at the fire. "But maybe he was disoriented from the blow to the head. Or cold, maybe, like hypothermia."

Griff nodded. "Whoever killed him had to get off the boat on shore, not on Turtle Island. So the boat must have drifted down the pond to Turtle Island, where it got caught in the roots, from a point somewhere up the pond where the killer got off," he continued.

"So, he couldn't have gotten off at the parking lot since that's downstream from Turtle Island?" Peg asked. She had turned from her meditation on the fire.

"Right. Here, hon," Phil said handing her a mug.

"Why would he get off in the woods instead of at the parking lot?"

"Less obvious than the parking lot, where somebody passing by might notice?" Phil asked, rather than answered. "Or—maybe because it's closer to wherever he wanted to go?"

"But there's nothing within walking distance in that direction except..." I paused.

"Except Doc's clinic and house," Phil finished the sentence.

"But didn't they say neither the clinic nor house had been broken into?"

Phil nodded. "Right. There was no sign of a break-in. Nothing missing."

Peg sat down on the sofa next to me. She sighed deeply. We'd been chattering on about Doc just to keep the silence at bay. I put one arm around her shoulder and squeezed. "They'll get some clues off the collar or the ransom note."

"Maybe," she said and stared into the mug she was holding two-handed.

I knew she was still thinking about the note. Detective Insley had been very careful as Peg and I watched him unfold the note with the non-business end of a pen. It was a word-processed sheet of paper with the simple message in all capital letters:

$20000 IN SMALL BILLS.
WILL CONTACT WHERE TO LEAVE MONEY.

What puzzled us was why the dognapper left this note at the Nest. Whoever it was must have known that Peg and I are close friends. That narrowed it down—not much, but some. Still, why not break into Peg's house? Why break into my house? I wondered whether whoever broke in know I wasn't here because of the show? That would really narrow it down. I had scoured my brain repeatedly trying to think who, besides the three other people seated around the coffee table, knew that a) Peg and I are close friends b) where I live and c) I wasn't home Sunday. Unable to come up with anyone, I shook my head. Unless it was just coincidence.

"You know, I really thought that whoever took Teke was motivated by jealousy—somebody like Evelyn Hitchens. It never dawned on me that it was just someone after money."

"They could be one and the same, Peg," Phil said.

"Yeah, it could be. We've been watching the Hitchens woman's place all this time, but nothing's been out of the ordinary," Griff added. "Her place is a lot closer to Peg's than to here. 'Course…Peg's place is kinda out in the open. This is a lot more secluded, being out in the woods and all."

"I guess I'd better get home," Peg said abruptly, putting down her mug and standing. "I have to take care of the dogs and then figure out where to get that much money."

"I'll go with you…" I began.

"No, you can't," she said sharply. "We don't know how or where they'll contact us. It could be here or my house."

"OK. You're right." I paused. "Listen, Peg, do you need money because, if you do, I can get some together."

"Me, too, Peg." Phil had risen to his feet when she stood up. "We'll manage it somehow."

"No, I think I can raise it, but thanks." She rubbed the back of her neck. "But if I run into trouble, I'll let you know."

Leaning over to hug me, she said, "Listen, I really gotta go." I noticed she was trembling. I hugged back.

"I need to keep moving, doing something. Phil, can you drive? I don't think I can drive right now."

"Sure, honey, sure. I'll get your jacket."

The eastern horizon was pinking when Peg and Phil disappeared down the lane in her truck. Griff stood behind me watching them through the kitchen door.

I turned back to the kitchen where Dawa and Senge sat watching me expectantly. Griff trailed me.

I finally asked the question that had been burning. "Did you and Thor pick up anything out there?"

"The guy went along pretty much parallel to your driveway, then he veered off toward Cattail Branch and over your fence just down from the main gate. Maybe he didn't know there's a gate further along the fence. Then Thor tracked him down the farm lane and along the shoulder of Swann's Pond Road to the bridge."

"So, he didn't drive up here?"

"Nope. He was definitely on foot."

"Strange, if he knew I wasn't here, why not drive up?"

"Dunno."

"Must've had a car there at the bridge. Not unusual for people to park their cars at the bridge while they go fishing. But you don't see cars there at night."

"Uh-huh."

My eyes popped open. They focused fuzzily and I realized that I was standing at the counter staring blindly at the coffeemaker. I must have dozed. The adrenalin rush, bolstered by caffeine, that had propped me up through the night, had suddenly evaporated. I was vaguely aware that my shoulders ached.

"You're dead on your feet. Get some rest," he said. "Listen. Do you want me to stay? If you don't feel safe, until you can get a new lockset on the front—I mean back—door, I can hang around..."

"Hang around, please," I interrupted. A moment later, I was enveloped in strong, warm arms. I gladly let my weight rest against him.

"I'm not much of a night person," I whispered.

"Mom is very tired," Senge said nestling his body next to hers.

"Yes, and afraid. The human who hurt Mom was the same one who lured Teke out of his crate," said Dawa from her pillow. "That is the third time I have smelled him."

"Well, what can we do, Sister?" asked Senge, sitting up to look at Dawa.

Dawa stretched out a paw and delicately tapped Abby's cheek. "Mom cannot smell like we can, Brother. If we see him or smell him or hear him, we will know him and we must tell Mom."

"Like we told her about the dead man?"

"Yes, Brother, for, as you know, 'little brooks make much noise'," *Dawa quoted and closed her eyes.*

Chapter Fifteen

Eleven o'clock the clock radio said. Lifting my head with a groan, I squinted toward the window to see if it was eleven o'clock in the morning or at night. Ah, morning.

The events of last night were muddled in my brain, and I struggled to put them in sensible order. They all came back with shocking clarity when I tried to raise up on my elbows. "Ow!" I fell back on my stomach.

My hand instinctively reached for Dawa's plush body on the pillow next to mine and, finding nothing, moved to my side in search of Senge. The dogs' absence alarmed me at some basic level, and I dragged myself upright, peering around the room through half-open eyes.

"Oh, there you are, monkeys," I said, spotting them sitting and staring up at the door knob. "Poor little ones, you must have to pee something awful. And I'll bet you're hungry, too." I slid off the bed.

In reply, Senge bounced to the bed and woofed while Dawa, more ladylike, roo'd from the bedroom door.

"C'mon sweet peas." I stood aside as they darted through the door and down the stairs. Halfway down the staircase, the sound of quiet snoring reached me. Peeking through the great room door, I spied the figure wrapped in an afghan on the couch with a large German Shepherd asleep on the floor in front of the couch. Back upstairs on cats' paws, I pulled a terry robe on over my nightshirt and a brush through my hair. I swished mouthwash around my mouth.

"Mornin'," he greeted me as I stepped down into the great room a few minutes later. Both Thor and he were now upright.

"Morning. Sleep OK?"

"Mmmm. Nice couch."

The Tibbies were arf'ing loudly at the kitchen door so I signaled a time out and hurried to open the dog door. They shot through the flap.

"He needs to go, too," Griff said behind me as he snapped a lead onto Thor's collar. "Back in a minute."

I watched Griff through the kitchen door. His shirt was rumpled and his hair stood off in spikes. As if he heard me thinking, he ran his fingers through his hair. I hung up the phone just as he returned ten minutes later. No contact yet, Peg had said. And no word from Insley either.

"Breakfast?" I offered. He accepted.

"How's your back?" he asked, walking up behind me.

"Sore as hell."

"Lemme see," he said, reaching for my shoulders. I flinched at the contact. He gently slid the robe down over my shoulders.

He grunted, and I felt the trace of his fingertips from right to left across my back.

"Nasty-looking bruise." His voice was husky. His hand rested on my back and then dropped away. He pulled the robe up to cover my shoulders and said matter-of-factly, "You know if he'd hit you just a little higher he could have fractured your neck or your skull."

I swallowed. "Phil said that's what he meant to do but that his aim was bad."

"You should get an xray today."

"It really doesn't feel that bad," I said, turning my head to glance back at him.

He nodded.

A short stack and three sausage links later, Griff pushed back his chair and declared that he had to leave as he was already late for work.

I followed him outside. The cold night had given way to a sweet-scented spring morning—one that, under ordinary circumstances, would have lifted my spirits. But a worry headache, fueled by sleep loss, roared behind my eyes and drove away all other feelings. Well, almost all feelings.

"If they call, take down what they say carefully. Do you have caller ID?" Griff asked. I shook my head. "Then hit *69 to see where the call came from and call Glen Insley right away." I nodded.

Hesitantly, he leaned down and kissed me on the lips. Just a little. Just enough.

With Thor settled on the backseat of his truck's extended cab, Griff climbed into the front and reached out for the door. "Stop worrying. I'll call you later."

"Thanks for staying, Griff. Really." I wondered if I should offer another kiss, but I didn't and he pulled the door closed.

I waved as he pulled away and stood listening as long as I could hear the crunch of tires on gravel. Two extra-strength Tylenol® later, I settled on the couch in the great room, phone at hand, Dawa at my head and Senge at my foot.

It seemed I had only just dozed off when the phone rang. I woke up with a jerk and looked sideways at the phone in my limp hand. My heart was already racing.

"Hi. May I speak to Mrs. Swann?" said the cheery voice on the other end.

Oh great, I thought. "This is Ms. Forrest Swann," I replied in the icy tone I reserve for telemarketers. Moments later I dismissed the unwanted caller with a brisk, "Thank you for calling but I am not interested" and settled back to my nap.

In what seemed like a minute later, I was awakened by a banging sound from the main house. Struggling upright, I squinted first at my watch—three o'clock—and then at dogs perched expectantly on the pillows of the sofa back. A driving rain pelted the great room windows.

I walked over and pressed my nose to a pane. My nose told me the temperature had dropped several degrees. The trees beyond the pane were swaying like waving wheat.

"Oh well, so much for the lovely spring day," I said out loud to the dogs, "Sounds like that shutter in the parlor has come loose again."

I trudged to the kitchen and shrugged into my slicker. Minutes later, the dogs watched me intently through the great room window as I struggled to secure the flapping shutter. Back inside, I shed my slicker in the mudroom and toweled off my face. Fishing my cell phone out of my bag, I called Peg's cell number and massaged my neck as it rang.

"Heard anything?" I asked without preamble.

"No. You?"

"Nothing here either," I said. "Are you having a downpour there?"

"Yeah and it's blowing a gale, too. I got whitecaps in the hopper," she answered.

I couldn't help but smile. "Same here," I paused while I settled the teakettle on the burner. "Peg, I just can't figure out why they would bring the note here. It's driving me crazy. I mean, a lot of people know we're friends. But, so what? Why not take the note out to your place?"

"Maybe because they know where you are but not me."

"What do you mean?"

"Well, I've been thinking about it, too. The address on Teke's tag is just a rural route and box number. I never got around to getting him a new tag after all the route numbers changed to road names because of the 911 project. And…there's nothing but my name in the phone book. So, I'm thinking that maybe they just don't know where I live."

"But I'm easy to find, right? Abby Swann of Swann's Nest with the big sign out on Cattail Road."

"Right."

"But, Peg, doesn't Evelyn Hitchens know where you live?"

"Sure. She came out here with one of her Poodles that time I taught a basic obedience class for the kennel club," Peg said. The light bulb came on. "Oh. So that means she's not the one behind this?"

"Who knows?" I said, pouring hot water into a mug of cocoa powder. "Maybe it's like Griff said—it's just because your house is so out in the open and mine's back in the woods."

"Well, for that matter, why go to all the trouble of breaking into your house, Abby? Why not just call me on the phone or leave a note in your mailbox?" Peg's voice broke. "And, Abby, if whoever it is wants money so bad, why not take something at your house? There's expensive stuff sittin' all over the place."

I dropped mini-marshmallows into the cocoa. "Well, maybe he—or she—doesn't know what my stuff is worth or how to sell it. I mean, cash is easier."

"Yeah, but why take my dog in the first place? Aren't there a lot simpler ways to steal money?"

She had me there. "I dunno, Peg.."

"Why take my dog?" she whispered again. I listened to her cry softly. I realized I hadn't heard Peg cry about Teke until now. In fact, I hadn't heard her cry since, well, probably since high school when she broke her ankle playing field hockey.

"Don't cry, Peg," I whispered back. "We'll get Teke back."

"What if they aren't feeding him?" she sobbed. "What if he's dead?"

For that, I had no answer.

Chapter Sixteen

It was getting dark out. I was getting anxious. Griff hadn't called. I didn't relish spending a night here alone. I wanted either Griff on the couch or a new deadbolt. I'd called Frank Hayes, Dad's carpenter—now my carpenter—about installing deadbolts on the back door and front door to the main house. I knew my purist father would turn over in his grave if he knew I was having holes drilled in the solid oak plank eighteenth century doors but I was in no mood for another unwelcome visitor. Frank had said he would be over tomorrow, but that still left tonight to deal with.

I found myself pacing the great room, doing what can only be described as "fretting" while ignoring Andrea Boccelli on CD. When the phone rang, I jumped a foot. Dawa and Senge jumped, too.

"Hello," I said tentatively.

"I lost your cell phone number."

"Griff," I said, the tension flowing out of my hunched shoulders.

"Anything going on?"

"Not a thing. Getting a little stir crazy, sitting here by the phone all day."

"I'm sorry I didn't call. I've been really busy today. Three accidents, two domestics and a bar fight. Want some company?"

"Yes, please." I was a surprised by my plaintive tone, so I hurried on with an explanation, "My carpenter can't come until tomorrow to put on the new locks. I don't feel safe."

"I'll be there in about an hour."

"Thanks, Griff."

True to his word, Griff arrived still in uniform and changed into jeans and T-shirt in the tiny half-bath off the kitchen. We shared dinner in front of the TV. I wasn't very eat-ish as they say here, but life has to go on.

Though Griff swore he had never allowed Thor to beg, Dawa and Senge soon remedied that shortcoming in Thor's training. We laughed at the three of them, the big dog flanked by the two little ones, sitting in a row, doing "tilty-heads" together. A round of dog biscuits followed dinner. It felt good to laugh.

We made small talk for a while. The usual getting-to-know-you stuff—where he grew up, where I went to college, what kind of music we like, how I got started in business, why he quit being a teacher to become a trooper, why our marriages broke up, why I decided to come home, what we do in our spare time.

It was very comfy—him tucked in Dad's overstuffed wingchair, feet propped on the ottoman and big dog at his side—me nestled against the pillows at one end of the sofa, legs curled beneath me, little dogs at my feet. By ten o'clock, I was powerless to keep my eyes open and my head up. I decided to call it a night.

Though I offered him one of the two immense guest rooms upstairs, Griff avowed the sofa was just right and, besides, a much better place to be if someone tried to break in.

"You don't really think…"

"No, I don't. But, really, the sofa's fine," he said. I thought he probably would be more comfortable on the sofa in front of the tube than in one of those lace-draped four-posters upstairs, so I didn't argue. Instead, I made up the sofa with fresh sheets, two feather pillows and a down comforter and pulled Teke's big plaid bed next to the sofa for Thor. I left them channel-surfing.

I half-woke myself snoring that night—something I do only when extremely exhausted—only to find the dogs snoring more loudly than I was. As I stared at the canopy, willing myself to drop off to sleep again, a faint beam of headlights in the distance traveled across the ceiling. Odd, I thought groggily and turned to my side. One of Dawa's velvety paws tapped my cheek, and Senge sighed deeply and contentedly.

I awoke with a lurch, squinting stupidly at the sunlight streaming through the wavy panes of my bedroom's east-facing window.

"What time is it?" I said out loud. No answer. No dogs lay in their customary places. Blinking several times and peering at the carriage clock atop the chest of drawers, I answered myself, "Seven thirty." I sat on the edge of the bed, my toes just touching the bed stairs. Leaning over, I tugged my robe off the blanket chest at the foot and stepped down.

Paws thundering from the hallway below scritched in a tight turn onto
the stairs. Thunk, thunk, thunk, they came up the stairs. They met me at
the door of the bathroom, dancing and bowing.

"Ah-ha," I teased as I hugged them good morning. "It's more fun
downstairs, huh? You fickle little things." They must have understood
me for, in a flash, they turned and bounded down the stairs to resume
their wild-dogging below. I could hear them play-snarling as they
wrestled up and down the hall.

The sunlight in the bathroom was unkind. I brushed my teeth,
scrubbed my face until it was bright pink, untangled my hair with a
dampened brush and gargled away morning breath. A touch of mascara
and smear of blush and I was ready to descend. Poised at the top of the
staircase, I thought better of appearing *déshabillé* and retreated to my
bedroom to put on jeans and a sweatshirt.

"What a beautiful morning," I said, gazing out onto the backyard
through the great room windows a few minutes later. A wisp of night
mist clung to the ground but the sun shone brilliantly through the newly
budded leaves of the trees.

"Yeah," said Griff from the kitchen. "Your thermometer outside the
window here says it's already up to 65 degrees."

"Really?" I said. "Gosh, I wish I could go for a ride."

"What kind of ride? You don't have a horse hidden out here
somewhere, do you?"

"Oh, no. I meant bicycle."

"Feeling better, are you?"

"Yeah, I'm sore but it's not bad. A ride would feel good."

"So, go."

"I can't leave the phone. They might call."

"I don't have to go to work until three o'clock today. I'll hang
around," he said from behind me now. "Here. Coffee. Drink." He was
in my personal space. I backed away a little as I turned.

"Oh thanks," I said, gratefully taking the mug. "You sure you don't
mind? I've been dying to get out for a ride."

"Go," he said with a wave of his hand. "I'll have some breakfast
ready when you get back."

"It'll be brunch by then."

"Whatever."

"OK, I'll just feed the dogs and go." The Tibbies, who'd been chasing each other in circles around the sofa—first one way then the other—heard my declaration. Senge dropped Dawa's tail, by which he had been dragging her across the floor, and whined. Dawa seized the moment to spin and deliver the final word—a cheek-chomp—and then she too looked up at me eagerly.

Twenty minutes later, I left the dogs sniffing around the daffodils and rescued my Fuji from its rack in the carriage house. I carefully seated the computer into its handlebar mount and tested the battery. The display came up.

I applied myself vigorously to the bicycle pump and squeezed the tires. "Nice and hard," I said to no one. A little oil applied to the chain and we were ready to go at last. Straddling the seat, I buckled my helmet and slid on my sunglasses.

My bike and I have traveled many hundreds of miles together, and we know each other intimately. I'm sure she was every bit as happy as I was to get out of the carriage house into the out of doors on a spring morning. We glided effortlessly down the light-dappled lane, the branch trickling alongside, until we reached the main gate.

As I walked the ironwork open with one hand and guided the bike through with the other, I planned my route. Fifteen miles, I thought, would be a pleasant ride this morning. By the time I'd closed the gate and re-mounted, I had in mind a circular route and, with a glance to my left, I pushed off toward the morning sun and set a good pace for my winter-lazy quads.

I was sucking air by the time I reached three miles, but it was clean, cool air. My jagged pace soon steadied. My breaths became deep and easy and my muscles warm. This is my favorite time in any ride, the time when I can relax and enjoy the scenery. Fields stretched as far as the eye could see—some newly plowed while others sported a vivid green carpet of rye. One field was freshly manured; I gulped deeply, upshifted and pedaled hard, trying to take only shallow breaths until I left it behind.

When I'd reached eight miles, I had zigzagged back and headed west. The sun toasted my back. I paused briefly for a few squirts of water and continued on. The ride was smooth, gear changes needed only as I descended and climbed from the bridges over streams.

I intently observed each house as I passed, picking out anything that had changed since I'd last ridden by in the fall. A few people, out in their yards cutting grass or planting pansies, waved as I passed. Slowing as I neared the Hancock farm, I wondered why Mr. Hancock had parked a tractor between the twin oaks in his front yard. I smiled when I saw the big white bunny in a bow tie seated atop the rusty old Farmall. So much had happened that I had completely forgotten that the coming Sunday was Easter.

At mile 12, I rejoined Swann's Pond Road, about three miles west of the Pond and once again turned east. I paused for several minutes to enjoy the beauty of a Zinmatic's arcs of water that captured the sun and spread a shimmering sheet of rainbow over a field. Passing the huge irrigator, the breeze brought cool mist to my face.

Someone had built a trophy house about a mile beyond Doc Twilley's clinic. When I'd last ridden this way in the fall, it'd been just a frame with a construction trailer alongside. Now, judging from the two SUV's in the driveway and the Dobie in the chain-link kennel out back, the new owners had moved in. Somehow, it looked out of place plopped in the middle of a cornfield. I pedaled on. Everyone wants their country acre. Soon there won't be any country acres left.

Doc's clinic looked busy. I wondered if they'd started taking appointments again. Slowing down to five miles per hour, I mentally catalogued the vehicles out front. The tan Camry with the Colorado plates must be Don's, I thought. There were also two pickups, a white Hyundai and a battered green Ford station wagon. As I passed, I glanced curiously down the pine-lined lane that led back to Doc's house behind the clinic.

Suddenly, my hands clenched the brakes. The bike stopped on a dime, and I whipped my head around. Hurriedly turning myself around, I backtracked and stopped at the head of the lane to Doc's house, just short of the parking lot.

"That looks like the same pickup I saw at Evelyn Hitchens' house," I said to my bike. "8-7-7 is the plate number." I rehearsed the number a couple times, so as not to forget. "Wonder why it would be up here, assuming of course that it's the same one?"

At that moment, the door to the clinic opened. I ducked my head and pretended to fiddle with my shifter cable, all the while watching over the top of my sunglasses. I recognized one of the vet techs, the redhead—what was her name? Jeez, she's looking straight at me, I thought. In a smooth move, I turned my head away nonchalantly as though looking curiously down Doc's lane and lifted the water bottle to my mouth to cover my face.

A door slammed and the engine came to life. I looked back. She was backing the black pickup. She's probably gonna turn east, toward me, since that's the way to town, I thought. Jamming the water bottle into its holder, I quickly pushed off. She'll see my face when she turns the truck, I thought. I wasn't quite sure why I didn't want her to see my face but, there it was, I didn't. Maybe she won't recognize me in sunglasses and a helmet, I thought. Rather than risk it, I stood and pushed hard, turning my face away from her as she stopped and waited for me to pass. My instincts were right—she turned east on Swann's Pond Road, toward the Nest.

Pedaling slowly in the opposite direction, I watched the truck in my rearview mirror until it faded into the distance. When I was sure she could no longer see me if she glanced back, I turned my bicycle around.

As I approached the clinic again, I observed it with heightened awareness. A black Lab stood in one of the runs at the back staring into the woods that were the clinic's backdrop. A drop box for lab samples sat conspicuously next to the front door. A shingle was off the roof. A blue bin from the same trash removal company I use sat at the head of the driveway back to Doc's house.

"It could have been a different pickup, but I've got a funny feeling it wasn't," I said and pedaled hard for home.

Chapter Seventeen

Igave the pond barely a glance as I went by, and have no recollection of bearing left on Cattail Road. My whole focus was on the black pickup.

I remembered Peg saying that the man in the pickup could be one of Evelyn Hitchens' sons. I remembered also that Griff never told me whose pickup it was although I'm sure they ran the plate on the pickup as well as the plate on Jackie Lynch's Jeep.

As I swerved a little too sharply into the lane at the Nest, I skidded on the gravel and put my foot down hard to keep from falling. At that moment, the orange newspaper tube caught my eye. The end of a rolled newspaper protruded from the opening.

"Oh, I forgot to pick up the mail and newspaper yesterday."

Dismounting, I walked the bike to the mailbox and retrieved my mail—just a couple bills—and then tugged at the morning paper. As the paper emerged from the tube, a crumpled flyer slid out and floated to the ground a couple feet away. I ignored it and fished yesterday's paper from the tube as well. After bungee'ing the mail and newspapers to my rack, I leaned over to pick up the flyer. Expecting to see an ad from a lawn service or an offer to pump out my septic tank, I flattened it against my thigh with my palm and turned it over.

LEAVE $20000 SMALL BILLS ON PORCH OF RECORDS CHURCH
10 AM WEDNESDAY.
COME ALONE. NO COPS OR YOU NEVER FIND DOG.

I experienced a moment of abject terror trying to remember if today was Tuesday or Wednesday, followed by immense relief when I realized it was only Tuesday. Sliding the sheet of paper under the bungee, I sped for home.

Griff made the calls. With Peg and Detective Insley on their way to the Nest, he and I sat on the sofa studying the note that lay before us on the map table.

"I'm sorry, Griff. Before I knew what it was, I'd smeared my hand all over it."

He shrugged, "They didn't get any prints off the other one. Probably nothing on this one either."

"Looks the same as the other note," I observed lamely.

He nodded. "This Records Church—where's that?"

"Old Mennonite church about ten miles from here, on Tindall Road out on the Neck, near the bridge over the gut."

"Oh yeah, I know where you mean. Plain white building that sits in a clearing the other side of the bridge?"

I nodded. "Nothing out there. All that land is part of the wildlife preserve I think."

We fell silent, petting our respective dogs. Dawa sat up on her hind legs and delicately placed her slippered forepaws on the edge of the map table. I looked at her with a scold in my eye as she knows she is not to lay paw on the all-purpose table that serves as my dining table most of the time. She rolled her eyes at me adorably and then stretched her neck toward the ransom note.

"Aack!" I exclaimed ungracefully, snatching the note away from her curious nose. "She'll snort on it," I explained, adding, "Tibbies always snort to clear their noses before they do a sniff." Sure enough, Dawa snorted on cue, still straining her neck to get a good smell of the paper I now held out of her reach. Senge whined.

"Maybe they smell Teke on it."

"I hope so," I said, dropping the note out of their noses' reach on the console table behind the sofa. "Lay down, sweethearts." Surprisingly, they obeyed.

"You know, Griff, something else happened on my ride this morning. That black dually I saw at the Hitchens' place was parked at Doc's clinic and one of the vet techs—I can't think of her name but I met her at the funeral—drove off in it. Headed in this direction."

"Are you sure it was the same one?"

"Well, no, I can't be completely sure," I admitted, "but I'm pretty sure. I got the tag—it was a black plate, 8-7-7. Didn't you guys run the plate of the truck that was at Evelyn's."

"Yeah, we did. It belonged to Douglas Hitchens, who is one of her sons. I'll check my notebook and see if that was the plate number you saw at the clinic."

"I wonder if the girl in the truck dropped off this note."

"I doubt it."

"Why?" I challenged.

"Because you said the note was behind today's paper."

"So?"

"So it must have got crumpled when the paper was delivered this morning. What time does your paper get here?"

"About six."

"So, the note had to be put there sometime before six this morning but after six yesterday morning 'cause it was on top of yesterday's paper."

"It might've been there a whole 24 hours?"

"Right," he said just as Peg's pickup emerged from the woods and rolled to a stop in the carriage yard.

"I guess this means they tell me where Teke is after I leave the money at the church?" she said after we'd shown her the note.

"Looks like that," said Griff.

"They could just take the money and never tell me where he is, couldn't they?" she asked.

"That's a possibility," Griff agreed.

I frowned at Griff over Peg's shoulder. "C'mon, Peg," I said, "Give me your jacket and come sit down. Phil will be here any minute, and Glen Insley's on his way."

After she handed over her jacket, Peg sank onto the sofa. She looked like hell. Her eyes were dull, and her lips were colorless. She looked like every ounce of blood had been drained out of her. I could tell she'd lost weight, weight she could ill afford to lose.

I began to ask Peg whether she'd raised the money but was interrupted by the crunch of gravel on the lane. For a moment, I stared stupidly at the white van that pulled up to the backdoor. Then, it clicked. "Excuse me just a minute."

When I met him at the backdoor and showed him the damage from the break-in, Frank Hayes was full of questions. I just said I was lucky not to have lost anything valuable. He wanted to talk about how he could repair the door jamb where the pry bar the intruder had used had destroyed some of the old wood. I cut him short with an apology and explanation that I had company in the great room. I asked him to do whatever was necessary to repair the backdoor and to make both doors secure. Frank had worked with Dad on many projects over the years and knew Swann's Nest as well as I did. I trusted him to do the job right.

By then, Glen Insley had pulled in with Phil on his tail. Griff met the men outside and brought them in through the kitchen door. I could hear them talking quietly as they hung their jackets on the pegs beside the door. I sat next to Peg and took her hand. It was icy.

The sound of Frank's power drill grinding into wood came from the front hall. As I closed the door against the noise, Griff brought Phil and Insley into the great room. They greeted Peg solemnly. Then they examined the note.

Peg spoke up, the strain as obvious in her voice as on her face. "I've already got the money. I want Abby to show me where this place is this afternoon. I'll stay here tonight—if that's OK with you, Abby?" she asked, looking at me as if I might say 'no.' I nodded.

"And, in the morning, I'll go out there by myself and leave the money. I don't want anybody else out there. I don't want anything to jeopardize my dog."

Glen Insley tightened his lips, but he said nothing. No one said anything.

"When I get my dog back, you can do whatever investigating you want," she added.

More silence. Glen Insley turned to me. "Griff tells me you saw a pickup meeting the description of the pickup we observed at the Hitchens' place. Plate number 8-7-7."

I nodded.

"That vehicle is registered to Douglas Hitchens, Evelyn Hitchens' son."

"Really? I've remembered the girl's name, the one I saw driving it. It's Katie Adkins."

"Why do you think this is important?" Griff asked.

"The day I ran into Doc out on the pond, which turned out to be the day he was killed, Doc told me that he'd never heard of Evelyn Hitchens. It's been bothering me ever since why Doc said he didn't know Evelyn but Jackie Lynch was out seeing her dogs."

"Couldn't Dr. Lynch have had patients that Doc didn't know about?"

"I guess so," I admitted, shaking my head, "but something just doesn't seem right."

"Maybe Doc forgot," Peg offered weakly. "You know Lorraine said his personality had changed. Maybe he had dementia or something."

"Yeah, maybe," I said. "But then I see Douglas Hitchens' pickup at the clinic today and one of the vet techs is driving it. Doesn't that strike you as too weird to be a coincidence? There's got to be some kind of connection."

Insley was leaning forward, his elbows on his knees, studying his shoes. "The address on Douglas Hitchens' registration is his mother's house. But he wasn't there when we went out to talk to her. She said he stays with friends a lot," he said in his deliberate way.

"Meaning?" Phil asked.

"Meaning...maybe he lives up here someplace. Maybe with this vet tech you saw in the truck. Maybe he's involved in this. Maybe he's doing it for his mother," Insley replied. He shrugged.

We all nodded except Griff. "C'mon, Glen. Aren't you stretching?" he said.

"Well, maybe," Insley said and stood up. "But I'll check out Katie Adkins anyway." He picked up the ransom note from the map table, pausing to pet Dawa who was sitting on her haunches and "praying" with her forepaws. After contemplating the note for another minute, he slid it into a plastic bag. "I'll be in touch," he said and left.

I sat looking around the glum circle of friends. Frank was now hammering vigorously in the hall. My heart was hammering, too. I'm still on an adrenalin rush from all the exercise, I thought. Suddenly, I involuntarily leapt to my feet, startling everyone.

"Sorry," I said feebly. "I, uh, this hammering is giving me a headache. I'm going to go upstairs and take an aspirin. Listen, just help yourselves to whatever and I'll be back in a sec." I waved to Frank on my way by and was halfway up the stairs when, on an impulse, I rushed back down and poked my head in the great room door.

"By the way, I forgot to tell you, Peg. I've got an appointment to take Senge down to the clinic. He's got this, uh, problem. Anyway, I won't be gone long. There'll be plenty of time to show you where the church is."

At the sound of his name, Senge lifted his head from where he was napping at Peg's feet and tilted his head. Dawa cut her eyes at him.

"Abby, wait," Peg called behind me. I poked my head back in the door. "What's wrong with Senge?"

"Um, it's just an odor problem," I lied. "Nothing serious."

Senge frowned.

"Funny. I hadn't noticed any smell," Peg said. "Maybe it's his anal glands. Come here, Senge, let me check you out."

"Right. That's what they think. Anal glands."

Peg reached down to pick up Senge, but I cut her off. "Senge, Dawa, come!" They obeyed and happily ran up the stairs to the bedroom with me.

"Mom thinks I smell," Senge complained between cat-like licks. "Tibbies smell good, not like other dogs."

"She doesn't really think you smell, Brother. She just said that. She's got a plan and she had to lie to get out of the house," Dawa said, glancing into the bathroom where the sounds of splashing could be heard.

"Really?"

"Oh, Brother. You can be so dense sometimes. Listen, you get to go with Mom. So, you've got to be really sharp and watch everything that's going on. It's your job to protect her."

Senge stopped grooming himself. "I do? It is?"

Dawa sighed. "Yes, Brother."

Senge contemplated this revelation for a moment and then asked, "Sister, did you get a good enough sniff of the note?"

"Yes."

"Did you smell the human with the liver?"

"Yes, Brother, I did," Dawa said, lying down with her chin on her forepaws. "It was the human who let Teke out of his crate."

Senge resumed washing his face with his forepaw, cat-like.

" 'A dog's tongue is his own cure,' " Dawa muttered.

Chapter Eighteen

I pulled into the clinic parking lot cautiously. The black pickup had not returned. Don's tan Camry was gone, too. In their place was a silver Town Car. The green Escort remained. The Hyundai was gone.

Poking my head through the door, only one other person, a man with a briefcase but no pet, was in the waiting area. Debbie Masten was behind the desk.

"Hi Debbie," I began and then, apologetically, "Senge has got a problem. Would it be possible for Dr. Lynch to take a quick look at him? I don't have an appointment."

"Well, we're not making appointments anyway, Ms. Swann," she said. I guess she must have seen my disappointed look because she relented. "What's Senge's problem?"

"Um, well, he's got this odor. Maybe it's his anal glands."

"OK, Dr. Lynch just got out of surgery. Maybe she can take a look at him. I'll check." With that, she disappeared down a corridor leading to the back of the clinic.

I glanced back at Senge, now standing in the driver's seat of my car with his nose pressed to the window. The man with the briefcase was observing me unabashedly. He smiled and nodded. I smiled weakly. Debbie re-emerged from the corridor.

"Mr. Boyd, Dr. Lynch can see you now. Just go on back down this hall, then turn right. Her office is at the end of the hall," Debbie said to the man with the briefcase. "If you can wait a little while, Ms. Swann, Dr. Lynch said she'd examine Senge."

"Oh, that's great. Thanks so much. I'm really sorry to come in without an appointment."

"No problem. You can wait out here if you want or go on in Exam Room 1. She'll be with you as soon as she can."

"OK, good. Um, is Lorraine here today?"

"Oh yeah, she's just cleaning up the surgery. Did you want to see her?"

"Oh, no. No. That's all right. Just wondering." I said, Lorraine being the last person I wanted to see. "Well, I'll go get Senge."

As I returned to the car, I realized that, now that I was here, I didn't know why I was here. I wanted to snoop around but I didn't know what to snoop for. "C'mon Senge. We'll just see what happens."

Minutes later, I was standing in the waiting room, watching Debbie through the corner of my eye as I pretended to study the bags of dog food on display. Senge was happily gnawing on a rawhide held between his forepaws, his eyes closed in ecstasy.

Debbie stood and pulled her jacket off the back of her chair. "Ms. Swann, I'm leaving for lunch now," she said. "Lorraine will check you out after Dr. Lynch sees Senge."

"Oh, OK. Thanks, Debbie," I said. Moments later, the ownership of the green Escort was established as Debbie drove away in it.

I listened intently but the clinic was eerily quiet. I sauntered over to the reception counter and, casually fingering a display of colored ID tags, surreptitiously observed the arrangement behind the desk. Computer, Rolodex, telephone, fax machine. Patient files in a vertical file cabinet along the back wall. The cabinet was open.

Suddenly, I made up my mind. Moving swiftly behind the counter, I scanned the files and located the "H's." Hitchens, Floyd; Hitchens, Ronald; Hitchens, Vernon. No Evelyn, no Douglas.

They said she had another son, I thought, but I don't know his name. I sighed.

I looked over at the computer. Quickly seating myself in the chair, I scanned the menu. I hit the option for setting up an appointment and keyed "Hitchens" as quietly as I could. I froze as a door closed somewhere in the clinic. Suppressing my instinct to run, I listened for any other sound. None came. The computer beeped and drew my eye back to the screen. Floyd, Ronald and Vernon came up. No Evelyn. No Douglas.

Doc was right. They aren't patients of the practice, I thought. Then, on a sudden hunch, I hit the escape key and the menu came up. A slight sound drew my attention to the corridor but I saw no movement, no shadow.

"Hurry up," I whispered to myself and, on a hunch, keyed in another name. A beep. Out of the corner of my eye, I saw Senge stop gnawing his rawhide and lift his head.

When Dr. Lynch emerged from the corridor into the waiting room a second later, I was standing on the far side of the counter, perusing a display of note cards with drawings of dogs on them. My hands were clutched behind my back to keep them from shaking.

"Hey there, fella," Dr. Lynch addressed Senge first.

He happily left his rawhide and dragged his lead across the room to meet her halfway. While she squatted to pet him, my eyes fell back on the screen where Katie Adkins' record was still displayed. I had had just enough time to read her address and note that six pets were listed.

My eyes slid back to Dr. Lynch just as she stood up. I smiled brightly. Realizing that I probably would croak like a frog, I coughed slightly and cleared my throat noisily.

"Thanks for seeing us, Dr. Lynch," I said struggling to control my shaky voice. My feet seemed rooted to the floor. Lucky for me, Senge began jumping up on Dr. Lynch and poking his nose at the pockets of her jeans. His misbehavior on cue somehow propelled one of my legs forward and then the other.

"Oh so sorry. Let me take him. Bad dog," I told him with my voice, while praising him with my eyes.

In the end, Senge was subjected to an anal gland cleaning. As Tibbies are extremely embarrassed by any untidiness in the nether regions, Senge was an unhappy little dog when we exited Exam Room 1. I consoled him as best I could by offering him the rawhide. He ignored it and punished me with doleful eyes and accusatory grunts.

I exhaled as I saw Lorraine behind the counter tapping away at the computer. She must have cleared Katie Adkins' record to do some work. I steeled myself to a chat with her.

"How's it going, Lorraine?" I sallied.

"Not bad. Yourself?" she answered, continuing her keying.

I leaned on the counter. "So what's going on here? Any word yet on what's happening with the practice?"

She shrugged and motioned me to come closer. "I think Dr. Lynch is talking to the sons about buying it but, hey, nobody's telling me nothin'. I just work here." It was obviously a sore spot with Lorraine so I left it alone. No doubt she was worried about her job.

A few minutes later, I'd left a check for the office visit on the desk and walked Senge out to the car. The Town Car was still there. It must belong to Mr. Boyd, the man who'd gone in to see Dr. Lynch before me but had never exited.

Senge roo'ed at me and I glanced down at him. He was impatiently waiting for me to open the car door so that he could hop in.

"Sorry, fella," I murmured. I unlocked it but re-locked it immediately. "C'mon, Senge. Let's go for a little walk first."

When he heard the "w-word," Senge began bouncing like a kangaroo. He is always up for a walk.

I knew, of course, that there were runs for exercising patients and boarders behind the small clinic, but I had never been around back. We headed toward two staggered rows of pines that formed a barrier between the lane to Doc's house and a narrow driveway leading to the rear of the clinic property. Senge gradually made his way along the row of pines, snuffling in the shats and marking the lowest boughs.

Luckily, the sidewall of the clinic was windowless. Leaving Senge sniffing at the far end of his lead, I peeked around the corner of the building. I was relieved to find the runs empty, since Senge would undoubtedly have barked at other dogs and they at him. Just this side of the runs, a Jeep that I recognized as Dr. Lynch's was parked by the back door. There was no other car. I wondered how Lorraine got to work.

Muffled voices caught my ear and, looking up, I realized that they came from a small window at the corner of the building. I stepped under the window and sharpened my ears. Dr. Lynch and a man, the mysterious Mr. Boyd presumably, were talking. Though I could make out only the occasional word, 'loan' was fortunately one of them. So, Dr. Lynch is trying to buy the practice, I concluded. No surprise there. Mr. Boyd must be a banker or maybe an appraiser or financial planner.

Looking around once more, I sidled back to the driveway where Senge was still methodically sniffing his way along the pine trees. Interesting though, I mused while waiting for him to finish, here was someone who, according to the other employees, didn't get along with Doc. She had tried to buy the business before but failed. Now that Doc was out of the way, she stood to gain the thing she wanted. I wondered if she has an alibi.

Somewhere inside the building, a dog began barking. Senge pricked his ears and barked in reply. I shushed him and hurried him back toward the parking lot.

Rather than go straight home, I decided to run by the address on Katie Adkins' record. Stone Beach Road, a typical country road lined by farm fields, was only about seven miles northeast of the Nest. I found that the address belonged to a doublewide trailer in a row of about six similar mobile homes.

I crept by, taking in as many details as I could. The doublewide was a fairly new model set on a bare lot. A canoe leaned against the apron next to the front steps. The black truck Katie was driving wasn't there, but a white Japanese mini-pickup and a rusted Camaro were parked beside one another in the gravel driveway. The Camaro was tagless, but the black and white Delaware tag on the small pickup read number 019.

What grabbed my attention were three chain link dog runs out back. They sat in a row, each with a large doghouse at one end. The center kennel was draped with a blue plastic tarp.

I drove a half-mile past the trailer and pulled over. Twisting around, I scanned the back seat. "I don't believe this," I said out loud, "No binoculars. I never remember to bring the stupid things when I need them." Senge tilted his head at me.

I made a U-turn and slowly approached the trailer again. Although I stared hard at the runs, my unaided eye detected no sign of dogs in them. Heedless of the risk, I decided to pull over on the shoulder and watch for a while.

After only five minutes, I grew bored, sighed and put the car in gear to leave. Ahead of me was the row of rural mailboxes for the trailers. Names made of sticky gold letters from the hardware store were on a couple of them. There was no name on the box for Katie's trailer; only the house number in metal figures on the post identified it as hers. I crept forward until I reached her box. Watching back across the road at the doublewide, I lowered the passenger window. Sliding my butt halfway into the passenger seat, I reached through the window and opened Katie's box. Lucky for me, Katie hadn't picked up her mail.

Chapter Nineteen

Gravel crunched under the tires of Peg's pickup as we pulled into the empty church parking lot. Records Church didn't look like a church—no steeple, no arched windows, no traditional trappings at all. It was, instead, a simple, rectangular one-story wood building, painted white, with clear glass windows. Only the sign along the road identified it as a Mennonite church.

In contrast to the church's man-made plainness, the surrounding grove of loblolly pine, dogwood in bloom, holly and hardwoods was pristine. The spring afternoon had grown warm, and the heady fragrance of rich, moist earth and new growth wafted over me as I lowered the window.

From where Peg and I sat, no entrance was evident. "Must be on the other end," I said, and we slowly rolled forward.

A carport set on metal posts sheltered double steel doors set into the far end of the building. Probably built as a convenience for churchgoers disembarking from their vehicles in inclement weather, it appeared to be a recent addition to the older structure.

"This must be what the note meant by the 'porch'," Peg said. I nodded. She turned off the engine. We got out and slowly walked around the church. Three picnic tables sat on a narrow verge of grass at the edge of the woodland. A well-used deer path broke the undergrowth and disappeared into the trees. The nearby trash barrel was empty, but raccoon tracks showed in the dried mud around the base.

The top of my head barely reached the sills of the windows but Peg, with her three-inch advantage, was able to stretch and peek inside. She declared it too dark inside to see anything. We also tried to peer into the small basement windows set into metal wells around the foundation, but they too revealed nothing.

"Well, I guess that's it," Peg said, her hands hanging helplessly at her sides, looking up and down the narrow road.

"Are you sure you can get here without any trouble?" I asked. I'd made her drive so that she could better remember the route.

"No problem," she said, still looking down the road as if expecting Teke to come along. "C'mon, let's walk down to the gut."

Five minutes later, we stood on the bridge over a small inlet, close enough to the coast to be tidal. The tide was running out and the branches of fallen trees jutted from the shallow black pool. Lily pads dotted the surface near the shore. Despite the slightly swampy odor, the view would have been pleasant were it not for innumerable beer cans, cigarette butts and fast food containers littering the approaches to the bridge. Graffiti defiled the bridge abutments.

"I guess kids hang out here," Peg observed. She turned to me, "You don't think whoever's got Teke is connected to the church?"

I shook my head. "I think that whoever took him picked this place just because it's so isolated. There's nothing from here to the coast—no houses, no store, nothing—so there's no reason for anybody to be out here unless they're coming to the church or going fishing at Tindall Beach."

She nodded and started back up the road toward the church.

We drove back to the Nest without saying a word. Griff and Phil were gone. A note they left on the table said they'd be back after work— about midnight. Peg dropped me off and then returned once more to Records Church, alone, just to be sure she could find the way without my help.

While I waited for Peg to get back, I curled up with the dogs on my bed and mulled over all the 'coincidences.' I hadn't told her about the bow-hunting magazine addressed to Doug Hitchens that I found in Katie Adkins' mailbox. It had given me a hunch.

It was common knowledge that Peg and I are friends, but there had to be a better reason why the two notes were left at my house rather than Peg's. I didn't buy the theory that it was because the Nest is hidden out in the woods and Peg's house is in the open. Peg probably hit the nail on the head when she said that whoever had Teke simply didn't know where she lived. Evelyn Hitchens certainly knew, but her son Doug probably didn't.

Doug had to know about Peg and Teke through his mother. She'd probably told him that Peg stood to make a lot of money out of the deal. Maybe it was Doug's idea to take Teke. Everybody was thinking this was about revenge, but maybe it was just about money, plain and simple.

Besides, I just couldn't see Evelyn skulking around, breaking into pickups and houses. It had to be Doug. It had probably been Doug trying to get Teke out of Peg's RV when something interrupted him and Teke was left loose. Then he'd tried again, and succeeded, at the speedway.

After he got away with Teke, he couldn't tell where Peg lived from the tag on Teke's collar. But his girlfriend Katie Adkins knew where I lived because that bigmouth Lorraine told her at Doc's funeral. That's probably why he left the notes at my house.

The more I thought about it, the more I became convinced that Evelyn wasn't involved in this at all. If she were, then she would have told Doug where Peg lived, and the ransom note would have been left there.

I glanced out the window. Peg had just pulled her truck next to my car in front of the carriage house. Sliding off the bed, I quietly closed my bedroom door and hurried across the room to the English washstand. I rummaged through the junk in the drawer until I found my address book. Flipping through pages until I found the number I wanted, I punched it in quickly. The carriage clock said three o'clock when Grace Bishop answered her phone.

"Grace, it's Abby Swann...Oh, I'm fine, thanks. Listen, Grace...No, we haven't found him yet...Well, yes, there have been some developments and we hope we'll have him back soon...Listen, Grace...Right...Well, we don't know...She's pretty bad off actually...*Listen* to me for a minute, Grace. This is important. I need your help."

That, at last, shut her up.

When four o'clock rolled around, I was staring in fascination at the numerals superimposed on the face of a young John Wayne in his cowboy persona. The long hand bisected his forehead and appeared to be holding up his ten-gallon hat. The short hand pointed toward his ear lobe. The hideous clock hung, crookedly, over the harvest gold refrigerator, circa 1972, behind the counter at Kenny's Tire Service. Kenny's was in Felton, a small town a few miles from the Nest.

"Can I help you, ma'am?"

"Uh, yes," I stared stupidly at the middle-aged man with a beer belly who'd appeared from behind the racks of tires crowding the tiny service counter. The name patch on his dark blue jumpsuit said 'Kenny.' I was momentarily at a loss for an ad lib. "I, uh, think my car needs an alignment."

"Is it pullin'?" he asked, squeezing his bulk behind the counter.

"Yes, I think so," I lied, "To the right."

"OK, we'll take a look at her. Which one is it?"

"The BMW," I said and pointed through the grimy window. "Keys are in her."

He nodded, squeezed back around the counter, and disappeared down the tunnel of tires towering over him. A door slammed at the other end.

My nose twitched at the inescapable odor of rubber that permeated the space. There was no place to sit. Or, rather, the only place to sit, a formerly tan vinyl-covered chair, was gray with ground-in grease. I opted to stand. My eyes swept the array of faded NASCAR™ posters plastered over every square inch of the wall not occupied by the fridge and John Wayne. I decided to take my chances outside.

Tucking an errant strand of hair under the green ball caps embroidered with a dog, I buttoned up my denim jacket. Sliding on my sunglasses to complete my hurried, unimaginative disguise, I exited into the tiny parking lot of the former gas station.

I had seen Doug Hitchens once, but I didn't know whether he'd ever seen me. Strolling over to the open bay of the garage, I smiled at Kenny and feigned interest in watching the work on my car, which, of course, needed no work at all. There was no sign of Doug. Losing interest, I continued on my seemingly casual ambulation, past the open bays, and peeked around the corner of the garage.

Crap, I said to myself, fighting the instinct to pull back sharply and draw attention to myself. Instead, I managed a controlled about-face back toward the bays. Doug Hitchens and Katie Adkins were standing not ten feet away. She must have pulled up in the black truck while I was inside the station. I leaned against the building nonchalantly, pretending to watch the work but, in reality, desperately straining to hear what they were saying.

At first, Grace had told me she didn't know much about Doug Hitchens. However, she had then proceeded to tell me where he went to high school and that her friends Fran and Art, both retired teachers who'd had him their classes thought he was a hothead. She also knew that he'd been in a bad car wreck three years ago, that he had several German Short-haired Pointers ("poor dogs"), that he was a mechanic by trade but lost his job at Wilson's Automotive because ("according to the rumors") he was drinking and, last but not least, that he now worked at Kenny's Tire in Felton.

I don't know if she was right about any of the other details, but Grace was right on the money about Kenny's. From the moment Grace told me where he worked, I had a hunch I might learn something by spying on him at work. And here he was, just around the corner, angrily and—lucky for me—loudly ordering his girlfriend, "Just take 'im back and stop yer bitchin'."

'Him' who and 'back' where, I wondered. Ohmigod, he's coming this way. There's no time to move. Just play it cool, I told myself.

"And don't forget to take Mom them perch I cleaned!" he shouted back at her as she slammed the truck door.

He passed me just as Katie threw the truck in forward gear and gunned it down Main Street. He looked back toward her—and, thankfully, away from me where I stood trying blend into the wall—and then stomped into the garage. That gave me another panic as I tried to remember whether he'd ever seen my BMW with the oh-so conspicuous "TIBBIE" license plate. Apparently not, because he passed it by without a second look and disappeared through a door in the back of the bay.

Kenny was more-or-less honest. He said that my alignment wasn't off by much, but he still charged me $75 to fix it. I was about to sign the check I'd shakily written, all the while glancing nervously toward the back of the station, when I suddenly grabbed the check and ripped it up.

"Oh, I'm sorry. I forgot. I brought cash," I said, tucking the torn pieces of the check into my pocket. Kenny was looking at me like I was crazy as I counted out three twenties, a ten and five one's and pushed them across the counter.

"Name?" he asked.

"Uh, Forrest. Two "r's." Ab, I mean, Ann Forrest," I replied, staring fixedly at the garish posters as Doug rolled a tire past me and turned down the tunnel of tires toward the garage.

"Thanks very much, Miz Forrest," Kenny said, handing me the receipt. "Come back again."

It was just after five o'clock.

Chapter Twenty

I phoned the Nest as I sped toward Stone Beach Road, but Peg didn't answer. When I called her cell phone, she told me she'd gone home to pick up Bits and Dapper and was now in her truck on her way back to the Nest. I told her something important had come up and that I'd be home as soon I could. She sounded slightly irritated and rightly so, but I was embarrassed to tell her that I'd left her alone because I was running all over the country on a hunch.

When I reached the doublewide Katie apparently shared with Doug and someone named Trudy Bozman, whose name had also appeared on the mail in the box, the black truck had joined the old Camaro and the white pickup in the driveway. I pulled off the road just past the trailer and sat thinking. OK, stupid, you're here. What now? How long had it been since I'd seen Katie at Kenny's—three quarters of an hour at the most? Had she already done what Doug had ordered her to do?

In the rearview mirror, I saw Katie climb into the black truck. She backed it onto Stone Beach Road headed in the opposite direction. As Katie rounded a bend in the road and disappeared from view, I turned the BMW around and sped after her. At the last possible second, I changed my mind. Instead of pursuing Katie, I swerved into the doublewide's driveway and parked between the pickup and the Camaro.

Slipping out of the car, I glanced around furtively and began running across the open ground behind the trailer to the dog kennels out back. A chorus of warning barks greeted me as several Pointers emerged from their igloo-shaped houses. No dog appeared in the middle kennel.

"Teke, Teke," I called, "It's Auntie Abby, Teke. C'mon boy. C'mon Teke," I called as I ran along the fence peering into each dog house.

He wasn't there. The dogs were barking furiously and throwing themselves against the chain link. I swerved away and sprinted back toward the trailer. A red, mud-splattered ATV was parked against the doublewide's back wall. As I cut around the corner, I nearly tripped over the upside-down canoe I'd noticed on my first visit to the doublewide. I stumbled up the concrete steps to the front door. Pounding my fists against the metal door, I shouted, "Teke. Teke. Teke, speak!" I stopped, turned my ear to the door and listened. No sound from inside. No barking. Nothing. I think I could have heard him through the flimsy metal walls, even if he were kenneled and muzzled.

Leaping from the top step, I ran to the idling BMW and, throwing it in reverse, peeled out the driveway, gravel flying. My eyes scanned the neighbors' trailers for signs of life. None. They'll see the tracks, I thought, as I shifted to 'drive' and sped in the direction Katie took. "Oh well, tough crap," I said out loud.

Needless to say, Katie was long gone. I'd gambled and lost. If Teke had been here, she had already left with him. Or, else he was someplace else and she'd gone to get him. Was she going to bring him here or move him someplace else?

Peg had beat me back to the Nest. I found her sitting in the dusky light, looking out the great room windows toward the old landing on the Creek. Bits and Dapper and the Tibbies were arranged around her. I switched on a table lamp.

"Peg, I've got some news," I said, making my way through the dancing dogs. Plopping on the sofa, I hurriedly spilled what I'd found out.

She listened without comment, without even looking at me. When I finished, she said, "So you think that Doug Hitchens took Teke and that he and this girl have got him hidden someplace and are bringing him back to their trailer tonight?"

I nodded eagerly, "I'm going to call Insley and get them to go out there and check it out."

"Wait!" She looked at me. "He could have been talking about something else, Abby, not Teke."

"Well, maybe," I conceded, "but he said 'him'—not 'it'—and *I* think he was talking about Teke. We should get Insley on this right away."

"No, I don't think so. I'm just gonna deliver the money in the morning."

"Peg!" I couldn't believe my ears. "You *can't* be serious."

"Oh but I *am* serious," she said and looked me in the eye. "They said 'no cops,' remember?"

"Of course they said that. What do you expect them to say—'bring cops along for the ride'?" I asked sarcastically. "Peg, we've *got* to call Insley."

"*No*," she repeated adamantly. "Look, Abby, even if you're right and they are the ones that took him and they're moving him somewhere tonight—all that means is that he's alive and they're probably gonna return him tomorrow after they get the money. That's good news, right?" She paused to take a deep, shaky breath. "I don't care about the money, Abby. I only care about Teke, and I don't want anything done that puts him at risk tonight. I don't want a bunch of macho guys going out there and maybe getting Teke killed."

"Oh, Peg, Insley's not that kind of cop. He's totally professional. You know he wouldn't let that happen."

"How do *you* know he's not that kind of cop?" she said, finally turning to look at me. "And even if he is totally professional, how do you know he could control what happens? This guy broke into my truck and stole my dog in the freakin' public parking lot at Dover with security cameras all around!" She was shouting now—something Peg never did. She took a deep breath and lowered her voice. "And he broke into your house. If they confront him, he could turn around and kill Teke."

"Peg, you're imagining some kind of Hollywood scenario."

"And maybe this is all *your* imagination, too," she retorted.

"He'd probably just get scared as hell when cops show up at his door, and it would be all over."

"Maybe. Maybe not."

I shut my mouth against the further protests I wanted to voice. Teke was her dog, not mine. I tried a different tack.

"Peg, I understand how you feel, but shouldn't we at least tell Phil and Griff?" I asked quietly. "They're in a better position than you and I to judge…"

"No."

"Peg, please."

"I said *no*." She got up from her post beside the darkening windows and walked to the kitchen door. Her back was to me. Bits and Dapper trailed her, their heads hanging, and sat down on either side of her.

"I mean it, Abby," she said to the kitchen. "Do nothing. Say nothing."

My head was hanging, too.

Peg and I made a sort of peace as the night wore on. She fed her dogs; I fed mine. I made something nondescript to eat. She ate hers without comment. Mine turned my stomach, and I scraped it off the plate into the garbage. I read the same page of *History of India* time after time. She switched on the TV but didn't appear to be looking at it. Instead, she sat in the floor and hugged the dogs.

When I couldn't stand sitting around anymore, I busied myself in the house. I mopped up the dust bunnies of Tibbie hair in the great room. I inspected the new locks and repairs in the main house and tested the keys Frank Hayes had left me. I made up the bed in the guest room for Peg and laid out fresh towels. But I kept finding myself back in the kitchen staring at the kitchen door.

When I couldn't stand another minute in the house, I escaped to the carriage house. I was fiercely tempted to get in the in the BMW and go snooping around the trailer again. Quashing the urge, I ferreted around in the dimly lit workshop until I found a new floodlight. Retrieving the ladder from its hooks, I clumsily installed the new bulb by the feeble light of the waxing moon. I put away the ladder and surveyed the carriage yard, now bathed in halogen glow. Switching off the new light, I leaned against the door in the darkened yard and hugged myself against the chill air, watching for the occasional headlights passing by on Cattail Road beyond the woods.

When I went in at nine-thirty, the TV was silent. Peg had gone up to bed. Wanting to wait up for the men, I conducted a short search among the CD's, and the pleasing strains of Debussy soon filled the great room. Dawa and Senge joined me and *History of India* on the sofa. For nearly a year, I've been reading this tome. As always, it worked its magic, and my eyes closed.

Car doors slamming in the carriage yard jolted me back to my senses. I squinted at the schoolhouse clock—midnight. That Dawa and Senge were alertly watching the kitchen door but had not bothered to abandon their comfy spots on the sofa confirmed that the car doors belonged to the guys. Right on time.

I assume Peg was awake because she hadn't been sleeping at all. But when she didn't come downstairs, Phil didn't linger long in the kitchen with Griff and me. Ham and he disappeared up the stairs, leaving Griff and I drinking Cokes in the kitchen.

"So anything happen today?" Griff asked.

I looked down and shook my head.

"She isn't going to tell him, Brother," Dawa said and snorted indignantly as she looked up at the two humans.

"Tell 'im what"? Senge asked through an immense yawn.

"Oh for Buddha's sake. About the man who's got Teke at the trailer, Brother! What else? Aunt Peg told Mom not to tell but I still think she should tell Mr. Griff."

Senge licked his lips. "Teke's not at any trailer," he said.

"What?"

"Teke's at the place where they...," Senge paused and shuddered.

"Where they what, Brother?" Dawa prompted impatiently.

"You know, Sister!" Senge said, embarrassed, and sniffed his nether parts tentatively to see if the evidence was still there.

Dawa snorted again. "I don't care about your behind, Senge. How do you know Teke is at the vet clinic?"

"Because I smelled him on the lady vet," Senge replied defensively. "You're not the only one with a good nose, Sister. And besides, he spoke."

"Teke spoke?" Dawa asked, her eyes round.

"Yep. After Mom and me went outside. I was enjoying some trees. I heard him bark inside the building and I barked back."

Dawa thumped her elbows against the floor as she dropped to the down position, causing the startled humans above to look down at her. She chewed her right forepaw in frustration.

"What's the matter?" Senge asked.

"Why didn't you tell Mom, Brother?" Dawa growled.

"I barked," Senge protested feebly but then hung his head. He knew that he hadn't done enough, that he'd been preoccupied with the good smells on the pine trees. "What would you have done, Sister?" he asked meekly.

"I don't know, Brother, but I would have done more than bark once," she snapped and leapt on his back, her jaws clamped to his ear. He accepted the punishment because he was ashamed.

"I'm sorry, Sister," he whined.

She chomped down again but then let go and slid off his back. She was still angry, but anger wouldn't help Teke. She licked the ear she had bitten. Senge happily licked her back, glad to be forgiven. For once, Dawa was proverb-less.

Thor watched the Tibbies from a down-stay next to Griff's chair, his chin on his forepaws. He hadn't followed all they said—Tibbies have a strange accent—but he'd figured out that Senge had not warned his mistress when he should have. He cleared his throat and rumbled through his lips, " 'He who has once burnt his mouth always blows his soup.' "

Dawa showed her bottom teeth in acknowledgment of the appropriate proverb.

Chapter Twenty-One

G riff and I sat up most of the night. I was tortured by wanting to tell him what I knew—or what I strongly suspected—about Teke's whereabouts but not wanting to break my promise to Peg. Eventually, I curled up in the Queen Anne chair under an afghan and dozed fitfully for a couple hours. I woke up with the sun. Griff was still snoring peacefully on the sofa.

Peg came in the kitchen just as I was putting the kettle on to boil. Her dark circles were as bad as mine.

"Did you tell Phil?" I asked.

"No," she answered accepting the mug I offered. "Did you tell Griff?"

"You told me not to."

She nodded.

I may not have told Griff outright, but I'd planted some seeds. While we'd sat around the kitchen table in the middle of the night, Griff had told me that Glen Insley planned to position unmarked cars near the turn to the road by the church. Since the road continued past the church and ended at the Bay and no other roads branched from it, Glen figured that the dognapper had to pass by that turn on his way to and from picking up the money.

I had asked Griff why the dognapper would be stupid enough to pick a place where he could be boxed in like that. Griff brushed off my question. "Criminals are usually stupid," he said.

I had persisted. I had told him that I thought the dognapper would find another way in, either on foot or by some kind of off-road vehicle or maybe even by water. I hinted that I thought the dognapper knew his way around the woods.

Griff had looked at me funny. "You don't think Evelyn Hitchens is gonna drive her minivan out there and pick up the money?"

"Do you?" I'd retorted but I couldn't look him in the eye, gorgeous though they were.

"No, I don't," he'd admitted. "Neither does Insley."

When I'd said nothing more, Griff grabbed my chin and made me look him in the eye, "What do you know about this, Abby?"

"Nothing," I had lied and then corrected, "Nothing I can say. I mean, nothing except what you already know. And you know as well as I do that Evelyn Hitchens didn't skulk around the parking lot in Dover and didn't break into my house. It has to be her son." I disengaged my chin.

"Based on what evidence, Abby? There's no proof this Hitchens woman *or* her son has anything to do with this."

"Has Insley checked out Doug Hitchens?"

"Yes. He's been interviewed. Glen said he came up clean. For one thing, he doesn't drive a Jeep. The surveillance cameras picked up a Jeep in Dover, remember?"

"Well, maybe he got rid of it."

"There was never one registered to him."

"Well, maybe it wasn't his. Maybe he borrowed it—from the girlfriend or *some*body."

"Could be," Griff had conceded.

"What about the girlfriend—this Katie Adkins—did they check her out, too?"

"Yeah. Nothing."

"Tell me something, Griff," I'd challenged, "Where's this Katie Adkins live?"

"Insley said she has a Magnolia address."

My mouth had opened to refute this obvious error but I shut it again. I was too close to breaking my promise to Peg.

"So, you're going to try to get him out at the church even though Peg doesn't want you to interfere," I had asked after a pause.

"Can I get some of that coffee?" Peg asked, interrupting my recollection of my conversation with Griff.

Coming back to the present, I scooped instant powder into her mug and added the boiling water. We sat companionably blowing and sipping, all the dogs under the table, until Phil and Griff groggily joined us a half hour later.

At nine-thirty, Peg left for Records Church with a lunch bag full of twenties and fifties. She was back by ten-thirty. No, she hadn't seen anyone, she told us. The road to the church and the church itself had been just as deserted as it was the day before.

The day dragged by. Griff left for work around two o'clock but Phil hung around.

At six-thirty, Glen Insley called. He told Peg that the paper bag had disappeared from the church porch. He confessed that they'd had Tindall Road under surveillance all the while, but no vehicles were spotted going in or out.

When Peg relayed this information, I couldn't resist muttering, "That's because he didn't come by car." One of the least admirable attributes of my personality is, regrettably, an 'I-told-you-so' tendency.

Phil frowned and asked me what I meant. Peg glared at me. I glared back.

"Because he's a hunter. He probably knows that whole area like the back of his hand. He came in either by boat down the gut or maybe by ATV, picked up the money and went home."

Peg was still glaring at me.

"I'm sorry, Peg," I said sternly but not unkindly, "but I've watched you sitting there staring out the window all day, hoping to see Teke wander up to the house. You don't know whether they're going to bring Teke back. It just doesn't make sense not to tell Phil what we know."

Dawa, always upset by any discord in her human family, stood on her hind legs and pawed at Peg's knee. Peg picked her up and buried her face in Dawa's soft white shawl. Dawa kissed her ear lobes.

By this time, Phil's face was about as red as his hair. Peg looked up, saw his expression and shrugged.

"OK, OK. Go ahead and tell him, Abby," she whispered.

In short order, I revealed all I'd found out by snooping. I summed up, "It wouldn't take long to cut across country by ATV from Stone Beach Road, where they live, to Records Church. Or he could have put the canoe in the gut and gone in that way. I don't know if they're going to return Teke or not, but I do think he's alive and that they moved him someplace last night."

Within a minute, Phil was on the phone to Glen Insley. Peg stared dejectedly into space. Always so pragmatic and purposeful, she seemed paralyzed by fear. On the other hand, I felt energized. Surely, *some*thing would happen now, I thought.

As it turned out, nothing happened. Phil left to meet Insley. Peg and I sat and waited until he called around midnight. They'd gone to the trailer but found it dark, deserted. The neighbors claimed to know nothing about the occupants of the doublewide and to have seen nothing all day. Phil told Peg that Doug's German Short-hairs were still in the kennel, but Teke wasn't there. Always mindful of dogs, she asked if he'd fed and watered them, and he reassured her they were well cared for. Still, it had been a dead end.

But Glen Insley hadn't stopped there. When he left to pay a visit to Katie Adkins' family in Magnolia, he sent Phil to meet Griff at Evelyn Hitchens'. Glen had reported that Katie wasn't at her parents' home but that the absent roommate, Trudy Bozman, turned out to be Katie's older, divorced sister. The doublewide was Trudy's, their father said, but he didn't know where either daughter was. He knew Doug Hitchens, he said, but seemed unaware that Doug had pitched his tent at the doublewide.

Meanwhile, Phil and Griff got Evelyn Hitchens out of bed. Though she was surly, Phil's professional judgment was that she was being truthful when she said she hadn't seen Doug for several days and denied knowing his whereabouts. This time, she readily gave permission for the police to search her home and outbuildings. They came up with nothing. Another dead end.

When she hung up, all Peg said was, "Phil says Griff and he are on their way back here. They'll be here in about an hour." The conclusion was unspoken but unavoidable. Doug and Katie had taken off for parts unknown, and Teke was nowhere to be found.

Chapter Twenty-Two

Exhaustion set in. I'm not the kind of person who can go without sleep indefinitely, and it just wasn't in me to pull another all-nighter. By the time Griff and Phil arrived, I was in the fetal position on the sofa, Dawa tucked under my arm and Senge behind my knees, dead to the world.

They must have sat up the better part of the night talking or maybe just waiting. I forced my eyes open at about seven o'clock Thursday morning. When I dragged myself into the kitchen, the scattered remains indicated they'd consumed cold cut sandwiches, corn chips and salsa, all my Dogfish Head beer and a pot of coffee—not necessarily in that order. I put on a fresh pot of coffee.

Upstairs, I instilled some eye drops and pressed a cool washcloth against my aching eyes for several minutes. Although I felt better after washing my face and drying it with a soft, fragrant towel, I couldn't summon enough energy to shower. Maybe after my coffee, I thought.

A sound from my bedroom, adjacent to the bath, drew my attention. I peeked through the door and found Griff sprawled across my bed, atop the comforter. He must have been too tired or sore to sleep in the Queen Anne chair again, and I had already staked out the sofa. Thor, stretched out next to the bed, lifted his head. "Sh-h-h," I motioned with my finger on my lips and quietly latched the door.

Still barely functioning a half-hour later, I stood by the great room windows overlooking the front yard, two-handedly gripping my second mug of coffee. It was, or would have been under other circumstances, a glorious spring morning—one on which I would have gladly set out for a long, long ride. But there was no question of that today. I had a premonition this was not going to be a good day.

Outside, the resident Canada geese were pecking around the budding azaleas. I felt a ping of annoyance. Though goose crap was a nuisance to clean up, I had to do it because I didn't want the Tibbies to come into contact with it. Who knew what avian diseases or parasites it might harbor? Thinking of the Tibbies, I turned around. Dawa and Senge were still fast asleep, unbudged, on the sofa. I smiled and turned back to gaze at the pastoral scene before me.

Geese. My mind wandered back to the day I'd sat in Uncle John's chicken house watching that flock of snow geese forage in the field between Uncle John's and Evelyn Hitchens' farms. Snow geese are such loud honkers. If a flock goes over the house, they'll wake you up from a deep sleep. At the mere thought of sleep, my eyelids slunk down over my eyes and I dozed for a blissful moment. I popped them open.

The same thing had happened that day in the chicken house. I'd dozed while watching the geese and then woke to find Jackie Lynch's Jeep parked at Evelyn's. 'Course I didn't know it was Jackie Lynch at the time. I didn't recognize her—the hooded person I saw could have been a man or a woman for all I knew. But Griff told me it was Jackie Lynch and her Jeep. I sipped my coffee.

Jeep. Jackie Lynch was in that Jeep at St. Michaels, too. She'd brought Teke and Peg back to the clinic in it. That was really nice of her. And it was really lucky she was there in the first place. Peg's RV couldn't have made good time, and my BMW wouldn't have held all of us with Teke lying down. Dr. Lynch seems nice. Too bad she didn't get along with Doc. Didn't get along with Doc, my mind repeated. I swayed and took another sip of coffee.

Doc. Poor old Doc. Dead and nobody knows why. 'Course he loved to fish in Swann's Pond. If he had to die someplace, I guess that's as good a place as any. What a stupid thought, I chastised myself.

Fishing. Doc sure loved to fish. I'd seen him out there fishing just that morning. They said he didn't die until that evening. I wonder if he'd been out there all day. He didn't usually stay all that long. Strange that they found his rod and tackle box in the cab of the truck. Why would he be out on the pond without his rod and tackle? And whatever happened to the fish he caught that morning? Wonder what kind of fish they were? Perch maybe? I looked down at my coffee. I don't really like coffee, I thought tiredly. I really prefer latte. I took another sip.

Coffee. Doc really liked coffee. Hardly ever saw the man without a cup. They found his thermos in the cab, too. It was empty when that trooper turned it upside down. So, he must've already come in from fishing and, for some reason, went back out on the pond. Why would he do that—why would he go out again with no rod, no tackle? It had to be the murderer. Whoever killed him made him go back out. But they said he wasn't robbed. If robbery wasn't the motive, why was he murdered? What would anybody have against sweet, old Doc? I sipped.

Sweet, old Doc. Course, Lorraine says he wasn't so sweet to the employees at the clinic. Wasn't sweet to Jackie Lynch either. But he was always sweet to me and my dogs. Funny, though, that he told me he didn't know Evelyn Hitchens. And isn't it strange that there was no file for Evelyn Hitchens at the clinic? Even if Doc didn't know her, Jackie Lynch was her vet. So, why wouldn't there be a file at the clinic?

Jackie Lynch. Evelyn Hitchens' vet. Makes house calls out there. Probably knows Doug Hitchens. Knows Katie Adkins from work. Knows me. Knows Peg. Knows Teke. Has a Jeep. Why wouldn't there be a file on Evelyn Hitchens at the clinic?

I hurried to the kitchen and retrieved the phone book from its drawer. My hand was shaking as I punched in the number.

"Uncle John? This is Abby Swann. Bill's wife's cousin. Remember me?"

Within a few minutes, Uncle John made the connection that had eluded me. He told me Evelyn Hitchens was a Lynch before she married. She had two brothers, Dewitt and Albert. The younger brother, Al they called him, had a daughter who became a vet. Al had died young and the girl was raised by her mother, whose name he couldn't remember but who was born a Massey. I thanked Uncle John, marveling at his ability to remember the interrelationships of people he barely knew. It was just like my Dad always said—everybody in lower Delaware knows everybody, and a lot of them are related to each other somewhere way back.

That relationship explained everything that had puzzled me. Evelyn Hitchens was Jackie Lynch's aunt. That would explain why Jackie Lynch was doing Evelyn's vet work *gratis*—maybe that's the reason there was no file in the office. That also made Doug her cousin, and Doug probably met Katie through Jackie Lynch.

In a flash of insight, I also knew without a doubt that it was Jackie Lynch's Jeep that Doug had used to steal Teke. Of course, I couldn't prove it. And the new question to plague me was whether Jackie Lynch had been in on Teke's dognapping all along.

My head started to ache. I abandoned my efforts to make sense of it all in order to feed my body. Not to be left out, the Tibbies oozed off the sofa. Rather than talk and dance in their usual manner, they sat quietly beneath the dog food dispenser in the pantry, blinking their sleepy eyes, while I filled their bowls. As I swallowed buttered oatmeal, they ate their kibble without enthusiasm and soon re-established themselves on the sofa.

A tall glass of orange juice seemed to revive my mental abilities. I seated myself at the great room windows and returned to my contemplation of the out-of-doors and of Teke's dognapping. The question at hand, I reminded myself, was the extent to which Jackie Lynch was involved.

"If Peg is right that the dognapper left the notes here at the Nest because he, or she, doesn't know where Peg lives, then Jackie Lynch had nothing to do with the ransom," I said to the Tibbies, who raised their heads and peered at me through half-open eyes. "She knows where Peg lives because she took her home after Teke's accident in St. Michaels. So Jackie Lynch can't be the dognapper."

I felt relieved to have exonerated Jackie Lynch in my own mind. She seemed to be a competent young vet. "She must've loaned her Jeep to her cousin Doug. Or maybe he just took it," I concluded out loud.

Something just beyond my mind's fringe, where I couldn't quite grasp it, was nagging at me. There was something I was forgetting—I was convinced of it. Yet, the harder I tried, the more elusive it became. Shaking it off, I decided to take the dogs out for a stroll down the lane to pick up the morning paper. Creaking floor joists and clanking plumbing told me my friends were stirring. Maybe everyone would be up by the time I returned.

They were. Griff was just hanging up the kitchen phone. Phil was leaning on the counter, and Peg had just come in from the great room.

"No sign of them," Griff reported. He rubbed his cheeks, bestubbled with a day's growth of salt-and-pepper beard. A good look for him, I thought.

I dropped the paper on the counter and glanced over the front page. A car accident featuring a mangled Jeep was the subject of the color photo above the fold. "Three hurt in 19-car pileup on I-95," I read the caption out loud. I-95 was upstate, so it was probably nobody we knew.

Everyone grunted. I moved on to the next article but my eyes returned to the photo unbidden. "Probably speeding," I murmured.

"Yeah, usually. Or drunk. Or both," Phil remarked.

Speeding. Jeep. 19. It suddenly came to me—the thing I'd been going crazy trying to remember. A speeding Jeep had passed me on Swann's Pond Road the night Teke was stolen. I could see that plate clearly in my mind's eye. The tag was black and white with the number 019.

Momentarily, I marveled that I could remember such minutia. Then again, he had really pissed me off—first by tailgating me and then by swerving recklessly around me and just missing the car coming head on. That dumb SOB could have killed all of us, I grumped to myself.

"I wonder," I murmured.

"Wonder what?" Peg asked.

Startled that I'd spoken aloud, I glanced around. "It's stupid, I guess," I began. Nobody contradicted me. "Well, the night Teke was stolen, a dark-colored Jeep passed me like a bat out of hell on Swann's Pond Road, at the bridge. Its tag number was 019. I've got a hunch that Teke was in that Jeep. I think Doug Hitchens was driving it, and I also think it belongs to Jackie Lynch."

They stared at me goggle-eyed. "Jackie Lynch?" Phil said dubiously.

I hurried on. "You see, I found out this morning that Jackie Lynch is Doug Hitchens' cousin. I think he was in her Jeep when he stole Teke."

"*What?*" Phil said.

Griff leafed through a notebook that he had produced from somewhere in his jeans. "The day she was out at Evelyn Hitchens', we ran her plate. The tag number on Jackie Lynch's Jeep is 338," he said.

I flashed back to Uncle John's chicken house. I remembered straining to read the tag on the Jeep but only being able to make out a 3 or an 8.

"Oh," I said, defeated. I looked at Ham sitting quietly at Phil's side. He was watching me intently with his lovely head cocked.

German Short-hair. Doug's German Short-hairs barking as I was running toward the doublewide. Jumping into my BMW and throwing it in reverse, the gravel flying as I sped backward out of their driveway. Looking forward and the last thing I saw before I swerved onto Stone Beach Road was the tag on the little white pickup—number 019. I blinked and came back to the present.

"019 is the tag on the white pickup I saw at Doug's doublewide. It probably belongs to Katie Adkins. Or maybe it's her sister's—that Trudy Bozman person, wherever she is," I said, leaning over to scratch Ham's chest. Ham wagged. "He switched the tags on the Jeep."

Peg was staring at me. "So where's my dog?" she asked, a hint of bitterness in her voice.

I shook my head. Unfortunately, I was fresh out of hunches about that.

Chapter Twenty-Three

Griff and Phil acted on the revelation that Jackie Lynch and Doug Hitchens are cousins and that it may well have been her Jeep used in Teke's theft. After a call to Insley, they hurriedly shaved and dressed while Peg and I fed Ham and Thor. They and their dogs were soon gone with a promise to call as soon as they found out anything. It was just before nine o'clock.

At noon, Griff called. He apparently asked to speak to me since Peg handed me the phone without a word, a hang-dog look on her face. When I clicked off a few minutes later, I looked up to find Peg analyzing my face. Evidently, she saw the bad news written all over it.

"Is he dead?" she asked in a tiny, frightened voice.

"Oh no, Peg, it's not Teke," I said and drew a deep breath. "It's Katie Adkins. They found her—shot—at Doc's clinic. She's dead. Killed sometime last night. Lorraine found her when she opened the clinic this morning."

"Do they know who did it?"

"Well, they think it was Doug Hitchens."

I led her over to the sofa and we sat.

"Griff said that, when Phil and he left here this morning, they went straight to the clinic. They figured Jackie Lynch would either be there already or would come into work soon. They were right. She showed up at the clinic right after they did. When they questioned her, she told them everything. She said Doug and Katie told her they spotted the cops at the trailer last night and took off, but the money you paid to ransom Teke was still in the trailer. So, they went to Jackie's house to get some money off her. They told her they were gonna leave the state, but she claims they didn't tell her where they were going. Anyway, she gave them some money."

I paused for breath. "When they left her house, Jackie says they were arguing about returning Teke—Doug didn't want to, but Katie was trying to talk him into it. Griff says that, after they left Jackie's house, they came to the clinic to get Teke and, whatever happened, Katie ended up dead."

"You mean Teke is at the clinic!" Peg hollered and jumped off the sofa.

"No, honey, he isn't. He was gone when Lorraine came in," I hurried on. "It seems that Jackie had been suspicious that Doug was involved in the accident at St. Michaels. And, then, when she heard that somebody in a Jeep stole Teke, she figured out that Doug had used her Jeep to steal Teke. Apparently, Katie had borrowed the Jeep to run an errand that day. Jackie told Phil and Griff that Doug went ballistic when she confronted him with all this but that she had convinced him to let her keep Teke at the clinic. She says she was trying to protect Teke from Doug and that she was gonna make sure Teke got back to you."

Peg sat down. "I can't believe he was at the clinic the whole time," she said in the tiny voice.

"Insley says they're going back to Evelyn Hitchens' and the girl's parents. And they've put out a BOLO for Doug's truck. They'll find him."

"I don't give a crap about him," Peg yelled. "Where's my dog? Where's my Teke?"

Peg was inconsolable. She cried until I didn't think she had any tears left and then she cried some more. Bits and Dapper alternated leaning against her and lying with their chins on their forepaws, their eyes swiveling this way and that as they tried to understand what had happened to their imperturbable mistress.

My neck and shoulders were so tense a quarter could bounce off me, but I didn't see much point in crying. I glanced over at my red-eyed friend, glued to the window, staring out as she had for most of the past three days. The thought popped into my head that my nosiness was to blame for Teke's disappearance from the clinic. If I hadn't sent the police to the doublewide, Doug and Katie wouldn't have been scared off and Teke might be home by now. I shook off the thought. Then again, he might not.

And how could I have been so wrong about Jackie Lynch? I was disappointed and not a little puzzled that she had known about Teke all along. To know that I'd been right in that clinic while Teke was in the kennel in the back was almost too painful to think about.

And what about that stupid Lorraine? I snorted. Why hadn't my loudmouth second cousin picked up that the Chessie in the kennel was Teke? Was she in on it? I instantly rejected the idea. Lorraine may be pushy, nosy and utterly irritating but she would never hurt an animal. Probably, as far as Lorraine was concerned, if you've seen one Chessie, you've seen them all.

As for Katie Adkins, I couldn't feel much for her. Based on the one interaction I'd witnessed, I guessed that Doug was probably nasty to her. If what Jackie Lynch said was true, that she had tried to protect Teke from Doug, then I supposed she deserved some pity.

Later that afternoon, Phil called to talk to Peg. He told her that they had some leads but that nothing had panned out so far. I suppose he must have tried to encourage her because she spent a long time listening without speaking and then said "OK, I'll try."

When she'd hung up, she turned to me and bluntly announced, "I'm going home, Abby. I need to be alone in my own place, in Teke's place, for a while."

Twenty minutes later, she was gone. The Tibbies and I watched her truck disappear down the lane, Bits and Dapper in their crates in the bed staring forlornly at us through the grates.

Griff sounded beat when he called me about six o'clock. He obviously didn't want to talk. "No news" was about all he would tell me. When he said he'd call me tomorrow, I deduced without comment that he was going home—his home. So, I spent the night alone—except for my Tibbies, of course.

Friday morning was a long time in coming. Dawa and Senge, in the manner of all their kind, sensibly slept soundly all night except when my thrashing disturbed them. By dawn, they were awake and lively whereas I was barely able to stagger down the stairs.

Ignoring my Bride of Frankenstein reflection in the mirror next to the kitchen door, I opened the dog door for the Tibbies and watched them scamper into the carriage yard. They perked their ears and looked delightedly from left to right to left, undecided which way to explore first. Something caught their eye to the right and they streaked out of sight.

Leaving them to play, I went hunting for food. The pantry was nearly empty of everything, including dog kibble. Likewise the fridge. So much had preoccupied me, I'd neglected the mundane chores of housekeeping. I resolved to visit the grocery store that morning and began jotting mental notes on what I needed. It wasn't going to be difficult—basically I could just walk the aisles and pick up one of each.

Jiggling the handle on the dog food dispenser, I managed to half-fill the dog bowls and sat them on the floor to await the Tibbies. After swallowing a vitamin with the two remaining ounces of orange juice, I wandered into the great room. The feature titles on the cover of a neglected *Southern Living* on the map table reminded me that the coming Sunday was Easter and today was Good Friday. I usually had Peg and some friends over for Easter Day dinner, but I had no spirit to plan a celebration this year.

A couple hours later I was unloading groceries under the unflinching scrutiny of Tibbie eyes. At their vocal insistence, I sliced pieces from a newly opened brick of Cheddar to supplement their meager breakfasts. While thus occupied, the phone rang.

It was Peg. I instantly felt guilty for not having called her first thing. She sounded a bit better. She was sorry, she said, for her behavior the day before. She didn't want me to think she was mad with me because she'd taken off so suddenly. I hadn't thought that, and I told her so. I agreed to bring the dogs down that afternoon and stay for dinner—something simple, we agreed, like freezer lasagna.

It occurred to me, as I hung up, that I hadn't heard from Griff since the night before. To my surprise, I was more than slightly irritated.

Chapter Twenty-Four

I was speeding south when I decided to leave the dual and take a leisurely drive cross-country instead. Once off the highway, I lowered my window and opened the sun roof. The fresh spring air scented with fragrant flowering plum instantly lifted my spirits. It also lifted Dawa's and Senge's noses, where they perched on the passenger seat straining toward the open roof.

"Good smells?" I asked. Senge snorted.

I wasn't exactly sure how to get to Peg's house, but I was sure I could find it with that built-in guidance system country people have. I jinked back and forth along the web of roads segmenting the freshly plowed and planted fields. Completely confident that I was headed in the general direction of Peg's house, I relaxed and observed the passing scenery. Unlike people who are content to passively drive through life in a daze, I am at all times a curious and keen observer of my surroundings. It's a trait that comes in handy most of the time.

A placid greenwater pond went by on my left. A bass boat floated on its smooth surface. Momentarily blinded by reflections off the water, I didn't see the angler. I felt a flutter of panic as I flashed back to the day I'd seen another empty boat on a pond. I blinked. There he was, standing in his boat, plying his line. The flutter died. I'll never see old Doc out fishing on the pond again, I realized sadly.

A half-mile along from the pond, I came to an intersection. A crudely lettered sign declaring "We'll miss you Charlie" tacked to a tree and faded plastic flowers bunched at its base commemorated an accident that had happened here long ago. I debated which way to go and then noticed one of those newly-posted 911 road signs—Horsey Road.

"I'm near Evelyn Hitchens' place," I said to the Tibbies. They stared at me, wide-eyed. I decided to turn right. Approaching Cedar Neck Road, I slowed the car and, unable to contain my curiosity, turned onto it. I soon faced a fork—left on Reynolds Road would take me to Uncle John's or right on Cedar Neck to Evelyn Hitchens'. "Let's go right," I said.

Dawa and Senge were sitting erect, their ears forward, staring intently ahead. Their foreheads were wrinkly. Dawa trembled. I knew they were sensing something—probably just my skittish emotional state. "It's OK, little guys. I'm just going to ride by. No big deal. Stop worrying."

Cedar Pond passed slowly to my left, and Evelyn's long driveway came into view. I pulled the car onto the shoulder and waited. A State Police cruiser was parked alongside the driveway on the grass. Good, I thought, they're trying to get information out of her. Another vehicle, some kind of SUV, was parked ahead of it. There was no sign of life. Losing my resolve, I u-turned the BMW and headed back the way I'd come, past Cedar Pond. A guy I hadn't noticed before was fishing from the bank, his license on his cap.

Fish. That day at Kenny's Tire, the only time I ever saw him, Doug had said something to Katie about cleaning fish. The dim recollection migrated to the front of my mind. Fish he caught here in Cedar Pond maybe? Or maybe my own Swann's Pond? What exactly did he say? Something about taking his mother some fish. Oh yeah—"don't forget to take Mom them perch I cleaned"—that's what he'd said. Why, of all things, would that remark about the fish pop back into my mind?

When I came to the fork to Reynolds Road, I slowed the car to a crawl. Which way? I could resume my ride to Peg's or I could take another detour. I glanced at the clock on the dash—it was just after noon.

"Let's go to Uncle John's. I'll bet Aunt Bessie would get a kick out of you two," I said and guided the car to the right.

Minutes later, as we crunched onto their driveway, Dawa was arf'ing and roo'ing—always excited by the prospect of a visit. Senge was busily sniffing. Clouds had covered the sun and the air had cooled. Don't like the Delmarva weather? Wait a few minutes and it'll change. I shivered and raised the window.

To my relief, Aunt Bessie was truly taken with the Tibbies. Answering my tentative knock with a gracious smile, she nodded pleasantly, wiping her gnarled hands on her bib apron, as I'd explained my relation to her through her nephew Bill's marriage to my cousin Bonnie on my mother's side. I mumbled my fabricated reason for stopping—to thank Uncle John for letting me watch the Hitchens place from the chicken house and for helping me figure out the Lynch connection to the Hitchenses. She accepted this explanation with a "Pshaw," a word I'd often seen in print but never heard pronounced.

Uncle John, it seemed, was somewhere out back. Why didn't I come on through to the kitchen and have something to eat? she asked me. And bring those cute little dogs, she instructed, pronouncing the word 'dogs' with a long oh in the way of native Delmarvans. I could smell chicken frying—perhaps one of the feckless creatures I'd met in the broiler house—as I followed her down the narrow, center hall of the farmhouse.

Dawa and Senge also smelled the chicken frying, of course, and made themselves even more adorable by dancing around Aunt Bessie on their hind legs and circling their clasped forepaws in the praying motion of their kind. While she brought ice tea and hot biscuits to the vintage yellow kitchen table, circa 1955, she lamented that her last little dog, Sparky—who'd been a terrier mix—had died a couple years back. She always loved dogs, she said, but she'd decided against another because she was getting on in years and didn't think she could manage a puppy. I observed that she could probably find a nice adult dog, already trained, at the SPCA—a dog who would just love to have a good home like hers.

"Well now, that's probably true. I'll have to think on that," she said. Lowering her considerable bulk into the chair opposite me, she beckoned the Tibbies, who gladly complied. She stroked their ears and pinched their cheeks, which they loved.

I heard the distinctive screech and slam of an old-fashioned screen door. "That'll be John," Aunt Bessie said.

When he came in from the screen porch in his stocking feet, having shed his boots somewhere out back, Uncle John was a little more suspicious, though no less welcoming, than Aunt Bessie about the reason for my visit. He, too, pronounced my thanks unnecessary, seated himself at the table and popped a biscuit in his mouth.

With his little blue eyes sparkling, he quizzed me on the events of the past few days. He'd seen the comings and goings over to Evelyn's, he told me, and wondered what was happening. I told him about Peg paying the ransom, the involvement of Evelyn's niece Jackie Lynch, the murder of Doug's girlfriend at the vet clinic and the disappearance of Doug.

"Well, I'll be," he and Aunt Bessie said over and over. I noticed they pronounced this expression the Delmarvan way, which best transliterates as 'L.I.B.'

"So, *that's* why the cops have been over there more of'en than not. They been lookin' for that boy," Uncle John said.

"Mmmm," was all I could manage in reply as I exercised my jaws on a biscuit, beaten and kneaded until hard as a rock on the outside but feathery soft and light on the inside. They were just like my MomMom used to make, I told Aunt Bessie.

"T'ain't nothin'. Onliest way I know how," Aunt Bessie said dismissively. She placed a heaping plate of crispy brown chicken, still sitting on its bed of paper towels, and a bowl of greens on the table and resumed incessantly turning the batch still sizzling in the pan.

"That boy weren't never good fer nothin'," Uncle John declared, "'cept huntin' and fishin', I guess. He were allus bringin' Evelyn something to eat."

"Yeah, I heard he'd been fishing lately. And somebody told me he was into bow-hunting," I said as I sprinkled vinegar on the greens.

"Ever' kind o' huntin' and fishin'. His brother Paul and him built a huntin' camp up in the woods when they was just kids. Always out there shootin'. Then it got to be drinkin', smokin', raisin' hell and Lord knows what else."

I shoveled a forkful of real mashed potatoes, not the out-of-a-box kind, into my mouth. The food was distracting me. I needed to focus and think. I put down the fork.

Even when he was in the middle of plotting to ransom Teke, Doug Hitchens had told his girlfriend to take some perch out to his mother. Something about that didn't jive. Would the kind of person who'd kill his girlfriend worry about giving his mother some fish? Somehow it seemed out of character. Or maybe not. Maybe killers are like that. I picked up the fork.

"Would you say Doug was good to his mother, Uncle John?" I asked, finally forking a little pickled beet that I'd been idly chasing around the plate.

Aunt Bessie joined us. She'd apparently decided the table was sufficiently laden to keep us nourished until supper time. This was, after all, just noon day dinner.

"She's about the onliest one he was good to," she interjected, spooning hot pepper relish from a canning jar onto her plate. "Here, try some of this. It's my own." She pushed the jar toward me, and I scooped out a tablespoonful.

"He was the orneriest young'un I ever did see. Always pitchin' fits. Spoilt rotten—that was his problem," Aunt Bessie continued. "Raymond was the oldest boy—he died young. Somethin' was wrong with him when he was born. Then came Paul and Dougie. Dougie was always close to his mother. Even after he got growed, he couldn't do enough for her. Like John said, he was always bringin' her somethin'—sea trout or freshwater fish in season, a deer every fall, muskrat in spring, crabs in summer—whatever he could catch. And Evelyn always depended on him to fix things or run errands, whatever she needed done. Paul wudn't that way. He lives in Bridgeville—wife and a couple kids, good job— but he don't dote on his mother like Dougie always did."

"You said he was ornery. What do you mean? Did he get in fights, stuff like that?"

Uncle John piped up. "Oh yeah. He's got a *bad* temper. Took after his mother I 'spect. She allus got hot under the collar over anythin' and everythin'."

"How about a drinking problem? Or drugs?"

"I hear tell he likes his booze. Don't know 'bout them drugs. I guess all the kids take drugs nowadays. But I think he got hauled in a coupla times for fightin'—whadyacallit, assault."

I mulled that over. If Doug Hitchens had a record for assault, why didn't the cops jump on him like flies on you-know-what? We paused to enjoy the food. I was getting full as a tick.

"Did he like Evelyn's dogs?" I asked.

"Oh, I don't think he cared one way or t'other about them poodles, but they was his mother's and so he helped her with 'em like he did everythin' else. Went to those dog shows with her and such like. But he always had his own dogs—huntin' dogs."

"Right. German Short-hairs."

161

Uncle John pushed himself back from the table. "Get me a cup of coffee, Bessie," he ordered and, unless I was mistaken, he winked at me. She left the table. "So where'd you hear tell about Doug Hitchens' German Short-hairs?"

Uncle John's question had to wait. I had just experienced heaven on earth in the form of Ant Bessie's spicy-sweet red condiment. "Lord, Aunt Bessie, this relish is wonderful. I almost swallowed my tongue. You ought to market that."

Aunt Bessie chuckled as she poured the coffee in Uncle John's cup. "Here, have another maffle of greens. Got plenty," she said, pushing the bowl toward me.

"Well, to be honest, Uncle John," I said, returning to the subject, "I've been snooping around. The cops didn't think Doug lived with his mother anymore but they didn't know where, so I kinda figured it out and then went over and checked out the place. His dogs were there."

I paused to form a thought and chew a mouthful, or maffle as Aunt Bessie called it, of greens. I swallowed. "From what you say about this Doug, I wonder if he's really taken off for parts unknown like everybody's assuming. I have a funny feeling he might still be somewhere around here, close to his mother."

Just at that moment, Dawa and Senge, who'd been patiently alternating between Aunt Bessie and myself in hopes of a piece of chicken, decided on a less passive approach to begging. Both barked loudly.

"Gracious me!" Aunt Bessie exclaimed and dropped her fork, which clattered onto her plate.

"Oh, I'm sorry, Aunt Bessie. Bad dogs! Shush!" I scolded. But as I frowned down at them, Dawa's magic eyes grabbed me. She sat upright on her haunches and twirled her forepaws, roo'ing at me.

"Oh, isn't she adorable!" Aunt Bessie said.

Having gained my full attention, Dawa abandoned her "praying" and dashed to the kitchen door. Senge followed. They both looked back at me, stamping their slippered forepaws with impatience. Dawa stared up at the door, trembling violently. She growled.

"Maybe they have to go out?" Aunt Bessie guessed.

"Right. I'll take them out for a walk," I agreed but I was suspicious. I had never known the Tibbies to abandon the prospect of a choice morsel no matter how badly they had to go.

The screen door had no sooner slammed behind us than the Tibbies took off like bullets toward the tractor shed. I had only a split second to grab their leads tightly or they would have torn them from my hands. Maintaining a death grip on the leads, I stumbled after the flying dogs. "Wait! Stop!" I called breathlessly to no avail, looking around for the barn cat or rabbit that must have crossed our path to motivate this reaction.

When they passed the tractor shed and started to cross over the yard toward the cornfield, I knew I had to get them under control. We were already in Uncle John's fresh furrows when I finally hauled them up short.

"What's the matter with you? Listen to me!" I shouted at them. But they paid no attention whatsoever to me. Staring straight ahead, they both strained and bucked at the end of their taut leads. It dawned on me that they'd done this only once—that was the day they led me to Doc's body—so maybe I should pay attention to them rather than the other way around.

"What is it, Tibbies?" I asked in a gentler tone and followed their unwavering sightline across the cornfield to the woods beyond the field. Those woods belonged to Evelyn Hitchens.

"Do you think Mom saw, Sister?"

"I am sure that she did not," Dawa sighed, "Human eyes are very weak compared to ours."

"Then why are we walking back with her? Why don't we make her go the other way?"

"I do not think she saw, Brother, but I think she understands."

"Oh, Sister, stop being so enigmatic, like some old lama!" Senge instantly regretted what he'd called her, but Dawa just laughed.

"If I was an old lama in my last life, little Brother, then you must have been a naughty monk."

Senge acknowledged that what she said was probably true, but he still didn't understand why Dawa had given up and he said so.

"Because Mom must cross the bridge which she herself has built," she explained, paraphrasing the proverb. *"Do you understand?"*

"Ah," Senge said in what he hoped was a parody of sagacity.

Dawa rolled her eyes and quoted another proverb from old Tibet, *" 'Any fool can say Ah. You need intelligence to say yes.' "*

Senge accepted the rebuke and trudged on. *"Little Sister, why do you call me little Brother, when our dam said I am the oldest of our littermates and much older than you, who was the last, by two full hours?"*

Dawa smiled. *"Though you are correct in saying that you are the oldest, I am also correct in saying that I am the oldest."*

"Huh?"

"Because, little Brother, I am an old soul and you are a sweet, young one."

Senge understood now why his little Sister was so wise. When they paused on the porch steps, he gently cleaned his sister's ears—a sign of love and respect among their kind.

Chapter Twenty-Five

"Well, this is unique," I said to myself as the Ford tractor I was driving bumped along the lane toward Uncle John's dump.

When the dogs and I had returned a half-hour earlier, I had explained my theory that Doug was holed up in his old hunting camp out in his mother's woods. Uncle John agreed it was a good theory. He'd eagerly described exactly where the camp was, but when I'd fished out my cell phone to call Griff, he'd protested.

"Them cops don't know nothin'," he declared, slapping the kitchen table with the flat of his hand for emphasis. "They'll just mess it up."

I began to respectfully disagree, but Uncle John further proclaimed that he would go check out the camp himself. Aunt Bessie clucked and said a few words about that, punctuated frequently with the phrase 'a man your age.' In the end, we agreed on a compromise—that I would go in Uncle John's place but disguised to look like him so as not to arouse suspicion in anyone who may be watching.

Though taller than Uncle John, who was all of five foot two if he was an inch, I was soon outfitted in a pair of his baggy overalls, his best camouflage jacket and a pair of his work boots with three pair of socks underneath. Tucking my hair under one of his John Deere hats, Aunt Bessie pulled the brim down as far as she could. But there was only so much we could do to make a thirty-something woman look like a seventy-something man.

"Here," Uncle John had said and thrust a blue bandanna at me. "Tie that around yer neck and, when you git out there, pull it up over yer mouth and nose. That's what I do when I'm haulin' manure."

"Manure?" I queried doubtfully, but spry Uncle John had already sprinted for the tractor shed, the screen door banging behind him.

Telling the dogs to be good for Aunt Bessie, I'd clunked along awkwardly after him. Unlike the rest of his clothes, the work boots were two sizes too large. Demurring at his suggestion—just a tease I'm sure—that I take the Ford behemoth used to plow and disk fields—I'd instead chosen a compact model that Uncle John said he used for hauling manure. It resembled one Dad had kept for brush-hogging and that I'd learned to drive as a teen.

Uncle John started the tractor for me and, when she was purring like a diesel kitten, he'd obligingly filled the bucket with chicken crap from the manure shed—to lend my disguise an air of authenticity, he explained in so many words. Pulling the kerchief up over my face, off I'd gone in the direction of his dump, which was conveniently located at the edge of Evelyn's woods.

As I rode along the dusty lane at the painfully slow pace of the tractor, I had plenty of time to think about a tale Uncle John had told me while we waited for the tractor to warm up. After swearing me to secrecy with a chuckle, Uncle John related how, a couple years back, there was another one of those rumors about a panther that had come north out of the cypress swamp and was on the loose in the Devil's Woodyard. While jawing about this particular panther with his fellow chicken farmers at the diner, he'd hatched an idea.

As the sun was "fixin' to set" one night later that week, he'd placed a 911 call to report a big black animal eating a chicken in a field off Cedar Pond Road. "It might be that 'ere panther they're talkin' about," he'd told the dispatcher. The troopers who'd responded studied the beast from the safety of the back porch. Egged on by Uncle John, they'd agreed that it appeared to be a very large black cat rather than the black Labs that panicked people usually mistook for the elusive panther.

The troopers had devised a plan of attack. Surrounding the beast, they had slunk across Uncle John's field, guns drawn and at the ready. Unperturbed by the advancing humans, the cat continued to eat its chicken, its yellow eyes glittering. As he watched the tactic unfold from his porch, Uncle John heard indignant shouts from the field as the cops had beamed their flashlights on the "panther" only to discover it was a giant-sized stuffed black pussycat with glass eyes. The dead chicken in its mouth, however, was real—another of Uncle John's authentic touches, I suppose.

"I had to go all the way to Wilm'ton to git that stuffed cat," Uncle John had said, his eyes gleaming in the darkened tractor shed.

You can never tell with any of Bill's family whether they're telling truth or lies. The telling of tall tales is a tradition among the Adamses, and they are very talented at fooling the gullible and the cynical alike. I myself had been duped many times. I resolved to ask Griff whether he'd heard the story about some troopers getting fooled in a panther hoax a couple years back.

By this point in my ruminations, I had drawn parallel to Evelyn's woods, and the dump was only a couple hundred feet ahead. Caught up in Uncle John's infectious enthusiasm for what he clearly saw as some kind of escapade, I now realized that I had acted rashly. I had no way to defend myself and no clear plan of escape. All I had was a dog whistle and a cell phone. The danger hit home with a jolt. A cramp of fear gripped my chest. I was facing a real panther, not some stuffed toy.

I seriously contemplated turning tail, but, for some reason, I continued to the dump and lowered the bucket of manure. Climbing down from the seat, I flexed my toes in the clunky boots and studied the surrounding woods while pretending to fiddle with something on the tractor. The hair on the back of my neck was standing up. What the hell am I doing out here, I thought.

Uncle John had called the place where Doug had his camp the Devil's Woodyard. Like most on Delmarva, the woods I was studying had once been cleared. Now, tall pines and hollies mixed with youngish oaks, hickories, poplars and sweet gums. It would have made a pretty forest, but the woodyard's understory was an impenetrable layer of brambles three or more feet deep. These were old, thick-stemmed, long-thorned briars—the kind that bite viciously and hang on tenaciously. I doubt anybody braved these barbs to pick the blackberries in summer. The place was well-named.

I couldn't see an obvious entry point, but Uncle John had assured me there was a deer path just behind the rusted hulk of a 1962 Chevy at the back of the dump pile. Walking along until I found the opening, I hesitantly turned sideways into the narrow passage.

It was soon abundantly clear to me why, as I'd sat atop the rumbling tractor, Uncle John had handed up a pair of grimy leather gloves with the remark, "Here. You'll need these." I was grateful that nearly every inch of my flesh was covered with some kind of tough fabric because the stickers sought out and lacerated every tiny bit of skin that wasn't shielded—namely my face and ears. Cussing, I turned up my shirt collar and tried vainly to draw in my head like a turtle.

To reach the camp, Uncle John had said, bear northwest toward an old oak. Thirty feet beyond oak's spread, the briars would clear and there'd be a slope down to a tiny stream. Turn and follow the stream northeast for about 100 yards, he'd said, and then cross over. The camp was along the stream a few yards further, in a patch of old growth forest.

I was sweating like a pig. Uncle John had warned me the woodyard was a maze. There were myriad critter paths through it. Indeed, a deer could have been lying in the brambles a foot away and I would never have seen it. Many of the paths I took dead-ended, so I was constantly doubling back. Every step was a battle. I longed to lift my arms to get them out of the way of the grasping briars, but what better way to announce myself than waving my arms over my head?

Not that I was any deerstalker, skulking silently through the sylvan surroundings. *Au contraire.* Uncle John's size 9 ½'s felt like snowshoes. As I trod upon and snapped the briars overbranching the path to keep them from grabbing my pants, I sounded like a 200-pound deer crashing through the forest. So I progressed ever so slowly, trying desperately not to attract attention to myself. Who was I kidding?

When I finally came to a place where the briars thinned out, I paused to wipe the sweat out of my eyes and catch my breath. Feeling exposed, I crouched and looked around. In the distance to my right, I spotted the gnarly arms of the old oak. Dense briars separated the oak from me. Quieting my labored breathing, I caught the muted babble of the stream straight ahead. The patch of briars between me and the stream appeared to be more passable than the patch between me and the oak. I reasoned that once I reached the stream, I could follow it easily to the campsite. So, despite Uncle John's directions to the contrary, I turned away from the oak and toward the stream. Why struggle more than I have to?

It was an easy hike, briar-wise, to the stream. I splashed across and headed northeast. My breathing had eased since ceasing my struggles with the brambles. Although my terror had abated somewhat, I remained acutely alert. Stepping carefully, I tried to place my hobbit feet on patches of sand, pine needles, or moss instead of crunching leaves or snapping twigs underfoot. I paused after each step or two to listen to the forest sounds.

Eventually, I reached a point along the stream opposite the old oak. According to Uncle John's reckoning, Doug's hunting camp lay little more than a hundred yards ahead. I very nearly jumped out of my skin when a squirrel leapt from the ground to a poplar just within my peripheral vision. He disappeared up the tree. I swallowed hard.

The sun came out. Though traveling along the stream bank was easy and quiet, I decided that I was too close to Doug's camp to travel in the open. I sidled into the trees for cover but was startled when they proved only a narrow verge and I stepped onto a narrow grass track only a few feet from the bank. Wondering why Uncle John hadn't told me about this old farm lane, I crept along the track just inside the trees bordering it. My neck began to stiffen and ache from constantly swiveling my head. I reached back and rubbed it.

Another bank of briars blocked my path. I groaned inwardly and stepped out of the sheltering trees onto the track to go around it. Dreading the prospect of returning through the briars from hell, I was tempted to just keep walking along the track. I wondered how far it went and where it came out. Creeping forward a few feet, I paused to scout in all directions. When I turned to my right, my heart stopped when I found myself staring directly into the headlights of a black truck—Doug's pickup to be specific. Lucky for me, the headlights weren't on and the cab was unoccupied. My heart lurched back to life.

Glancing down, I could see tracks where the tires had mashed the new grass. The truck had been driven in from the opposite direction and then backed into this cavern-like opening in the bank of briars. Observing more closely, I realized that this particular bank was man-made. Using a stand of saplings and sumacs as a framework, Doug had built a blind out of briars and tree branches. Tarps draped over the truck and covered with leaves and branches camouflaged the pickup from above.

I'm not ashamed to admit that I completely lost my nerve at that point. Maybe I hadn't truly believed my own theory, deep down, until I stood face to face with proof positive that there was, indeed, a real panther in the Devil's Woodyard. I ducked into the blind and, squashed against the driver's door, fished my cell phone out of a pocket in the overalls. I punched 911.

It took me several minutes of urgent whispering at the dispatcher before I made her understand that all she needed to do was to tell Trooper Glen Insley that I'd found Doug Hitchens' truck hidden just off an old track that runs parallel to the stream through Evelyn Hitchens' woodlot and that I had every reason to believe the man himself was holed up in a hunting camp nearby.

"Tell him that Uncle John Adams can direct him to the camp. OK? And tell him to get his butt out here *fast*," I hissed and pressed the "End" button.

Though mildly comforted that, somewhere, Glen Insley was being summoned, I knew at a gut level that he wasn't going to be any help to me. My one absolute certainty was that I wasn't getting any closer to that hunting camp. No sir-ree. Sorry, but I'm just not that brave. The only question on my mind was whether I should lay low until the cops came or try to get out of the Devil's Woodyard on my own.

Chapter Twenty-Six

In retrospect, I might have been smarter to stay put. Instead, I'd stepped out of the blind onto the track. That's when it hit me. Well, it didn't *actually* hit me; it *almost* hit me.

Moving from shade to sunlight, I'd been momentarily dazzled and, blinking, I'd turned down the track in the direction of Uncle John's and away from the hunting camp. After only a few steps, a sound behind me made me turn my head. A white deer with a brown patch on her rump had bounded into the center of the track. As she stood gazing at me with those great doe eyes for a fraction of a second, I caught a glimpse of a dark form in the underbrush behind her. Springing from the track in one leap, she crashed into the woods opposite and disappeared in an instant.

It's hard to explain, but in the next moment, I was staring down at an orange-fletched arrow that had thwunked into the track about ten feet ahead of me. This was no toy from a kiddie bow-and-arrow set but something a bow hunter would use—in other words, something Doug Hitchens would use.

My left upper arm was burning. I was rubbing it and still staring stupidly at the arrow when my brain finally clicked. Whether I actually said them out loud or only thought them I will never know, but the words "God almighty" came out of me. The next thing I remember is lifting my right leg and leaping into the cover of the woods exactly as the white doe had leapt.

I sped along the verge of the grassy track, just inside the trees, praying but not believing that it would take me to Uncle John's unimpeded. After all, if I could have followed the track to the camp, why would Uncle John have sent me to the maze? A cruel practical joke perhaps? Still, the track had to come out somewhere and I was going in the right direction. I kept on running. I didn't dare look back.

My chest was aching. My feet were stinging. My arm was burning. But I was still running as fast as my legs would carry me. To my right, the grass track was petering out, its smooth green surface pocked by young clumps of briars. I slowed to a stop and, gulping air, I hugged a shagbark at the edge of the track. Peeking around it, I neither saw nor heard anyone in pursuit. Small comfort. Looking back the other way, my second worst fear was realized. The track ended just ahead in a wall of briars, too high to see over and too deep to smash down.

I swerved to my left, still in the general direction of Uncle John's but now headed toward the maze, back the way I'd come. I searched for an opening through the wall of briars. I could not plunge in just anywhere; if I lost my footing, I would be mired and helpless to fight back.

I could just see over the wall now and, ahead, it seemed to get even lower. I could only hope that my sense of direction was still good. If so, I should reach the maze shortly. Right now, even briars from hell looked like the better of the available alternatives. At least, I knew I could get through the maze.

Just then, I heard a sound—something like a strangled yell—from the woods to my left. I flung my legs out behind me, dropped to my belly, and wiggled sideways under the nearest arched canes. I was gasping. Certain that the sound would give me away, I clapped my hand over my mouth and listened hard. I distinctly heard footfalls in the dried leaves. They were northeast of me. They stopped. I lay paralyzed, straining my ears. It could have been an animal, not Doug, I thought. Even a squirrel is loud in a quiet woods. I listened harder.

I think ten long minutes—and ten years of my life—passed before I tentatively wiggled from under the briars and came to my knees and then my feet. Still crouching, I watched and listened several more minutes. My eyes and ears ached from the strain. The forest was dead silent—no twittering birds, no scampering squirrels, no nothing—and that's no good.

Still, I felt I had no choice: stay and get caught or run and maybe get away. Sure that the maze lay just ahead, I set off at a crouched jog. About thirty feet on, the wall of briars finally thinned and I veered to the right on a deer path through the wall. The patch that lay beyond must be part of the maze. I hoped I would come out of it somewhere near Uncle John's dump and the blessed blue tractor.

I heard a sound. I whipped my head around and glimpsed a shadow in the forest behind me. My brain said 'animal' but the rest of my body said 'Doug!' I set off at a dead run, my arms pumping. The briars tugged at and ripped my clothes. Something grabbed my hand and held me. I gasped and fell backward, my legs yanked from under me. It still had my hand. Twisting, I rolled to my knees, ready to fight. I shook my head in disbelief. It was only a thick blackberry cane that had snagged my glove. I growled and snatched my hand away. I felt my flesh ripped by the vicious thorns that had pierced the leather. The cane kept the glove.

Scrabbling to my feet, the briars tore at my cheeks, and I instinctively closed my eyes to protect them. When I'd finally struggled upright and opened them, the seemingly endless maze lay ahead of me.

My run through the maze was a blur of pain. When I at last stumbled out of it, bloodied and exhausted, I tripped over a hardened clod of dirt and fell flat on my face. The wind was knocked out of me, but I managed to lift my head, spit out the grit and look around. I was sprawled crosswise a furrow. Tiny corn plants sprouted around me. From my ground level vantage point, I could see Uncle John's dump where the blessed blue tractor waited patiently. It was a good 300 yards away. His house was a speck in the distance. I had to cross a lot of open ground to get to either and I was worn to a frazzle.

Gasping as I scanned the horizon, I spotted a long row of round bales probably a hundred yards straight ahead. Since Uncle John doesn't have livestock of the four-footed variety, I surmised they must belong to another farmer. In any event, they would shield me from the Woodyard and give me a chance to rest. Half crawling, half running, I made my way across those 100 yards. As it turned out, the bales were lined up along a lane separating two fields.

As I cowered behind them, I thrust my swollen hand into the pocket where I'd left the cell phone, praying that it was still there. It was. The battery was low—probably only one call left. My hands were shaking so badly that I could barely press the number. As luck would have it, I got Peg's machine instead of Peg. I told the machine where I was and that the cops were on their way to get Doug. I asked her to call Uncle John Adams and let him know I was OK. After that, I slipped to the ground and leaned my back against the bale to rest.

I must have drifted for a moment because, when I came to, I was very disoriented. Rubbing my sticky, burning cheeks, I wondered how long I had been sitting there in a stupor. I'd forgotten my watch that day, but it looked to be about four o'clock. The sun was gone again, behind clouds that had rolled in thickly. I could smell rain on the way.

Reconnoitering on my hands and knees, I spotted no sign of life. I considered my options. One: I could follow the lane I was on—it probably ended at Reynolds Road—and return to Uncle John's along the public road. Two: I could cut across the wide open fields within sight of anyone in the Woodyard. I didn't like those options. Instead, I decided to follow the lane hidden behind the bales to within striking distance of Uncle John's chicken houses and then sprint across the field to the driveway that ran from his chicken houses to the farmhouse.

Carrying out my plan, I had almost reached the nearest of the chicken houses, the No. 3, when I sensed a commotion across the field. I stopped to listen. As I scanned the edge of the Woodyard, a line of troopers emerged single file from the briar maze. They fanned out to flank a tall trooper with a K-9. My eyes seemed veiled—probably by dirt and sweat—but I peered hard. I was sure I recognized Griff and Thor. This then was the result of my 911 call. They were tracking Doug out of the woods to... .

Ohmigod, I thought. To Uncle John's. If Doug had run this way, chasing me, he might be hiding in one of Uncle John's outbuildings or, worse, he might have invaded the farmhouse.

In retrospect, I didn't really analyze my next move carefully. I figured I'd just hole up somewhere out of the way, not call any attention to myself, and let the cops finish their job, as I trusted they soon would. I had been headed for the No. 3 chicken house, so I just kept going until I reached it. I slipped inside by one of the doors near the end of the long building.

Thankfully, the house was empty of birdlife. The catchers had come and hauled away the chickens by tractor-trailerfuls. Uncle John had crusted out the house, and it was ready for the next shipment of chicks from the hatchery.

With the curtains raised and no lights on, the house was pitch dark. Leaving the door slightly ajar for light, I squatted beside it to rest. Without the cackling of the chickens and the clicks and gurgles of the feeders and drinkers, the house was silent. My rasping breath was the only sound in my ears.

When I caught my breath, I rose and peeked through the door. Though I craned my neck, the angle of the house prevented my being able to see what was happening across the field. I decided to find a better vantage point and began to slink along the inside wall of the house toward the far end. The further I drew away from the cracked door, the less I could see. Although I'd noticed that the feeder and drinker lines had been raised so that the floors could be crusted, I clung to the wall for fear of falling over something else unseen. By this point, my body ached so badly that I thought one more fall would finish me.

I'd made it almost halfway down the house, futilely feeling for a light switch along the way, when a door I'd just passed creaked open. I froze. A shaft of gray light fell over me. The inside screen door was thrown back toward me. The man entering blocked the light. With only the chicken wire of the screen door between us, I found myself face to face with Doug Hitchens.

"You bitch," was all he said in the startled second before he lunged for me.

He grabbed air, of course. I was long gone.

I'd probably run only twenty steps when my forward foot struck. I knew what it was, but too late. I tried to lift my rear leg sideways to clear the obstacle but Uncle John's boot seemed to weigh ten pounds. My toe caught and down I went, sprawled over the wood-and-wire partition that spanned the house to keep the chickens from piling up at one end. I guess I threw my arms out because they were folded under me and crushed when my chest, followed by my chin, cracked against the hard dirt floor.

The wind was knocked out of me again, but, by some miracle, I didn't lose consciousness. I was sensible enough to know that Doug had also tripped over the partition. I didn't look but I could hear him cussing as he tried to get back on his feet only a few feet away from me.

Elbowing my body forward, I dragged my feet off the partition and raised myself to my hands and knees. Doug was still cussing. I vaguely remember being astonished that my legs were holding me up—I was absolutely convinced they'd both been broken in the fall—as I sprinted to the far end of the house and clutched at the last screen door.

I had just flung open the outer door to make my escape when Doug grappled me. His grip felt like iron. A feeble "Help" came out of my mouth as I twisted, clawing at the air where I thought his face was. I kicked out twice. Don't misunderstand. This wasn't any kung fu kick—I don't know any martial arts. It was just sheer terror and plain gut reaction. Yet, one of the kicks connected. He doubled over, and I tear-assed through the door.

I didn't get very far. From the intense pain, I surmised that the twist and kick had hurt my already sore back. Hobbling along the outside wall, I desperately looked for an escape route. Doug was still groaning behind me, but I knew I couldn't run from him anymore. I had nothing left. If and when he recovered, he would get me.

Reaching the end of the chicken house, I leaned against the feed bin stanchions and looked out over the field where I thought I'd seen the cops. I blinked in disbelief. No one was there. Where'd they gone? Where were Griff and Thor? Did I hallucinate them? The salt in my tears scalded my scratched cheeks.

I think I was on the verge of passing out from the pain—or maybe the terror—when, in the distance, I heard the voices of dogs. Not one dog but many dogs—the booming bark of big dogs and the familiar ear-splitting shrieks of my fearless little Tibbies. An eerie stillness came over me. My breathing calmed. The blood stopped roaring in my ears, and I sensed my heart rate slow. I could feel blood and strength flowing into my enfeebled hands and legs, and I stopped shaking in my boots.

I glanced up at the feed bin shining high above me and reached a decision. Pulling myself up stiffly, I scaled a few rungs on the feed bin ladder. Stretching up, I could now see the troopers converging on the No. 3 chicken house. Griff and Thor were in the lead. I dropped my forehead against a rung and closed my eyes in relief.

"If you think you can get away from me, you goddam stupid bitch," Doug growled from below me, "you got another think comin'."

I opened my eyes and looked into Doug's contorted, blood-suffused face below me. His hands, the knuckles whitened, gripped a rung of the ladder just below the one where my feet rested. Even the whites of his eyes were aflame.

"I got that interfering old bastard. I got that fucking bitch. And I'll get you, you... ."

I pulled myself to the top rung and screamed for help. The cops were at a dead run now. They could see me above No. 3's roof, clinging to the feed bin ladder. I was thinking that all I needed to do was hold out a couple more minutes when I felt Doug's hand close around my right ankle. He jerked my right foot off its rung.

I heard Griff yell, "Come down or I'll send the dog!"

Doug had an iron grip on my left ankle now. Despite my kicking at his head with my free leg, he dislodged my left foot. I dangled from the top of the feed bin, my arms burning and weakening fast, while Doug grasped at my jerking legs, trying to yank me off the ladder.

"Get 'im!" Griff yelled.

An instant later, Doug screamed and fell, pried off by the 85-pound German Shepherd who'd leapt and embedded his teeth in Doug's calf. My feet flailed until they found a rung.

"Out," Griff commanded, and Thor released the leg. Doug was rolling on the ground below, screaming and clutching his leg, as the troopers swarmed over him.

I clung shakily to the ladder for what seemed several more minutes while Doug was hand-cuffed and lead out of the way. Then, supported by a dozen coaxing hands, I slowly descended the ladder and wobbled to a nearby patch of grass where I sank gratefully to the ground.

Griff blanched when he knelt next to me. I didn't realize it at the time, of course, but I looked a lot worse than I felt—and I felt pretty damn bad. They tell me that my hands and face were swollen, striped with cuts and scratches and caked with dried blood, dirt and chicken crap. My hair was a nest of briars and leaves. What was left of Uncle John's clothes were ripped and filthy, and the cap, gloves and bandanna had long since disappeared.

"Thanks, Griff," I whispered hoarsely, sliding one of my lacerated hands into his. "I don't think I could've hung on too much longer." I mustered a grin at my unwitting pun.

Griff smiled and shook his head. "If you can still joke, I guess you're gonna be all right." He squeezed my hand. I flinched.

A paramedic appeared from nowhere and asked me where I was hurt. I didn't know how to answer him. "Pretty much everywhere," I said with a shrug, "from the top of my head to the bottom of my feet."

I turned to Griff. "He killed Doc Twilley. He said so."

Griff nodded. "Yeah, we figured that out. We had witnesses that put Doc at down at Trap Pond most of the day, but we couldn't figure out why he was killed out on Swann's Pond. Lucky for us, Jackie Lynch knew more than she was saying and she finally gave it up. She said that, when Katie and Doug came over to her house last night to get money, Katie was terrified. Doug had already beat her up some. He was yelling at her–you know, the typical abusive behavior, blaming her for everything that had gone wrong—and it came out what had really happened to Doc. Jackie already knew that Doug had taken Teke, of course, but she claims she didn't know about Doc until last night." Griff let loose my hand so that the paramedic could look it over and then continued.

"Apparently, on his way home from Trap Pond, Doc must have stopped by the clinic and recognized Teke in the boarding kennel. Unlucky for Doc, Katie and Doug drove up before he could call us. Katie told Jackie that old Doc confronted them, hopping mad, and pissed Doug off. Jackie says Doug's never been the kind to back down—you know, to say, hey, this is out of control, I've been caught, it's over. Instead, he pitched a fit. He forced Doc to drive over to Swann's Pond and put the boat in the water. Doc must've put up a fight out on the pond 'cause the medical examiner found some bruising that indicates they grappled. Then, Doug hit Doc with his gun—the same gun he used to kill Katie—pushed him overboard and left him to drown."

"Ow!" I shouted. The paramedic had probed the rip in my left sleeve and found where the arrow had grazed me. He started cutting off the tattered remains of Uncle John's shirt sleeve.

"We recovered the gun. The dumb bastard hid it in his old room at his mother's house. There was dried blood on the butt that we think will turn out to be Doc's."

Just then, the revving of an engine caught our attention. A familiar red pickup was bouncing across the field from Reynolds Road at top speed, raising billows of dust behind.

When she got as close as the troopers would let her, she slammed on the brakes, cut the engine and leapt from the cab—all in one smooth motion. At a word from Phil—whose red head I hadn't even seen until now—the restraining hands fell away, and she strode toward where Doug Hitchens slumped, handcuffed, against a cruiser. He straightened up. She hauled off and punched him in the face with all her strength.

"You son of a bitch," she shrieked. "Where's my dog? What have you done with my dog?" She punched him again.

Chapter Twenty-Seven

I'd hitched a ride back to Uncle John's farmhouse with the paramedics but refused to go to the hospital with them. There was nothing wrong with me, I'd insisted, that soap, shampoo, peroxide, triple antibiotic and time wouldn't heal.

"Tut, tut, tut" and "My, my, my" was about all that Aunt Bessie could say as she helped me shower and change back into my own clean clothes and, in so doing, discovered my many cuts and bruises. The worst had been my feet. When we'd finally pried off Uncle John's boots and socks, my feet were a mass of bloody blisters.

But that all happened two days ago. My feet were much better now. To prove it, I wriggled my stubby toes in the warm sunshine of Easter Sunday afternoon. Daffodils bordering the brick patio bobbed their buttery heads in the breeze. From the comfort of my lounge chair, I watched the dogs—all seven of them—romp though the front yard of the Nest. A male Eastern bluebird watched them worriedly, dipping back and forth between his house, tacked to a poplar trunk, and a nearby Bradford pear in brilliant white bloom.

Peg walked over. She leaned over to hug me and then handed me the glass of wine in her hand. She pulled up the iron garden chair next to me and sat down. The dogs were chasing each other down to the old landing and back.

"Dinner will be ready in a half hour," she said. I nodded.

While I'd slept nearly all day Saturday, with Dawa and Senge on duty as my bed dogs, Phil and Peg had shopped for Easter. While Griff brought me meals and kept watch, they'd been puttering in the kitchen and dining room.

When I'd finally hobbled downstairs, with Griff's help, on Easter Sunday morning, Peg related Aunt Bessie's story over breakfast.

It seems that from the moment I'd left on the tractor, Dawa and Senge had taken up positions on the back porch of the farmhouse. Though Aunt Bessie had tried to distract them with fried chicken, they never wavered and remained glued to their spots, watching and waiting. At about four o'clock, the Tibbies had started frenzied barking.

"She didn't know but maybe you were coming back up the lane but she looked out and didn't see you. So, she went out on the screen porch. She said that the Tibbies were jumping against the screen so hard that she was afraid they would rip right through the screen door. But when she reached up to hook the screen door, she looked down the porch steps and who should be standing there but my Teke—just as calm as he could be." Peg paused in her narrative to hug the Chessie leaning against her chair.

"She said that he was all full of briars and stuff—sort of like you were," she paused and smiled, "but that she knew who he was. She just opened the screen door and said, 'C'mon Teke' and he walked right up the steps onto the porch and lay down like he knew he was safe."

"Funny thing is she heard the phone ringing while she was out there with Teke, but she let Uncle John get it. It was me. I'd just picked up your message and was calling to tell them that you were OK and that the cops were after Doug. Then, five minutes later, Phil called to tell me that they were tracking Doug out at Uncle John's farm. That's when I drove up there. I still didn't know Teke had been found."

"Obviously not, judging from the walloping you gave Doug Hitchens," Phil said, squeezing her around the waist.

"It's strange but I heard the dogs barking all the way out at the No. 3," I said. "right at the end, when I thought I was done for, that I couldn't go another step, I heard dogs barking. Lots of dogs. Dawa and Senge, of course, but I heard big dogs, too." I paused and sighed. "The barking sort of gave me a little boost, enough to climb up the feed bin ladder anyway. I knew you were close by. I figured that if I could get up to the top, you could see me."

Griff looked at me quizzically.

"What?" I asked. "Why are you looking at me like that?"

"Oh nothing, I guess," he said, "It's just that I was right there at the No. 3 but I never heard any dogs barking. Not even Thor." He shrugged.

That evening, Peg served up an elegant dinner. Though it was against her down-home nature, she dressed the dining room table in linen and lace and set it with my china, silver and crystal, just as I would have done. A tiny Easter basket brimming with jelly beans, chocolate malted eggs and marshmallow bunnies graced each place. A ham, beautifully glazed with bourbon sauce, formed the centerpiece. Carrots swimming in honey, new potatoes glistening in their jackets and the first spinach steaming in sweet butter awaited our forks.

Before we fell to, Peg thanked us all for our parts in bringing Teke home, her eyes glistening with tears. "To best friends," she said and raised her flute in a toast. It was excellent bubbly.

The dogs joined us as we settled in the great room after dinner. From the kitchen, Peg produced slices of hummingbird cake and a silver coffee pot.

"I wonder what's going to happen to Jackie Lynch," I asked, sipping my coffee.

Phil and Griff shrugged simultaneously.

"It's up to the court," Griff said. "She knew about Teke—even had a hand in concealing him—that much is clear. She says she didn't know about Doc but, I dunno, I got a feeling she'd guessed." He paused. "On the other hand, she did cooperate."

"Only when her back was against the wall," Peg commented.

"True. But there's nothing new about that. Happens all the time," Griff said. "They'll probably give her a break for testifying against Doug Hitchens. It'll be a cold day in hell before that SOB sees the outside of a jail cell."

Since his arrest at the No. 3 chicken house, Doug had been held without bail for the murders of Doc Twilley and Katie Adkins.

"But why did she get involved in the first place?" I asked. I still couldn't understand how I could have misjudged her.

It was Phil's turn. "Well, she says that the Hitchens woman was mad as hell about losing the contest to Peg and Teke. She'd been agitating about it for months—wouldn't let it go. Then, after the aunt read about the St. Michaels shoot in Grace Bishop's column, Jackie says she started spouting off about going over there. The day before the shoot, Jackie overheard her aunt tell Doug to take her to St. Michaels. Jackie says that's the real reason she went to St. Michaels that day, too. She knew that her aunt was irrational enough to try to get revenge and that Doug always did what his mother told him to do. She says she was afraid something was going to happen to you or to Teke."

"And it did," I said. "So Jackie Lynch had good intentions at first and Evelyn really was behind all this?"

"Well, Evelyn denies it. She says it was all Doug's idea to steal Teke. She says she had nothing to do with it and didn't know anything about it. So she says."

"Motherly love," Peg commented.

"If Jackie Lynch knew her kin well enough to be worried about something happening to Teke, why didn't she come forward when he was stolen?" I asked.

"Blood's thicker than water. The aunt had apparently helped her with her vet school expenses. I guess she figured she owed her aunt enough to keep her mouth shut. And she claims that's why she kept Teke at the clinic—to make sure nothing happened to him. She may have suspected that Doug killed the old vet over Teke, but she says she didn't know until Katie told her. She claims she'd planned to come forward with what she knew on Thursday. But when she got to the clinic that morning, we'd found Katie." Phil said.

"Just why *did* he kill Katie?" Peg asked.

Phil shrugged. "They were arguing at Jackie's house. Katie told Jackie that ransoming Teke wasn't part of the original plan. They'd come up with that idea after Doc found them out and Doug had killed him. They'd asked for the ransom only so they could get away. But the ransom was at their trailer and, as you know, we were at the trailer when they went home Wednesday night."

He continued after a sip of coffee. "Anyway, they spotted us and got away, but they didn't have any money. So they went to Jackie for help. Jackie says Katie wanted to leave Teke at the clinic and take off. But Doug was enraged. He wanted to go back and get Teke. Jackie assumes he was going to, uh," Phil paused and glanced sidelong at Peg beside him, "do away with Teke in some way. By the time they left, Jackie thought Doug had calmed down. She says she tried to convince Katie to stay with her and let Doug go on his own. But Katie insisted on leaving with him. Jackie says she was under the impression they were headed down south."

"But, they ended up back at the clinic anyway. From what everybody says, Katie really did love animals. Maybe she was killed trying to protect Teke. Only Teke could tell us that," Griff said, leaning over to pet Teke where he lay next to Peg. "Isn't that right, fella?" Teke lifted his head.

We sat around digesting cake and information for a few minutes. Peg suddenly glanced at her watch. She stood and announced, "Oh, it's time for the big surprise."

"What surprise?" Phil asked.

"Just wait and see," she said smugly. She switched on the TV and slid a DVD into the recorder.

At quarter after seven, Teke's first commercial aired. The theme was Delmarva's natural bounty and featured scenes of Teke with the wild foal on Assateague National Seashore, eagle spotting at Blackwater National Wildlife Refuge, retrieving a duck near St. Michaels and dolphin watching off Cape Henlopen. Three official state animals— Maryland's calico cat, Delaware's "blue hen" and Virginia's foxhound— made brief but light-hearted appearances with Teke. At the end, a spectacular sunset over the Chesapeake was the background for Teke's dogspeak invitation to visit beautiful Delmarva.

"What's all the whooping and hollering about?" Senge said, raising his head to look at the humans.

"It's Teke, Brother. He was on TV just now," Dawa said excitedly.

"Oh," Senge said, settling back down and smacking his lips. TV didn't hold much interest for him. No delicious smells.

"That was a good retrieve, Teke," Bits said and twirled in place to emphasize his point.

"I could have done it better," Dapper sniffed. He delivered an exaggerated yawn.

Ham rolled his eyes and whispered to Thor, "Der Retriever können es einfach nicht ertragen, wenn ein anderer besser ist als sie selbst."

"It's rude not to speak English," Dawa remarked. As the only bitch in the pack, she was allowed to correct their manners.

"Psst," Senge whispered in her ear, "What did Ham say?"

"He said, 'Retrievers are so competitive'," Dawa replied.

"Oh," Senge said. "Gee, Sister, is there anything you don't know?"
Dawa winked and smiled.

Meanwhile, Teke sat quietly alert next to his Mom. He hadn't left her side since they'd been re-united on Aunt Bessie's porch.

"What happened day before yesterday, Teke?" asked Senge, "Tell us all about it."

Teke shrugged and, dropping to his left, rolled over for a belly scratch from his Mom. "The man had me in a crate in his camp, but the latch was loose so I pushed it open and escaped. He was looking for me when I saw Aunt Abby find the place where he had hidden the truck. The man saw her, too, and got his bow."

Growls went around the circle of dogs—all except Senge.

"What's a bow, Sister?" whispered Senge.

"It's a killing thing, little Brother. Now shush," Dawa whispered back.

"I'd spotted a white doe resting in the underbrush. The man didn't see her. I called an apology and flushed her from her hide. She sprang just as he fired. She surprised the man, and his arrow missed Aunt Abby."

Grunts of approval went around the circle of dogs.

"I prefer birds to deer," Teke observed sagely, rolled over and sat up. "I could smell Aunt Abby was very afraid. She ran. The man followed her and I followed him. When she hid under the briars and became still like a possum, I made noise. I drew the man away and then I circled back and followed Aunt Abby." He paused to lick his paw where a thorn had scratched it.

"The man was stupid if he cannot tell a human from a dog," commented the taciturn Thor.

Grunts of assent went around the circle.

Dawa crawled to Teke on her belly. "Your real name is Tikam. That means 'Defend her!' " Dawa explained for the benefit of the others. "Senge and I thank you for defending our Mom."

Teke ducked his head in acknowledgment of her gratitude. She groomed his ear.

"What happened next, Teke? Huh?" urged the impatient Bits, stomping his forepaws.

"I heard the Tibbies call," he looked down his muzzle at the snub-nosed faces smiling up at him. *"I recognized those funny accents of my little friends."* He grinned toothily. *"So, I followed their voices across the field and came to a house where a nice lady brushed the briars out of my coat and gave me chicken to eat."* He circled twice and curled up, his story over. Teke was a dog of few words.

"Then I tracked the bad man and caught him with my teeth," Thor bragged. He puffed out his chest and pulled back his lips slightly so that the others could admire his teeth.

Congratulatory grunts went around the circle of dogs.

Following Teke's lead, the big dogs all circled and curled up to dream and twitch about the exploits of Teke and Thor.

"I wish I were a big dog so that I could catch a bad man with my teeth," murmured Senge, gazing at the sleeping Thor admiringly.

"Ah, Brother, 'we must each walk according to the length of our step'."

"Is that another proverb, Sister?" Senge sighed, stretching his rear legs behind while pulling himself forward on his elbows.

"It is, little Brother, and this is the lesson it teaches. We Tibbies have our gifts just as Thor and Teke have theirs. The depth of our intelligence and the height of our awareness are of much greater significance to us than length of teeth or height at withers. And we must behave as our natural gifts demand."

Senge meditated on Dawa's words for several minutes. *"So, the bad man Thor caught was the one we saw lure Teke out of his crate with liver,"* he paused to lick his lips, *"the same one who took Teke away?"*

"Yes," she said as she circled and lay down on her side. *"He was the man we smelled at the truck the day we found Doc in the pond and the man who walked in our house and left his smell on Teke's collar and the paper."*

"I smelled him on Aunt Peg's hand when she came home with Mom," Senge said proudly.

"That's right, little Brother. Aunt Peg punished him with her fist."

"Sister, when you made me leave the good chicken," Senge paused to smack his lips at the memory of Aunt Bessie's fried chicken, *"and we ran*

across the yard toward the woods, I didn't really see Teke. I didn't really see anything."

"I know," Dawa said and turned onto her back, extending and flexing her forepaws. "It takes practice to see so far, so deeply. Don't worry. You'll be able to do it someday."

"There's one thing I still don't understand, Sister," Senge said, resting his chin on his forepaws.

"What's that?"

"We can't bark as loud as big dogs,, Sister," he said. "So, how could Teke hear us all the way across the field? And how could Mom hear us down at the chicken house?"

"How indeed, little Brother, how indeed?" Dawa murmured and closed her magic eyes to dream of high monastery walls in old Tibet, where the sound of Tibbies barking carries very, very far over the land.